Cajun
Moon

Cajun Moon

GIGI GUNN

URBAN BOOKS

http://www.urbanbooks.net

URBAN SOUL is published by

Urban Books
1199 Straight Path
West Babylon, NY 11704

ISBN-13: 978-1-59983-060-5
ISBN-10: 1-59983-060-4

First Printing: April 2008

10 9 8 7 6 5 4 3 2 1

Printed in the United States of America

To the resilient People of Katrina, wherever they may be.
New Orleans remains in our hearts and on our minds . . . still.
What she was . . .
What she is . . .
What she will be again . . .

A tout moment, votre vie n'est que rèsultat de vos dècisions.
(At any given moment, your life is the sum total of all your choices.)

~ Creole Proverb

Chapter 1

Nudging out the setting sun, a Cajun moon rose high in the sky and cast an eerie golden orange glow over the French Quarter and the sign, RARE FINDS—COLLECTIBLE TREASURES AND ANTIQUITIES. Sassy stepped out onto Royal Street into the thick, humid air. She closed and locked the door of the shop before glancing up at the moon. The lunar ball hung so huge and luminous it looked like a fiery planet about to crash into the skinny streets. She dismissed that old folks' saying, that the Cajun moon was a bad moon rising, as she headed north to Bienville Street. She had others things on her mind as her heels clicked on the pavement and her bouncy, chestnut hair punctuated every step by tapping her waist. She felt an insouciant jaunt to her gait as she made her way to the only man in her life for more than eighteen years. *Roulon "Roux" Robespierre,* she thought, and smiled to herself with naughty anticipation. Mentally, she thanked her boss for entertaining out-of-town guests so she could close up early and surprise Roux.

A glint of moonlight bounced from her third finger, left hand where a three-carat diamond solitaire had lived for over five years. That was her doing; she didn't think

Roux was ready for marriage. A man that successful and easy on the eye had to get the play out of him before he settled down for life. And that's how she wanted him—for life. She planned to marry only once. Divorce was out of the question, so she had to be sure about him because she sure couldn't trust other women worth a damn. Of course, she smiled wickedly, she couldn't blame them either. He was a bona fide "pretty boy" with his bronzy copper skin, the color of his nickname . . . roux, the basis for all the rich sauces around New Orleans. His mother had been the beauty of all Louisiana and he was a male equivalent of her so much that they called him an immaculate conception. Very little of his father showed in him; his mother was fair, but his father's brown, colored his complexion in that tantalizing copper. His mother's hair fell like a curtain and you couldn't pay a wave to live there, but his father interjected his kinky hair so that Roux ended up with curls so big and silky that even the nuns liked to grab a handful. His mother's blue eyes mixed with the father's black ones gave Roux his unparalleled hazel eyes with copper flecks, topped by a mass of eyelashes, all offered on an altar of high cheekbones. He was "cute" as a boy, but with that body he grew into "handsome" by adolescence. His mother had stayed a beauty until the day she died. The day that Sebastien's Funeral Home refused to bury her. The day Roux swore to hate the Sebastiens as long as he drew breath.

As she turned on to Bourbon Street, Sassy wondered what made her think of all that. She looked ahead and saw the sign in the distance, SASSY'S, in bright, hot-pink neon letters; the color clashed with the golden orange of the Cajun moon. But after five years, she still got a jolt when she saw her name emblazoned atop the Bourbon Street club. SASSY'S, the "in" hot spot, and Preservation

Hall, the little club where old timers cut their jazz teeth, were antithetical, but "must-do" bookends for the perfect New Orleans' French Quarter experience. Sassy threaded through tourists whose open plastic cups brimmed with diluted beer. They shuffled along the streets of her hometown, gawking at the nude shows while mounted policemen tried to keep them orderly in this modern-day Sodom and Gomorrah. Nature's mugginess commingled with the crowds' liquor-breath, overworked deodorant, and funky perfume all rode the sultry wave of a typical autumn night in N'awlins—the native pronunciation. While most of the country enjoyed Indian summer, New Orleans felt like it had been dipped in a vat of boiling water, then wrung out to dry—hot and steamy with humidity thick enough to chew.

As Sassy walked, a jumpin' trumpet from one club gave way to a smoky sax of another, and the cacophony of music and revelers poured into the street, creating a loud, carnival raucousness. If the French Quarter was party central of the western hemisphere, then Bourbon Street was its pulsating core.

Sassy couldn't wait to reach the club with its quiet, understated elegance. The Cajun moon sank lower, dusting its gold-orange patina over all the pedestrians and buildings that lit Sassy's way.

In the back of a black limo, an exquisitely dressed man put aside his laptop and folded a copy of the *Wall Street Journal.* He eased back the monogrammed cuffs of his tuxedo shirt and read the face of his twenty-five-thousand-dollar diamond-studded watch. *Twenty of,* he thought. He pressed the privacy button and, as the glass disappeared into its well, directed his chauffeur, "Take Royal."

"Yes, sir," the driver answered. "This music too loud for you, boss?"

The man listened to Wil Downing sing "Bewitched, Bothered and Bewildered," smiled, and answered, "No," but thought, *How ironic.*

How long had it been since he'd stopped by Rare Finds just to get a glimpse of her as she closed up—as she walked to Roux's? The man may not have seen her in weeks, but she was always there—in the back of his mind, in the front of his mind, as he worked, as he played. Her image was always close to his heart. He was on his way to pick up his date for the opera this evening, but he could spare a few minutes to glimpse the woman he wished he were escorting tonight . . . any night— anywhere. Sassy Crillon. How many years had he been in love with her? *Too long,* he thought, as Wil vocally expressed his sentiments.

He remembered the first time he'd seen her. Even though he was years older, he was struck by her long rope- braids, looped and caught by two ribbons, and her intelli- gent, defiant eyes hooded by Bayou-thick eyelashes. But it was her skin, a buttery, golden copper, like maple syrup poured in a stream of sunshine, that captivated him and let him know that she was going to be a real heartbreaker when she grew up. The braids evolved into a ponytail, which revealed an exquisite freckle on the back of her neck. He remembered how that ponytail sat high on her head but still touched her waist when she walked— to her mother's beauty shop, to ballet class, to Mardi Gras parades—and he was always amazed at how she could jump double Dutch without getting her hair caught in the ropes whenever he "happened" to see her. When she was in junior high, he found himself at her track meets, one face among many who'd watch that ponytail flip from side to side, pacing her gait, as she crossed the finish line to break records and claim her medals. In high school, she was a cheerleader whose crazy-phat legs, developed in dance and secured by athletics, were now guaranteed to please anyone who had the good fortune to gaze upon them; as they performed complicated steps in syncopated rhythms at basketball games when she cheered for the All-American point guard, Roux Robespierre. She was the epitome of class, style, and grace. Despite her dynamite body, she never displayed it in low-cut tops or by wearing fabrics that clung to her curves or rode up into tight wrinkles. "Mocha ya-ya," guys would call to her from the bleachers. He'd even heard a grown man in the stadium reverently remark of her, "Every rich man's dream and poor man's fantasy."

The man watched as Sassy chased her dreams and Roux chased her—got her early and has kept her ever since. He would have thought her too young to date, but Roux and her parents apparently didn't. Game over, and the man hadn't even known it was being played. The trophy was being "Roux's girl." The man planned to bide his time until she and Roux broke up . . . but they never did. He wasn't in New Orleans consistently enough to make a play for, get, and then hold Sassy.

Between boarding schools, summer vacations abroad and in the Caribbean, college, the business world and beyond, he'd seen, done, and had everything he'd wanted. The world and all its treasures were his for the taking, but no matter where in the world he was, whenever his heart and mind turned to New Orleans—to home—Sassy was a big part of it. When he was younger, he'd get home, grab his cars keys and then search for her. Just to see if she was still the same. That she was, all right. That she hadn't magically become available. Until he glimpsed her, he wasn't really back in N'awlins. While away, Sassy became "home" to him. With her obvious goodness, strong values, and loyalty, she represented everything he wanted and, despite all his wealth and position, would never have. He didn't care about other guys—but Roux—no guy could go up against Roux for Sassy and win. And this man was used to winning. It didn't look like he was going to get his chance—not in this lifetime.

The man chuckled wryly, and thought, he wasn't the first or the only man to ever love a woman who didn't know he existed.

Sassy hurried towards Roux's bar, SASSY'S, smiling at how she'd surprise him. She'd never known another man, never desired one. He was every man to her.

She pushed open the door with the elegant "S" in gold script and entered the crowded, smoke-filled club. She greeted the bartender who slid her a glass of her usual white wine. She thanked him and began to look for Roux. She sauntered through groups of patrons, who were transfixed by the vocalist at center stage, before glancing over at the pool table area. The smoke began to wreak havoc with her nose and eyes.

She decided that Roux must be either in his office or at home. She gulped down her wine and set the glass on a nearby table. On this night, she was pleased that Roux's world was so self-contained. His club and office were in this building, and his apartment was just across the adjacent parking lot in the other building he'd bought; the bottom floor used for storage, his apartment on the top two floors. As she turned to go to his office, she spotted his profile off the dark hallway which led to the bathrooms. "Ah, there he is," she said to herself. She treaded through the standing-room-only crowd, and when she finally reached him said, "Hey, handsome."

"Sassy!" Roux choked. Startled and flushed, he held his stomach.

"What's the matter? Don't you feel well?" she asked, stepping toward him.

Roux's mouth was open, but nothing came out.

Just then, Maxine Dupree rose from a kneeling position and, wiping the sides of her mouth, greeted slyly, "Hey, Sassy."

In a split second which seemed like a slow-motion forever, Sassy realized that it wasn't his stomach Roux was holding at all. The look of triumphant pleasure on Maxine's face and the guilty horror scrambling across Roux's confirmed it all. Sassy backed away, freezing this betrayal in her mind.

"I'll be got-damned," Sassy said sotto voce.

"Sassy, baby. Wait. I can explain. It's not what you think. Really—" Roux said, walking toward her, zipping his pants.

Sassy's icy glare stopped Roux's advance. A sharp chill ran up her spine and yanked the breath from her body. She gasped for air and shivered in the cloying heat. The taste of bile rose in her throat yet her mouth was parched; she couldn't garner enough spit to curse him. Her stomach churned, her head split and she felt her world crash off its axis and rotate into a surreal, hellish nightmare. Her mind could not comprehend any of it, but her body took over, spun itself around, and began to run. She felt faint, like she was going to throw up, but her body ran. People everywhere were in her way.

"Sassy! SASSY!" Roux yelled.

She could hear him call her over the noise. She

glanced back and saw him running behind her. She didn't want to hear it. Not again. The bar became a conspiring labyrinth—the more she ran toward the exit, the farther away it seemed, like she was on a treadmill going nowhere. Her heart felt as if it were going to burst, and she'd explode into a million smithereens and never be found. She finally made it to the door and slammed open the plate-glass door with the gold "S" into the brick wall. Shards flew into a zillion pieces as she ran into the street.

The melee and confusion caught Roux at the door. Perfunctorily, he checked to see if any of his patrons were hurt by the flying glass, as he kept his eyes on Sassy. A lady was cut on the knee, another bleeding from her arm. Roux went to curb and yelled, "Sassy!"

Cars screeched to a halt as she dodged them and ran down the middle of Bourbon Street, cutting through an alley onto Toulouse Street. The Cajun moon laughed at her, mocked her, chased her. She couldn't get away from it! It began to rain, and Sassy ran. She ran onto Royal for four blocks, then cut over onto Dumaine Street, running like a crazy woman; trying to outrun the truth, the betrayal. The heinous vision of Roux and another woman. She was crying, or was that the rain? The wine gurgled in her empty stomach, jostling around and making her dizzy, but she wouldn't stop running. She was running out of breath, but she couldn't stop.

As the limo stopped in traffic, the man glanced over to the right. Caught in the red-orange glow of the Cajun moon was a woman silhouetted in its center. She was running full-speed, mowing down everyone in her way. Even before he could see her face, he knew that gait. He knew the hair flinging from side to side. As she got closer to the street he could see she wasn't slowing down. She was heading for oncoming traffic. He jumped from the car and ran towards her.

As Sassy reached Chartres Street, she turned around to see if Roux was still in pursuit. Not watching where she was going, she ran *swack!* into a wall and collapsed.

The impact almost knocked the man off balance, but he had caught her in his arms.

"You want me to call 911?" the driver asked.

The man unraveled the hair concealing her face and examined her.

"No. She seems all right. Just got the wind knocked out of her. Help me get her into the car," he ordered. "She just lives a few blocks over on Clemenceau Street. We'll take her home."

The man held her in the backseat, not believing his good fortune. Had he ever believed that he would ever *touch* what his heart only dreamed of? That he'd ever *hold* her? His unobtainable dream. Her hair cascaded over his legs, and the brittle streetlights spotlighted intermittent glimpses of her. She was wet and breathing hard, but she was as beautiful up close as she'd been from afar. She wore little makeup—lipstick and eyeliner that had begun to run down those exquisite cheekbones. He reached for his handkerchief and dabbed at the black streaks under her eyes. He was emotionally torn between wanting to hold her forever and wanting to hurry up and get her home before she woke up. He didn't want to meet her this way. He knew she wouldn't like the pretentiousness of the limo, the driver, and the tux.

He couldn't remove his eyes from her. Her flawless skin set in all the cinnamon-coppery tones in which he'd decorated his bedroom. If he couldn't have her in the flesh, he'd wanted to be surrounded by all the colors of her rainbow. Now, he just wanted to savor every moment as the gift it was just in case he would never hold her again. He didn't want to waste this precious time wondering what had distressed her and sent her running down the street. But he knew. Only one person could affect her this way. Only one person was ever that close to her. Roux Robespierre was her one Achilles heel in life. With him, all her good sense went out the window, and Roux'd had years to cultivate and brainwash her, and make her dependent on him. When it came to Roux, Sassy turned a blind eye and a deaf ear to anything negative.

"We're here, boss," the driver announced as he lit from the car and went around to open the door.

The first floor of the house was lit with the revelry of a party. The second floor, her apartment, was dark. The driveway led to a gate anchored on either side by a formidable rod-iron fence. The rain now poured in steady torrents, concealing the moon as the man twisted the gate's bell. An enormous black Great Dane with a white diamond marking barked ferociously.

Inside, Cyril complimented Dante on his fuchsia scarf and heard the bell followed by Killer's bark. It was a minor irritation until he saw Sassy draped in this stranger's arms. His eyes filled with alarm, and he rushed to the gate with the key and said, "Omigod! What happened to her?"

"Just open the gate, please, so I can take her upstairs," the tuxedoed man commanded and thankfully noted that this was not her employer/landlord. "Stay with the car," he ordered his driver, then he whipped around the first floor and began to climb the gallery stairs to the second floor.

Cyril was in hot pursuit, asking inane questions that the man ignored until he reached the top of the flight and hesitated, not sure where to go.

"Straight ahead," Cyril directed, and the man headed for the middle room with the exposed brick walls and the French door windows.

"Pull the covers back," the man said, as lightning flashed across his face.

Cyril obeyed and turned on the overhead light.

The man laid Sassy gently on the bed and swept her wet hair away from her face before feeling her forehead and taking her pulse.

"Are you a doctor?" Cyril asked.

The man ignored him, removed her shoes, and arranged the sheet around her before he switched off the overhead light and turned on the lamp by her bedside. He added another pillow to raise her head, then adjusted the French doors so that rain was held at bay but the fresh air circulated freely around the room. He stood at the foot of her bed and looked at her—still for the first time since he entered.

"What happened to her?" Cyril asked again. "Where's Roux?"

"I don't know," the man answered quietly. "She'll be all right. She fainted. Can you stay with her until she wakes up?" He flashed coal-black eyes pointedly at Cyril.

"Yes," Cyril answered, as if accepting the assignment of a lifetime.

"She should wake up any minute. I don't want her alone until she wakes up. Understood?"

"I understand," Cyril responded, eyeing the man's exquisitely tailored tux draped over a taut, well-built body, accented by a white cashmere-and-satin opera scarf. He wasn't handsome like Roux, but he was commanding, sensual, impressive and, unfortunately, very heterosexual.

"You'll stay with her until she wakes up?" the man tested, as his chauffeur came up the steps to get him.

"Yes. Who are you?"

He yanked back his French cuffs to check his watch and answered, "Just a good Samaritan with tickets to the opera." He looked at Sassy, turned and left just as another man with a fuchsia scarf whipped around his neck came up the hall behind the driver.

"Good evening," the man in the fuchsia scarf said to him.

The man just nodded.

"Is Ivanhoe back yet?" Cyril asked Dante, as they watched the man and his chauffeur disappear through the iron gate.

"No. Who was that masked man?" Dante, who'd stayed downstairs with his manicured finger poised over 911, asked Cyril.

"The Lone Ranger and Tonto, honey."

A few hours later, Sassy's eyes struggled to focus on the images before her. Finally, Ivanhoe's weathered and comforting face came into view.

"Welcome back, chère," he said, stroking her brow.

"What happened?" Sassy asked.

"Depends on who you ask, chère," he said, exchanging a cold compress with Cyril.

"I remember running. I ran into a wall."

"Was he ever, chère. According to one houseguest, a black knight in a black limo saved you, Rapunzel. Cyril says he was a black Prince Charming. I say that Cajun moon speared something fierce between you and Roux. I don't know exactly what, but he was so anxious and contrite . . . very un-Roux-like."

"Ummmhumm. Didn't take a rocket scientist to know he stepped in it big time," Cyril said.

"He's been back here twice and even sent flowers, chère. I sent him packing. I'll sic Killer on him if you want," Ivanhoe offered.

"You always had a sixth sense when it comes to *affaires de coeur*. Thanks," Sassy said weakly as she looked at Ivanhoe and Cyril, both different shades of rich brown. "The two blind mice," she said with a smile.

"We prefer being your Fairy Godmothers, thank you very much," said Cyril.

She chuckled, then winced.

"You hurt somewhere, chère?" Ivanhoe asked.

"Only my heart." She looked at Ivanhoe Fauchon, who was her boss, landlord, and friend and said, "It's broken. Along with my pride. I feel like such an idiot."

"Someone as good-looking as that Roux was bound to do it," Cyril interjected, and then died under Ivanhoe's reprimanding gaze.

"It only took him twenty years," Ivanhoe offered sarcastically, as he began stroking Sassy's hair with the ornate brush he'd given her for Christmas five years ago. "You want to talk about it now or later?"

She turned her head away from them. The rain had ceased and the mocking moon laughed at her outside her French door. "Maybe later," she said without looking at him.

Ivanhoe dismissed Cyril from the room with his eyes and said, "All right. Whenever you're ready, chère. I'm here for you."

Ivanhoe put the brush down and patted her hand before he turned to leave. Sassy grabbed his soft, bejeweled fingers and he sat back down on the bed. She looked into his aging but still-handsome face and said, "I caught him getting a blow job in the hall at SASSY'S."

"Whaaa? Ugh. No class. Did you know the lowlife heffa?" he teased.

"Maxine Dupree. She was in grade school with us."

"Probably been after him ever since."

"Well, she got him tonight. Or rather, tonight's the first time I caught him—with his dick in her mouth."

"Sassy, let's not stoop to their level, please," Ivanhoe warned.

"They could have taken that lowlife crap upstairs to his apartment instead of the public, common hallway."

"Common people do common things, chère."

It was so unlike Sassy to curse, Ivanhoe thought. In all the years he'd known her, he could count on one hand the number of times she swore. She was far more upset than even she knew.

"Besides he wouldn't take that skank to his place, chère. I bet she or any other woman has never been up there. Even in his horny little mind, Roux wouldn't betray the sanctity of his apartment—you-all's—apartment with such vulgar shenanigans. This was just a quickie in the hall, nothing more."

"Don't defend him!" She rose up on her elbows. "Why would he even feel the need to do this if he truly loved me? One thousand women could parade butt-naked in front of him and he should love me enough to just-say-no!" She plopped back on the pillows. "The bastard!"

"Far be it from me to explain the psyche of the hetero male, but you know the man loves you, Sassy. For a lot of years."

"I don't understand that kind of 'love,' and I don't have to. Not anymore. He goes through these little breaches of faith every few years and I'm sick of it. I thought he'd stopped. But this was the last straw." She began to laugh. "Get it? The last straw—in her mouth."

Ivanhoe watched the laughter unsuccessfully mask her pain.

"I'm through with all of it, and him." Angry tears began to flow from her eyes and flowed like the River Niger for a few days.

Sassy awakened with a jolt. Her eyes opened in the two AM pitch-dark, then warmed to the familiar surroundings of her dark room. The ceiling fan spun quietly, catching and then converting the warm, humid air into a gentle breeze. The lunar rays spilled through the glass of the French doors. She turned on her side and slid her hands over the cool, empty sheets. Her open hand turned into a balled fist as the searing pain of being alone attacked her heart. She'd played by all the rules, done all the right things, and this was what she got in return? Her worst nightmare was reality, but after two days, she was out of tears. Her emotions had run rampant; she wanted to cut off his penis and send it to Maxine with a note: *Here, enjoy.* She wanted him to limp around with a nub for the rest of his life. She wanted to torch his club and watch it burn. She wanted to key his signature truck and take a Louisville Slugger baseball bat to both headlights. She hated him. She loved him. She was pissed at him, but more so, she was pissed at herself. For being so trusting. For being so stupid. "When people show you who they are, believe them," her daddy used to say. Roux was being Roux, and she was being naïve and stupid. Well, the naïve Sassy had to go, and a new, savvy Sassy had to take her place.

She swung her feet off the bed, set them on the chilled tile, and padded to the kitchen. She poured a glass of grapefruit juice and drank it slowly as she looked through the French doors that overlooked the iron-filigreed balcony onto Clemenceau Street. She eyed her answering machine, which Roux had filled with apologetic nonsense until she'd cut it off. In the funnel of the streetlight, she checked her caller ID to make sure Willowbrook Sanatorium hadn't called about her mother. Only Roux's number glared back at her.

Her eyes scanned her spacious, spartanly furnished apartment where, thanks to Ivanhoe, the rent was dirt-cheap and hadn't been raised in over five years. Between work and Roux's, she hardly spent any time here. Roux preferred being in air-conditioned comfort close to his club. He'd had her decorate his house and invited her to move in, but she'd always insisted on keeping her own place. She was glad she had. Now this was her only address.

She took another sip of the tart liquid as she surveyed its assets. The gallery-like kitchen had two doors, one that led to the living-room and dining area, and the other to her bedroom with the exposed brick walls and the bathroom with the porcelain, claw-footed tub. She did her exercises in that bathroom in front of the long French window and under the skylight, controlled by the pull chain. When she opened the French door of her living room and those of her bedroom, the twelve-foot ceilings captured any coolness and kept her house ten to twenty degrees cooler than the outside temperature. She didn't need air-conditioning, and she didn't need Roux.

Through the open doors, she spotted two lovers on Clemenceau returning after a night out, snuggling, and cooing, and going inside apparently to fall asleep wrapped in each other's arms. She let her bare feet lead her back to her bedroom and the ample window seat in front of her favorite view. The moon bathed the backyard in silver. The wisteria-wrapped cistern looked like a behemoth from a horror movie, and lush bougainvillea devoured the back wall. She watched fireflies blink gold as they flitted in midair and listened to crickets' and night frogs' mating calls. Tea olive and night jasmine perfumed the air as Sassy closed her eyes and placed the cool glass of juice between her breasts. It was going to be her only sensation for a while.

She tried not to think about him, but when she did, there was one thought: *Why?* That was her only question. Why? There was no answer.

She sipped her juice. She'd have to go back to a time when there was no Roux Robespierre.

She tried to remember the first time she'd ever seen him. Seemingly, he'd been there since day one. They were all poor in the Gert Town section, but Roux always had money to treat them to sodas and moon pies after school. He had given Sassy her nickname after the first time she skipped school. He'd been cutting school regularly and neither his mother nor Sister Superior knew where he went or why. Sassy saw beneath his masked joviality and one day asked him why he played hooky and where he went. He aimed his hypnotic hazel eyes at her. Stared at her—through her, and said, "No one ever asked me *why* before."

The next day he waited for her outside the fence and challenged her to come with him. Sassy's curiosity, and being on the verge of some tremendous revelation, caused her to throw caution to the wind, take the hand of Roux Robespierre, and skip school.

They'd caught the St. Charles Street trolley and ridden in silence to the Garden District, a section of town she'd never been to, but Roux knew exactly where he was going. Down the cobblestoned, tree-lined streets with magnificent houses on both sides, they walked as Roux silently introduced her to a whole new world.

Abruptly, he stopped across the street from the most impressive property on the block, leaned against a tall fence and eyed the huge, ornate house, bigger—one hundred times bigger—than the shotgun houses they lived in. Sassy asked him three times who lived there, but he never answered her. He just stared at the three-story stone house wrapped in black rod-iron fencing that contained a garden rivaling those she had only seen in magazines at her mother's beauty shop.

Five minutes later, a long, sleek limo left the covered portico and snaked down the curving driveway to the iron gates and stopped, as if challenging their being there. Sassy knew that not only were they skipping school, but they were somewhere they didn't belong.

Sassiere's heart beat nervously as she'd urged Roux to go, but he stood fast, calmly, claiming his right to be there. The car rounded the curve in front of them. The chauffeur ignored the pair, but the big-nosed boy in the backseat eyed them both—beady, cold black eyes darted from Roux, to Sassy, then back to Roux again, until he was out of view. It was spooky.

Roux picked up a rock and hurled it at the trunk of the car. He missed.

Sassy asked him who that was and he hissed, "Nobody," as he looked back at the house.

Sassy followed his gaze to an upstairs window and saw the curtain fall, as if someone had been watching them. She just knew the people in the house were going to call the police, and she pleaded with him to go. He wouldn't until she promised, right then and there, that she would *never* speak of this again. "Don't make me sorry I let you in," he had threatened.

They walked back to the trolley stop and, despite her attempts to talk to him, rode in silence until they reached the French Quarter. His demeanor changed and he asked her brightly, like they were on the school playground, what she wanted to do. He offered to buy her lunch. Sassy told him she didn't appreciate the way he'd treated her, asking her to come along, making her promise to never speak about it and then ignoring her. "I wrecked up my perfect attendance for this? And you think you can talk to me any old way and smooth it over by buying me lunch?" she'd fumed.

He was noticeably startled by her attitude. Girls never talked to him like that. "Well," Roux had said, "I didn't know you were so—Sassy. Sassy Sassiere."

She drained the last of her juice, and thought, that's how it all began. She was eleven years old when she skipped school for the first time. When she had her first "date" and first taste of freedom in the middle of the day in the French Quarter, and Roux gave her the name *Sassy*. Following Roux's lead, everyone began calling her Sassy, except her mother and the nuns, until after she graduated. There were a lot of firsts since then—all compliments of Roux Robespierre; the first man she ever loved—the first man to ever trash her heart. For no good reason. She was tired of trying to make sense out of nonsense. She couldn't afford to throw good time after bad.

Sassy got up and glanced at her reflection in the moon-drenched mirror. "Ugh!" She looked bad, felt bad, and smelled even worse. Stuck in the frame of the mirror was a picture of her and Roux at the Jazz and Heritage Festival. She plucked it from the frame and looked at their smiling images. "A big lie," she said and tore it up.

She then looked at the framed picture of Roux next to her bed. She popped him from the ornate metal and shredded it into colorful mosaics before tossing it in the trash. She repeated the exercise with pictures of him from the living-room étagère, then with the wicker-wrapped image of him in the bathroom. She let the paper sift through her fingers into the toilet bowl and flushed.

"Where you belong," she said.

She then proceeded to purge him from her house. With hands on hips, she stood profanely in the middle of the room looking for any renegade traces of him. Suddenly, the three carat diamond engagement ring grew heavy and began to burn her third finger left hand. She wrenched it off and went to toss it out back across the garden wall, but the reflection of the silver moon bounced off its brilliance.

"How much is this puppy worth?" she wondered aloud.

It would be cathartic to pitch it, but that was an emotional response. Over the last few days, Roux had stripped all the emotion from her, leaving only the practical. All her responses to Roux had been based on emotions, and what had it gotten her? This practical, savvy Sassy wasn't about to toss thirty thousand dollars over a garden wall. She could pay for her mother's care for a few months with this loot. She'd pawn it tomorrow.

Sassy looked around at her exorcized apartment, physically clean of all Roux remnants. She smiled as she remembered what her daddy used to say: "Things work out best for the folks who make the best of the way things work out."

She knew getting over Roux wasn't all going to be this easy, but this was a start. She was liking her Rouxless self. She was reclaiming her life and becoming a practical, independent woman who was taking responsibility for her own destiny. She'd never done that before. She never had to. There was always Roux telling her how to feel, what to think, and what to wear. Most of what she thought or felt about herself and others was through his lens.

She flopped back in bed and flipped her long braid over her shoulder. She scratched at her scalp furiously, and the braid just hung there. The weight became heavy, cloying, annoying, and suddenly she couldn't stand it. It was Roux who loved this albatross of dead hair. It was he who didn't want her to cut it, who liked to see it bounce and jump as she walked, or stream in the wind as he drove, or cascade over his body as they made love.

"Well, dammit, he can have it," she said, as she began to hunt for a pair of scissors. I'll lay it on top of his belongings and send it to him, she thought. Then she stopped.

"That's an emotional response, Sassy," she told herself. *Be practical,* she thought. *Let a professional do it. No reason for you to go around looking like a crazy lady just because you and Roux broke up.* "Wouldn't they just love that? To think that losing Roux made me lose my mind."

She smiled in the darkness. For the first time in her thirty-three years, she liked being the sole proprietor of her thoughts, feelings, and actions. "You go, girl," she self-validated, and fell back into her bed.

Sassy awoke later that morning, washed herself and her hair, and swallowed a bagel, boiled egg, and juice before she went to the pawnshop. She deposited the check for the ring on her way to her mother's old beauty shop. None of the stylists wanted to cut her hair, but finally a new operator agreed. Sassy gave her the name and number for Locks of Love, who made wigs for cancer patients, and Sassy sat in the chair.

Sassy watched the young, bird-faced girl hold the braid in one hand and begin to cut with the other. The sound of metal against hair silenced the entire shop. With every shearing cut, Sassy felt liberated. Free. With every rotation of the scissors, Sassy felt movement away from Roux and her old ways, into a new phase of being.

After the woman cut it a few inches all over, Sassy looked at her reflection in the beauty-shop mirror and smiled. She grinned, tipped the stylist generously, and wore an irrepressible smile as she did her last errand before sauntering into Rare Finds.

"Well, well, well," Cyril said as Sassy entered the shop. "Ivanhoe, come look see our new and improved protégée."

"You like?" Sassy asked as she twirled around, sporting her new short do.

"Oh, Sassy! Say it isn't so," Ivanhoe protested as he covered his heart in shock and then fell dramatically over the counter. "You cut all that gorgeous, luxurious hair. How could you!"

"Straight or gay, what is it about black men and hair? I needed a new, less dated look. Something easy to care for. I can't fool with all that hair while I'm on the road."

"Road?" Ivanhoe tested.

"You've been after me for years to do estate-sale buys. Well, I'm ready. I have no reason to stay close by now. Estate sales, transport buys, appraisals, even coordinating out-of-state auctions. You said I'd be good at it." She rounded the corner and riffled through the stack of mail. "You were right about me teaching the course at Tulane. You pushed me into that guest lecturer series, and now I'm teaching my own art history course twice a week and going for my master's degree. I have you to thank for that."

"I am brilliant, aren't I?" Ivanhoe agreed, then continued, "But are you sure, chère?"

"I am. I'm ready to explore what the world has to offer me."

"Ah, and the men . . ."

"One project at a time. It'll be a *great* while before I'm ready for another relationship. I'm gonna work on me first."

"He's gonna be a doozy when he comes, chère. You've only known one man in your *entire* thirty-plus years."

"Thanks for pointing that out," she said, drolly. "And you call yourself friend?" She went in the back to lock up her purse, and he followed. "One thing for sure," she continued. "I'm going to be in total control next time."

"With thoughts like that, there may not be a next time, *chère.*"

"Then so be it. But speaking of control and freedom," Sassy said, no longer able to contain her excitement. "Come here." She crooked her finger, led them to the front window, and pointed.

"What?" Ivanhoe looked up and down the street.

"What parked out there looks like me?"

"A car? You got your own car? That red convertible Cabriolet," Ivanhoe identified.

"Yep. An Audi. It's used, but it's new to me."

"Get out!!"

"Now I can come and go when *I* please."

They both laughed and danced around the fact that Roux didn't like foreign cars, didn't like red cars, and didn't like convertibles. But Sassy did.

"I'm scared of you, chère." They slapped five. "My baby's growing up," he teased and dabbed at fake tears as Sassy flounced to the back and picked up a stack of inventory slips. "You have been *tres* busy this morning, chère."

The shop bell tinkled.

"*Bonjour,* madame," Cyril gushed and sashayed over to one of their best customers.

The bell tinkled again, and Ivanhoe went out on the floor.

He returned to Sassy moments later. "Showtime," Ivanhoe said.

Sassy looked up at him.

"I'm afraid with Killer not here in our stockade, I have less control," he sighed. "Roux's here."

"What?" She'd told him on the phone she did not want to see him.

"I can call the cops if you like," Ivanhoe said.

Sassy grimaced, breathed deeply, straightened her back, and said, "No. I didn't do anything wrong."

This was the hard part, she thought. *Seeing* him. It was one thing to make resolutions at three AM alone in the dark with Ben and Jerry's for backup, but quite another to come face to face with the gorgeous dog in the flesh. She parted the tapestry curtain and walked to face the man she'd loved, unconditionally, all her life.

She watched his jaw drop at the sight of her short hair as she greeted the customer, "*Bonjour,* madame."

"Ah, Sassy. Your hair is cut off," the madame noticed in her clipped French accent. "I like it. It is indeed 'sassy'."

"Thank you," she said as she pulled at the natural curls, trying to get them to reach her neck. "Roux," she acknowledged, fighting the intensity of his hazel-eyed gaze.

"You cut your hair off."

"I think that's been established. Why are you here?" As he raked his hands through his brunette curls, Sassy realized that now they both had about the same amount of hair on their heads.

"Can we go somewhere and talk?" Roux asked.

"No, we cannot. I am working, and I told you there is nothing to say."

"Sassy. We need to talk," he said in a hushed tone.

"There is nothing to talk about, Roux. You did all the talking you ever needed to do three nights ago. I finally heard you loud and clear. You are not ready and will never be ready to be a one-woman man. It is not in your nature. I accept that. You made your choice and I've made mine."

"Bravo," he said. "That's quite a little speech. How long did you rehearse that?"

"You arrogant *bastard*—"

She hadn't meant to say the one word she knew would set him off. But he had hurt her, and maybe, unconsciously, she wanted to hurt him back.

Roux stared at her, tensing and releasing his jaw as hurt welled up in his eyes.

"I'm going to let that slide," he finally said.

"How very white of you."

His eyebrows knitted in confusion, his hazel eyes relaxed, and he asked, "Sassy, what are we doing?" He stepped towards her and she stepped back. "Can't we just talk this out?"

"There is *nothing* I have to say, Roux. And there is *nothing* you can say to justify your actions three nights ago. It is *over* between you and me. I wish you and whomever all the best. I mean that sincerely—but it won't be me. Not now. Not ever again."

"You are the only woman I have ever loved. That I can ever love."

"Then you should have taken better care." Her nose began to burn and she fought the tears which brimmed in her eyes but, defiantly, did not fall.

The shop bell tinkled, and the lunchtime crowd spilled into the well-adorned shop.

"Excuse me. I have customers."

"What about your mother?" He asked her retreating back.

She turned to him without coming closer. "She is *my* mother. I will take care of her."

"How?" he asked.

She ignored him.

Roux stood there for a while and watched Sassy conduct her business. She'd never been so cold before. She was enchanting to her customers, who complimented her on her lack of hair. He watched her explain the attributes of a Ruby Flash Berry set; the long elegant fingers that used to stroke his body to perfection glided over the red rim of the bowl. Another customer asked about an Etruscan vase; her hands slid up and down the vase, two fingers disappearing into the dark cavity, and all he could do was think about how much he missed her touch. Then he noticed. Her ring was gone.

"Sassy, where is your ring?" he interrupted her with a customer.

"Excuse me. I am working," she said tightly.

"I want to know what you did—" he challenged her and then stopped when he realized all eyes were upon him. He was loud, losing his cool and blowing his suave image.

Sassy cut her eyes and returned to explaining the artifact to her customer.

Roux stayed in place but couldn't stop looking at her. She'd taken off her ring. He couldn't stop thinking of how badly he had really messed up this time. But she'd come around, he reassured himself. She had before, and this time wasn't as bad—at least not to him. He couldn't live without Sassy; she'd been a part of him since he was twelve years old. He could never trust a woman like he trusted Sassy. *Yeah, she'll come around after she calms down,* he thought. She had to. She couldn't afford not to. This little job and teaching her one course at the university couldn't hold a candle to his money, couldn't even pay for her Maman's stay at Willowbrook. He'd give her time to realize what she was giving up—maybe by then her hair would grow back and everything would be as it should.

"Ah-hem." Roux heard over his shoulder and turned to see Ivanhoe glaring at him.

Punk, Roux thought, but flashed his award-winning Robespierre smile and made his way to the front door onto Royal Street. "See you, Sassy. We'll talk later."

She rolled her eyes at him like he was a smelly stranger harassing her for her last dollar, brilliantly hiding the searing pain. She bit back tears because it hurt when you'd given your all, plus a big chunk of your soul, and it still wasn't enough to keep him faithful. There was no hurt like the hurt when your best wasn't good enough.

Chapter II

"Which do you think would be worth more?" Sassy asked her class of the two Aleutian ceremonial masks on the overhead gel. "The mask made of wood, or the one made of bone?"

"Bone!" the class unequivocally agreed.

"Wrong!" she answered playfully before continuing. "The wooden one is very rare and, to a collector of Eskimo art, could be worth between eight thousand to twelve thousand dollars, while the one of bone was done in the 1930s for tourist souvenirs. It's worth about three hundred." She cut off the projector. "Now, what does that tell us?"

"Things aren't always what they seem!" a student offered.

"Bingo! You get an 'A.' You-all think of this last lesson as you navigate your weekend. Class dismissed." She turned to erase the board. "Don't forget. Exam next week!"

She answered the queries of a few students before locking her slides in the classroom closet and gathering up her briefcase. She sauntered down the hallowed halls of education denied her in her youth and marveled at the clichéd truth—it's never too late. A newly minted thirty-three-year-old finally finishing up her master's degree, teaching as an "expert" in her field, and it all felt so good. So right. So timely. She probably had the look of an accomplished, astute woman of the world, but just as her class had surmised, things aren't always as they seem.

"Have a nice weekend!" the dean said, breaking her train of thought.

"Thanks. You too," she replied to him as she walked from the cool halls of Tulane into the cloying, thick air and sunshine.

Sassy inhaled deeply before traipsing down the brick path towards her red Cabriolet chariot, the symbol of her new freedom and independence. She smiled from the inside out.

Suddenly, her vision was blocked by a man approaching her from the other end of the long walkway. His gait and the distant look of him seemed remotely familiar, but as he got closer, she realized she had never seen him before. His clothes hung on his body as if they were specially tailored to showcase his powerful shoulders and toned physique. He walked with cool, confident ease but with every step he took towards her, she grew more uncomfortable. His eyes held hers with a disturbing intentness that never faltered, yet it felt as if they roamed all over her body with a familiar intimacy. Did she know him? Did he know her? She broke her gaze after noting his neat natural that framed a cleanshaven, café au lait face with high cheekbones, a strong jawline and lips . . . which parted to say, "Good afternoon," as he passed her.

Sassy opened her mouth but nothing came out. She felt a strange calm envelop her at the nearness of him, quickly replaced by yet another jolt as their shoulders were inches from one another. Her senses were working overtime trying to keep up with the energy emitted from this stranger.

When she reached her car she looked back and saw the man being welcomed by the dean. As her heart restored itself to a natural rhythm, the dean and the man turned to enter the building, but she saw the man give a backward glance to see if she was looking at him. Sassy dove into her car and sat there for a while, trying to compose herself. What the heck was that? She wondered, and made a mental note to ask the dean who the man was.

Aidan could barely keep his mind on his meeting with the dean and the Board. What an unexpected treasure it was to see her. When on campus for varying reasons, he used to walk by her classroom, where her students seemed to be as enthralled by her as he was. He was only supposed to be there for a few minutes, but he found himself staying until the end of her class. He'd watch her leave and walk to Roux's signature black Range Rover's open door; he had her on a short leash. It was hard to watch the woman you loved and thought deserved better walk to and drive off with someone else. But now, Sassy had her own car and, it seemed, the freedom to come and go.

The dean asked him a question, which Aidan answered, and his thoughts immediately defaulted to Sassy again. He hadn't been so close to her since he'd held her in the limo and taken her home. She was unconscious then, but today when she aimed those deep chocolate eyes at him he wanted to grab and kiss her. He longed to tell her, "I've loved you all my life. Let me show you how much. I'd never hurt you. I'd treat you like the exquisite woman you are." He had to settle for, "Good afternoon," but his mind was already gearing up for a campaign to say, "I do" later. Aidan knew he had to move swiftly before she forgave Roux and went back to him or before other guys got wind that finally, Sassy Crillon was a free agent. Sassy couldn't possibly know all he had in store for her— for them.

It was only the second time he'd ever remembered gazing *into* her eyes. The first time was at the Jazz and Heritage Festival when she was about fifteen. She'd dropped her purse. They had both picked it up simultaneously—more his grip than hers. He released his hold. She smiled and hurriedly said, "Thank you," as she ran to catch up with her girlfriends. He stood and watched her ponytail flip over that little freckle on the back of her neck until she and her friends disappeared into the crowd. He savored that first meeting and the "thank you," born of good manners rather than genuine gratitude. Now he had the opportunity to change that. He wanted to make her happy—ecstatic, so she'd thank him for the rest of their lives. She was like the rare antiquities sold at Rare Finds. A buyer can want an *object d'art* badly, but until it becomes available, there's nothing you can do but admire it from afar. But now, Sassy was, and he wanted her now more than ever.

Aidan was anxious to leave the meeting and automatically began massaging his ring finger with his thumb. It was his habit to spin his great-grandfather's heirloom ring with his thumb when deep in thought, be it a business deal or boredom. He hadn't missed it right away. After he'd taken Sassy home, he was far too excited to really notice it was gone until after the opera when Michelle Micheaux wanted to keep the night going to its usual conclusion; he had needs but no appetite for anyone but Sassy. The ring wasn't there for him to spin.

He'd looked in the limo, on his valet and armoire at home, near his shower by the weight bench—all the usual places—but the heirloom signet ring was missing. He could always commission a jeweler to make a replica, but the prospect of winning Sassy outweighed his concern for the ring. If the gods deemed that he had to lose the ring to gain Sassy—so be it. He would be willing to give up even more to win her love. He'd had material riches all his life, but without someone special to share them with—without Sassy—he considered himself poor. Having her in his life would make him rich beyond his wildest imaginings.

The man's effect on her played about the fringes of Sassy's mind as she went home to pack a few things before setting out again. The weekends without Roux proved to be the hardest. Unless it was Mardi Gras, the Jazz and Heritage Festival, or some other Big Easy do, the weekend had been their time. They'd visit Maman at Willowbrook or be off to Thibodaux, Roux's favorite haunt along the Bayou Lafourche, where they'd lounge during the day, party all night, make love, sleep, and start all over again. Doing without his loving was a hard adjustment. The way he used to run his eyes over her body, followed by his hands where his eyes had been. He would tickle, taunt, and titillate her to orgasm with just a look and the promise of more. He was that good. She wondered, how do you live without what you can't live with?

"Stop!" Sassy said aloud. "Just stop it." She broke her train of thought, just as she'd heard some self-help guru proclaim was the best way to get over a man.

Sassy fed Killer and let him out to romp in the courtyard before she took off. She pointed her car towards

Lake Charles, leaving the city, all her troubles, and the mysterious man behind her in the rearview mirror. Cooler air circulated around her and through her, infusing her with a sense of relaxation and adventure. The sun kissed her cheeks and the wind tousled her hair as she sang "Little Red Corvette" along with Prince. Rubber ate up asphalt as she sped through the countryside, slowing as she wound her way onto the two-lane highways. She stopped at a colorful roadside stall because she could; Roux never wanted to stop, he always wanted to race straight through. She bought fresh, sweet peaches, vine-ripened tomatoes, an almost-ripe cantaloupe for Ivanhoe, juicy Bing cherries, and a bouquet of sunflowers, her Maman's second favorite flower, after gardenias. A few miles further, she gassed up at a filling station and relished putting in her *own* gas into her *own* tank and the attention of the three guys. She rubbed her exposed neck. Had she always drawn attention? Or was it her short haircut, sporty new car, and no Roux around? Absently, she wondered what kind of car the mystery man drove. Something sleek and cool like he was, she concluded. Sassy smiled, liking that she could think about any man she wanted without feeling like she was being disrespectful to Roux.

Four and a half hours later, she turned through the stately gates of Willowbrook, a former plantation mansion, which had the look of a country club instead of the sanitorium it was. Despite its pristine-white brick, antiseptic cleanliness, and perfectly appointed rooms, it was still an expensive gilded cage. As she parked and walked toward the columned verandah, Sassy took little comfort knowing it was the best place money could buy in all of Louisiana.

Sassy stood at one wide white column looking down

into the green knoll which surrounded the lake. Forlorn patrons dotted the grassy carpet, waiting for their loved ones to visit and let them know they had not been forgotten. She wondered how much time she had left with her mother. Maman's body was shutting down. The lupus, complicated by heart disease, diabetes and recent kidney failure, was taking its toll daily on her flesh and spirit. Her mother had been such an active, vibrant woman, who kept the family together with mother-wit and her beauty parlor after her father died. It was hard for Sassy to watch the slow decay and degeneration of the Maman she once knew.

"Hello, Maman," Sassy greeted from behind. With a kiss to the cheek, she presented the bouquet of sunflowers.

"Sassiere," her mother said, never liking nicknames. Her own name was Alouette and she never answered when her own friends used to call her "Ally."

"Aw, thank you." She tried holding the bouquet in her frail, gnarled hands.

"How are you today, Maman?" Sassy asked as a nurse whisked the flowers away.

"Fair to middlin', chou-chou. And you?" She looked up at her daughter. "You cut all your hair off?"

Sassy reached up and pulled at the curls near her neck. "Yep. You like it?" she asked, already knowing the answer.

"No, I don't. Folks trying to grow hair, buying hair, wearing other peoples' hair, and you cut yours off. I saw a no-haired girl get out of a red car. Was that you? Whose car is that?"

"Mine. It's something isn't it? I bought it this week. I always wanted a red convertible." Sassy often asked and answered questions, supplying additional information so as not to over-tax her mother.

"You drove here all by yourself? Where's Roux?"

The question just hung there.

Sassy had known it would come up, she just hadn't decided how she was going to answer it. "He's working, Maman," she said and glanced beyond the lake to the bayou, grateful when the nurse returned with the sunflowers in a vase. "Thank you," she said to the nurse.

"Do you want another blanket, Madame Crillon?"

"No. I'm fine," Maman said, waiting for the nurse to leave. "So, new haircut, new car, no Roux. What's else is 'new' in your life, chou-chou?"

Sassy looked into her mother's knowing eyes, then looked away.

"My body may be rotting away but my mind still works."

"I know, Maman." She sighed deeply and said, "Roux and I broke up."

"Is it bad?"

"Yeah, it was bad, Maman. As bad as you can get."

"No. You still alive and healthy. So it could be a lot worse. Take it from someone who knows the value of health." She stopped before she continued, "And Roux . . . well. He's a complicated man. A victim of his own gorgeousness and inability to 'just say no.'"

"Yet another making excuses for Roux," she snapped. "Whose side are you on? I'm your daughter. When I say it's bad and it's over—then it's bad and it's over, just take my word for it." Her mother fell silent.

Sassy felt badly but she couldn't say she was sorry. Her mother and father had always loved Roux too much. Anyone would have thought he was their son, placed in between her and her older sister, CoCo, and Sassy was the interloper. Her father had always called Roux the son he never had, and relished adding, "That Roux is no pansy. He's all man. A man's man." Sassy knew women who'd look the other way for the ten percent of the time their man was unfaithful, knowing that he'd be theirs ninety percent of the time. But Sassy wanted a hundred percent man—or no man. She was selfish that way.

"Some time you want too much, chou-chou," Maman said, as if reading her daughter's mind. "So some time you're going to be alone,"

"That's fine, Maman. Some time or all the time I'll be alone. At least I can look at myself in the mirror with some pride and dignity." She rubbed the back of her neck. "I can't be miserable just to make a man happy," she said sotto voce, then continued, "Just don't expect to see me and Roux back together. What he's done *this* time is beyond understanding. That's the end of it."

"It happened during the Cajun moon, didn't it?"

"I don't know," she lied.

Sassy only saw her mother once every other weekend, and she didn't want to argue because she didn't know which of these visits with her would be their last. She didn't want to discuss voodoo-hoodoo and she didn't want to discuss men—any man. Not Roux and not her daddy, who Sassy thought hung the moon. She loved her daddy, but he was one of those ninety percent men, which apparently he and her mother worked through. But Sassy didn't want her children getting the best of the man she married.

"I just don't want you to end up alone like me," Maman said, breaking the silence.

"What am I, Maman? Chopped liver?" she hissed.

"You're my daughter," Maman identified. "But you don't even have one of those."

Sassy took a deep breathe and released it slowly. "I'll be all right, Maman. Now. Let me brush your hair. Would you like that?"

Sassy undid the knot of black-and-white hair her

mother used to sit on in her younger days and began to brush it gently. Thankfully, the string quartet began to play under the sweeping fronds of the big willow tree as nurses flitted to groups of visiting relatives bearing trays laden with tea and canapés.

"Hors d'oeuvre, Madame Crillon?" the nurse offered.

Maman looked at the putrid, pale sandwiches and said, "Ugh!" She waved the nurse away and remarked, "What I wouldn't give for a pig foot and a bottle of beer."

Sassy laughed. "The song or the food, Maman?"

Mother and daughter engaged in surface banter until the setting sun and a slight evening chill graced the bayou air, signaling that it was time for the patrons to go inside.

"I got to get going, Maman. You need anything?"

"Just for you to find some happiness, chou-chou."

"I'm working on it, Maman."

"I know you think I'm hard on you, chou-chou. It's just that I thought I'd have you all married and settled down before I died—"

"I'm a grown woman," Sassy said as gently as possible, thinking that she too had thought her life was settled. "You and daddy did a good job. I can take care of myself." Sassy wrapped the blanket around her mother's lap so it wouldn't get caught in the spokes of the wheelchair, and she began to roll Maman to the verandah.

As they waited for a nurse to come and retrieve her, Maman asked, "What you going to do now?"

"Well, I'm going to get into *my* car, get something to eat—"

"By yourself?"

"Should I starve because I am 'by myself?'" When her mother didn't answer she continued, "Then I'm going to drive back to the Lidoyen Inn between Indian Bayou and Evangeline to attend an estate sale tomorrow morning."

Maman grunted her disapproval.

The nurse came over, and Sassy bent down to kiss her mother good-bye. She looked into rheumy, coal-black eyes and said, "I'll be all right, Maman. Please don't worry about me. You just concentrate on getting well. I love you."

"Humm. Love you too," Maman managed as the nurse turned the chair and the wheels bumped along the bricks of the south portico before disappearing through the two-story French doors.

Sassy did as she had told her mother. She stopped and ate before signing the register at the Lidoyen Inn. She looked at her lonely, singular name in black ink staring back at her, mocking her: *S. Crillon.*

"Is this all, *Miss*?" the bellman asked.

"Yes," she said, turning from him to the jubilant faces of loving couples who didn't even know she existed. She used to be one of those happy, self-absorbed couples, she thought.

"You here for the big Winthrop sale tomorrow?" the bellman asked as the tiny elevator groaned to the third floor.

"Yes." She followed him to room Number Twelve at the back, which overlooked a pond. She looked out of the window where more couples walked hand in hand, nuzzling and cuddling.

"Ah-hem," the bellman cleared his throat.

Sassy realized that he was waiting for a tip, which she offered. "Here you are. Thank you." She hoped it was enough. Roux took care of all driving, carrying the bags, paying for the meals, rooms, tips, gas—everything. Being alone was new territory for her. Sassy showered alone when she was used to company. She toweled off alone when she was used to help. She lotioned herself alone when she was used to a massage, which led to lovemaking before they ordered room service and made love again before falling asleep.

"Stop!" Sassy said aloud and plopped at the vanity facing the mirror, wondering who this short-haired, alone woman was. Did she know her? Did she even like her?

She walked to the night stand, picked up the remote and began surfing the channels . . . *In the Heat of the Night, Matlock, Andy Griffith.* With each click she felt farther and farther away from home—from the comfortable and familiar things she knew and loved—from herself. God, she missed him. God, she hated him. Heaven help her, she loved him. Would part of her always love him? Would he always pop into her thoughts? Would she always compare every man she met to Roux?

She clenched her teeth and pursed her lips, fighting the urge to cry, but despite her best efforts her nose burned and tears slid down her cheeks. He was there waiting for her—all she had to do was go to him, and he'd be glad to take her back. Their reunion would be wonderfully perfect—erotically satisfying, until the next time he messed up. *But maybe this time he's learned his lesson,* she thought. For the first time in his life, Roux Robespierre was scared. She could see it in his clear eyes, hear it in the timbre of his voice. Maybe he could be faithful for keeps this time. Maybe his doggin' days were over.

The savvy Sassy clicked the remote off and watched black claim the TV screen. She was finished with "maybes." She still couldn't be sure of him—of them. She was sure of herself, what she wanted and what she didn't want. She was the only one she could count on now. She breathed in and out three times. Deep down in the quiet, practical core of her, she knew—as sure as the sun would rise in the east and set in the west—he was going to mess up again. Not today or tomorrow or even the next two years, but it was coming. It was his nature.

"Hurt me once, shame on you. Hurt me twice, shame on me," she recited—one of her daddy's sayings. "And three times is just plain retarded," she self-admonished.

She blew her nose and went to turn down the bed. She looked at the naked third finger on her left hand. Had she ever expected to see it bare again? Well, life goes on. And so would she. No matter how hard or how lonely, she'd rather live without him than with him and his occasional women. She had that right. She had that choice. And choose she did.

She whipped back the comforter, and two chocolate mints stared at her from the pillows. She laughed sadly, then said, "More for me." She unwrapped and popped one, then the other into her mouth. "It takes a damn good man to beat having no man at all," her daddy's words danced in her consciousness and, only at that very moment, did she truly feel for the first time: "I'm gonna be all right."

Once at home, Sassy handed Ivanhoe his cantaloupe, and he handed her tickets. Sassy opened the envelope and read, "San Francisco? For me? I've never been to San Francisco. I've never been on a plane before!"

"Hummm. No thanks to you-know-who. Well chère, Fairy Godmother has plans for my little black Cinderella."

"Oh, Ivanhoe!"

"Upstairs on your bed, I took the liberty of getting you a few things, 'cause you've never been anywhere and it can get nippy there. Go pack."

"Oh, thank you, thank you, thank you!" She hugged him and ran up the stairs.

"It's no ball gown," he called up after her. "But I know you've been eyeing it for some time. Enjoy!"

Sassy grabbed up the designer pants suit she'd been looking at for weeks and spun around in a complete turn. Not only was it too pricey for her income, but Roux hated her in pants. He liked her to show off her legs, especially in shorts, and he had no use for her in jeans or slacks. But now Sassy could wear what the hell she pleased with no comments from the peanut gallery.

"Thank you, Ivanhoe!" she yelled downstairs.

Ivanhoe let a self-satisfied grin claim his knowing face.

Sassy had just the sandals to match this outfit. She lay flat on her stomach and let her hands pull them out from under her bed, and she touched something curious. She pulled at the object then opened her hand.

There in her palm was one of the most exquisite signet rings she had ever seen. A diamond "S" on a bed of rubies inlayed in eighteen-, maybe twenty-four-carat gold. Her trained eye concluded that its workmanship and setting placed it circa 1850s to 1880s. What was this artifact doing under her bed and how long had it been there? She always liked to hold treasures like this and imagine their history, but right now, besides having an "S" for Sassy, this old ring could not compete with the new adventure of going to San Francisco. She was the luckiest girl on the planet.

Early the next morning, in her designer ecru pantsuit, Sassy glided through the airport following the skycap with her luggage to the gate.

"This is sooo exciting," Sassy enthused.

"Don't act like the N'awlins hick you are, chère," Ivanhoe teased. "Act like you're *born* to it."

"To the Manor Born." Sassy obeyed matching his aloof
air as she genteelly threaded her arm through his.

"'All the world's a stage', chère," Ivanhoe quoted Shake-
speare. "Work it."

He exchanged their tickets for a "Have a nice flight"
from the stewardess.

Sassy maintained her aloofness until they were ensconced in first class and the seatbelts were clicked
around their respective waists. She looked out the
window and her stomach lurched with delightful butter-
flies as they taxied and took off. She felt like she was
flying free and easy. She looked down and saw New Orleans being reduced to doll-sized buildings.

"You like?" Ivanhoe asked her.

"It's amazing. The clouds look like cotton candy." She
turned to him and said, "Thanks, Ivanhoe."

"Psh! We have to transport that rare Etruscan urn."

"Not both of us. I really appreciate it. My first flight
ever, and in first class to boot."

"Well, you deserve it. Po' thing, never been out of
N'awlins."

"I've been to Thibodaux and Willowbrook, remember?"

"Oh, excuse me. Never been out of Louisiana," he
qualified. They were interrupted by the flight attendant
who wanted their drink choices and gave them menus.

"It's been a rough few weeks," Sassy admitted.

"It's probably gonna get rougher before it gets better,
chère. But you'll be all right as long as you don't see the
handsome devil."

"See him or no, I'm through. I can't—I won't go
backwards."

"That's the spirit, chère. I bet Yvette had a natural
born hissy-fit."

"She doesn't know."

"How can your best friend since dirt not know? What do you-all talk about during your weekly chit-chats?"

"The baby. She's so excited and I don't want to rain on her parade. When she asks about Roux I say he's fine and ask a baby question and she's off explaining plans and process. She wants Roux and I to be godparents."

"Well, of course she does. She's been looking forward to being your maid of honor since she nominated you two as the 'Perfect Couple' at Theodore Roosevelt High School senior year. You-all won too, so she wasn't the only one who thought so."

"What a laugh."

"It was true for a lot of years, chère."

"Was it?" Sassy shot him a sad-eyed glance. "But that was then and this is now. It's just that—" She hesitated, not wanting to whine.

"Talk to me. Spill your guts. Like spoiled crawfish étouffée, it's best to get it out of your system, chère. It's a long flight, and first class is hermetically sealed. No one can hear us," he whispered conspiratorially. "And even if they could, who gives a flying fig."

Sassy chuckled, then fell silent. Absently, she massaged her left-hand third finger and thought she'd get a ring guard and wear her newfound signet ring in its place.

The drone of the plane filled the cabin.

"Okay. I'll start," Ivanhoe forged ahead. "Roux was your first love. Your first everything, you two have a lot of history and your lives are all intertwined so you don't know where you begin and he ends. You're not sure whether it's love or just habit, chère. N'est-ce pas?"

Sassy shook her head.

He sighed, chuckled, fell silent, then said absently, "With the affaires de coeur, there's always a certain amount of fear and comfortableness that makes you stay when you know it's time to go." He looked wistfully, unseeingly, past her out the window.

Sassy figured he was no longer just talking about her and asked, "You've felt this way?"

"Plenty of times," he scoffed it off. "You think the first time you fall in love that no one has ever felt like this before. That you'll never be able to take another breath without him. Can't stand to see another sunrise without him. You'd rather die than live without him, but you're too chicken to take the drugs you've been saving up for weeks. And blowing your brains with the handgun you keep in your nightstand drawer would leave an ugly corpse." He chuckled wryly, then mused, "Other people come and go in and out of your life, but they're never quite like *him.*"

Silence claimed him again.

"How long ago was it for you?"

"Eons. Eternity. Another millennium, *chère.* "

"You still think of him?"

"Can't help it. He gave me my shop. I was so young when I met him. I worked for him. He was an older, very wealthy, married-with-children gentleman. I was four-teen when my sanctified mother put me out of that tired, little shotgun house 'cause I was more woman then she was. I was seventeen when I found him. My world didn't start rotating till I heard his voice each morning."

"He took advantage of you?"

"Quite the opposite, chère. I knew who and what I was since I was five." He smiled at her mischievously, and said, "But he didn't. Oh, Lord, he was sooo straight and narrow, very macho. But one day I handed him a plank of wood—our eyes met and Lawd—that was the best ever!"

"Scandalous!" Sassy enthused.

"Oooh, it was." He stopped and removed nonexistent

lint from his cashmere sweater. "I learned all sorts of things from him—quality in clothing, appreciation for all music, antiques, good food, fine wine—I taught him a thing or two too. But—"

"What happened? His wife found out?"

"I haven't told you this story have I?"

"You've probably never told this story."

"You're right about that, chère. I've never uttered a mumbling word." He sighed and folded his manicured hands in his lap. "It was ugly, too. She walked in on us in the workshop. We were just a-going at it, and we looked over and she was standing there in the doorway, watching us. Mouth open, like we were TV or something. I guess it was pretty hard to take if you didn't know your husband swung both ways. Hell, he didn't know himself until he met me. She didn't scream or anything. She just closed the door and left."

Ivanhoe became absorbed in his own scene.

Sassy waited.

"I had quarters over the carriage house," he continued. "And I heard all this shouting and ruckus coming from the main house. The next day, the wife and the little boy went on a trip to Paris. I was to be gone when they returned. So he set me up with the man at The Antique Shoppe."

"He passed you around like that?"

"No. The shop owner wasn't gay, just a sweet old man in need of help and company. I lived over the shop—you know, where the upstairs storeroom is now. I still saw 'My Love' every chance he got. But the wife knew, the way she would know if I were a woman messing around with her man. She moved out of his bedroom, which just meant more for me." Ivanhoe stopped again and massaged his fingers. "We tried to stop for his son's sake—"

"His son knew?"

"Never did. In fact to this day I don't think anybody knows but me, the wife, and now you."

"Is he still living?"

"No, died years ago. But one Christmas, after the owner of the shop retired and moved across the river to Algiers, 'My Love' gave me that shop, free and clear, as a present. I became my own boss at twenty-five. Not bad for a Gert Town queer whose family disowned him at fourteen, huh? 'My Love's' only stipulation was to name it Rare Finds because that's what I was to him. His rare find. What a world, huh, chère?" He stopped speaking, then added, "When we made love he always whispered '*Ne me quitte pas, ne me quitte pas.*'"

"'Do not leave me,'" Sassy translated. "How romantic."

"Well, it got kinda *Backstreet-ish* when he asked me to look out for his sons. Just to watch over them."

"Have you?"

"From a distance. They don't know me, and I don't want to know them. But I know who and where they are, and they're okay. They wouldn't need a thing from me; they were already filthy, funky rich. But it's nice to see a bit of 'My Love' still walking around N'awlins."

"Who are they?"

"You know better," he dismissed.

"Yeah, I do. That's one thing about you, Ivanhoe. You are a man to be trusted. I'm glad you're my friend, confidant, and Fairy Godmother," she said, resting her head on his shoulder.

"If I could make the hurt go away for you, chère, I would."

"I know. Time is all I need."

"And a new man."

"No way. I can't imagine starting up a relationship now. The baggage I have."

"You may just find a porter, chère," he quipped, then continued, "Then, take it from there. Who's this Prince Charming who brought you home that night you fainted?"

"Cyril and friends are trippin'. I don't know about any man in a limo bringing me home."

"How'd you get there?"

"I dunno. Just like I don't know what your houseguests were drinking or smokin' that night either. He was probably just a Rasta in a cab, but you know how prone they are to exaggerating."

The stewardess lay their covered meals on the linen tableclothes, and Sassy raised her head from his shoulder and remarked, "Real silverware." Ivanhoe just smiled as she bit into the sole meunière and said, "It's good. But not as good as yours, of course."

"Of course not," he said, in perfect Bette Davis-ese. "Little is."

Ivanhoe sipped a flute of champagne, and wondered who this mysterious man was who brought her home. There are only a few black men in N'awlins who fit the description that Cyril pegged for Sassy's Knight in Shining Armor. One stood out, but his height, complexion and the car were all wrong. Ivanhoe didn't want to think about any of it now—it was all too Biblical. He had his designs set on partying in San Francisco where he'd ruled the Castro District for two decades. When he put the "Ho" in Ivanhoe!

"Hooooe!" Ivanhoe's entourage yelled the way they used to greet their old friend back in the day. "I said, Hoe!

Hoe!" The sound echoed and bounced off the cavernous
airport walls. Ivanhoe introduced Sassy to his friends and
shooed them off to get the car. As they left they chanted,
"Hoe is here, hoe is here!"

"Got a little fan club going, huh?" Sassy said.

"What can I say? I got it like that," Ivanhoe said, trying
to sound young and hip.

Sassy laughed as they descended the escalator.

They retrieved their bags and, while waiting for the
car to circle, Ivanhoe asked again, "You sure you don't
want to stay with us?"

"And miss a chance to stay at the Fairmont? No way. I
can take you-all two, three at a time, but a whole tribe
of you is too taxing for a hetero girl. Draining—like
being in the beauty parlor all day long."

"You better be glad I'm not the sensitive sort. But you
will go to the gallery opening tonight and on the cruise
tomorrow?"

"Let's take it one day at a time. I'll go to the gallery
tonight, but we only have two full days, and I don't want
to waste it on a boat in the bay with gays."

"You are sassy today, Miss Thang."

"You've been here a million and one times. This is my
first, I want to do the touristy things. It's an adventure.
Why don't *you* go with me?" she teased and watched
mock-horror strike his eyes.

"Do San Fran with a straight girl? Puleeze. Now that
is pathetic."

"So we understand each other."

The car pulled up, Sassy and Ivanhoe rode to a friend's
house for late lunch and early drama before they dropped
Sassy off at the Fairmont.

"We'll come back and pick you up at six," Ivanhoe told
her from the car's open window.

"Okay, Mom," Sassy said, as he tweaked her nose playfully before the bellman came to get her bag.

Sassy followed the man to the desk where she registered, claimed her key and followed him upstairs with her one bag. He opened the door showed her the amenities while she went to the window and looked at the San Francisco skyline. The hilly terrain with the houses propped up was as breathtaking as the expanse of the clear blue sky. She smiled, then tipped him.

"Thank you. Enjoy your stay," he said, touching the brim of his hat as he backed out the door.

Sassy was getting used to being alone, and she liked the company she kept—herself.

She opened the window, allowing the salty, crisp air in to claim the room. She lay across the bed in a stream of cool sunshine, napped for forty-five minutes, bathed, dressed, and when Ivanhoe called, went downstairs.

She sashayed toward him in an elegant black slipdress which discreetly showcased the contours of her body. The strappy peau de soie heels, which perfectly accented her shapely legs, clicked across the marble floor. With a black silk purse nestled in one hand, she adjusted the fringed shawl over her bare shoulders.

"Sassy. You are a vision, chère," Ivanhoe said in awe.

"Yeah, right."

"No. Really. I'm not used to seeing you from a distance. It's like I'm a stranger seeing you for the first time. Now that you've gotten rid of all that hair, I can see *you*—your cute little figure, your face. Those pretty-pouty lips, those high cheekbones, and that flawless golden cinnamon skin. You are a beauty!"

"Why thank you, but you are embarrassing me."

"Maybe a little blush in the hollows to really accentuate those pronounced cheekbones. Make them more Cruella de Vil. Take out just a few of the eyebrows underneath to heighten your natural arch the arch on top—"

"I thought you said I was a 'beauty.'"

"So am I, but I still need to 'enhance' what Mother Nature bestowed upon my person. Everybody needs a little help every now and then."

"Can we go, you crazy man?" She said, pulling the shawl up over her silky-bronze shoulders again.

The gallery, debuting Ivanhoe's friend's work, was small crowed and the artist's work way too modern for her taste. Sassy retrieved a flute of champagne from a traveling waiter's tray and mingled with the guests as she tried to make a meal out of watercress sandwiches and shitake spring rolls. After circling the space once, she joined Ivanhoe and his group discussing the use of color and matter when—she thought she saw him—dressed in all black; the mystery man from campus who'd met with the Dean.

This would be too eerie, she thought as she sauntered over to where he was—but he was gone. She let her eyes surreptitiously roam the room for him with no success. She rejoined Ivanhoe's group, and he reappeared. Without moving, she inclined her head to one side of Ivanhoe then the other to see if that was in fact him. The man turned to the side—it wasn't him. Was she inventing him? Was she wishing to see him again?

"Who do you see?" Ivanhoe interrupted her thoughts as he turned around to scan the crowd.

"Nobody. Just looking."

"Good for you, chère." He winked and sipped his champagne. "Good for you. Taylor, come." He waved a woman over and continued, "This is my assistant I was telling you about. Sassy, this is Taylor Coleridge-Sykes. She's looking for a restorer," he said to Sassy. "She is the best," he said to Taylor.

"Really?" Taylor asked.

"I started out as a restorer but—" Sassy began.

"She still has the touch," Ivanhoe interjected, bouncing himself off of Sassy's arm. "Like riding a bike, chère."

"I have a picture of my great-great-great grandparents that's in need," Taylor said. "I could use several local people, but if you come with Ivanhoe's endorsement and can work onsite, the job's yours."

"Where are you located?" Sassy asked.

"In Napa. At the ranch my great-great-great grandfather built. But over the generations it's become a winery. Coleridge Vineyards, although we kept the ranch's original name, Kismet."

"Her great-greats were among the first blacks to settle in Napa," Ivanhoe reported. "Grandpa was free, fell in love with grandma and bought her." Ivanhoe spread manicured and bejeweled fingers across his heart and sighed, "Ain't that romantic?"

"That's the second greatest love story I've heard this trip," Sassy said with a wink to Ivanhoe.

"They were special and did so much for their community. I'd like you to at least see the painting. Ivanhoe, bring her to the party tomorrow night. I'm giving my husband a not-so-surprise birthday party, please come, Sassy," Taylor invited.

"It's just a couple of hours up the road," Ivanhoe pressed. "You can still have the next full day in San Fran to yourself. Have you ever been to a vintner's?"

"No," Sassy said evenly.

"See, yet another adventure," Ivanhoe urged, then drained the flute of liquid.

"Then you'll come?" Taylor asked. "And I won't press you about the painting. I promise."

"All right. Thank you."

"Great. Let me go find my husband, Cody. I want you to meet him," Taylor said.

When Taylor left, Sassy pinch-twisted Ivanhoe's arm and seethed, "Thanks," through her clenched teeth.

"Ow! Like you had a hot date or something. You might not go for the painting, but maybe there'll be a man or two to squire you around town." He massaged his arm where she'd assaulted him.

"For all of the one day that I'll have left? You keep chipping away at my 'vacation.'"

"You have all day tomorrow until I come get you at about five so we can get to Kismet in plenty of time. I want to be there when they set out all the good eats. Last time she had lamb chops with onion marmalade—"

"Gee thanks, there's oh so much I can do until five," Sassy said sourly.

"I promise I'll let you alone the day after that—all to yourself."

"Napa," she hissed and cut her eyes. "There's nothing for me in Napa."

"You never know, chère," Ivanhoe enthused. "You just never know."

Chapter III

The following day, Sassy lazily rolled over into a shaft of warm sunshine and read the digital clock. Ten-thirty. She executed a few feline stretches facing the San Francisco view before calling Le Boutique and room service. After a quick shower, she ate and set out on a walking tour of the City by the Bay.

Energized by the invigorating crisp air, she visited Pier 39 and spent three touristy hours absorbing San Francisco before her built-in radar steered her to Antique Row. She meandered in and out of the shops for another hour before she realized she had less than one hour to get ready for the Coleridge party in Napa.

At the appointed time, in a backless, shimmering, copper tea-length dress with a flirty ruffled hem, Sassy approached Ivanhoe in the lobby.

He shook his head in utter disbelief and said, "Ah, I can't stand it. You are stunning. You should have cut your hair years ago, chère." He twirled her around once, then crooked his arm artfully for her to take. "You are wearin' that dress, girlfriend. A symphony in bronze you are. I don't remember it?"

"I had it sent up with my room service this morning from the boutique in the lobby, along with masking tape."

"What? To keep your bosoms from dropping out?" he teased as they walked through the lobby.

"I want to put tape over your mouth so you won't take up any more of *my* free time in San Francisco."

"I'm a proud papa, what can I say?" He rolled his eyes. "Now, masking tape?"

"I wanted to wrap it around a ring I found so I could wear it, but I didn't have time tonight."

"Chère, no one is going to be lookin' at any ring with you in that getup. If I were a straight man, you'd be in trouble, chère. You look so good, I'll pay for it."

"You did. I charged it. You see, I didn't know I'd be spending all my time attending parties."

"Sassy-girl, you are living up to your name this evening. And I said I'd leave you alone after tonight. All day tomorrow is yours. My word is bond."

"Humph. We'll see."

Ivanhoe settled in behind the driver's seat with Sassy riding shotgun. He steered the car north as they talked and watched the sun melt into the distant mountain, finally plunging them into an unfamiliar pitch. Once they passed St. Helena's, Ivanhoe slowed as he turned onto an unlit two-lane road.

Sassy helped him navigate as her vision was consumed by mostly dark space and the occasional outline of a huge house in the distance. "There, on the left."

Ivanhoe turned between two stone pillars connected by an iron-lettered arch, which read COLERIDGE WINERY.

"Ooh. This is so *Falcon Crest*," Sassy said as Ivanhoe followed the glowing lanterns and eased around the curved driveway. Then the house popped into view. "Good God!"

"We're in high cotton now, chère." Ivanhoe said, pulling into the space between a Jag and a Bentley.

The house glowed in the blackness like a welcoming embrace. The expansive verandah's columns were wrapped in the twinkle lights that also lit the path aimed towards the stone steps and home.

"I'd love to see this in the daytime," Sassy said, looking at the curved expanse which, she surmised, must be even-rowed vineyards.

They circled the gleaming fountain of the curved drive, and as they ascended the steps, the pungent smell of organic earth gave way to the aromas of sumptuous edibles.

Ivanhoe chimed the bell, and Taylor opened the door.

"Sassy. Ivanhoe. I'm so glad you came," Taylor greeted warmly. "Welcome. You remember Cody."

"Hey, good of you to come," Cody echoed as the maid took their coats. "Still nippy out there?"

"Oh, yes," Sassy said.

"Come and meet my children," Taylor said, ushering the guests to the family room.

After all the introductions and chit-chat, Sassy took a glass of Coleridge Chardonnay and Taylor up on her invitation to enjoy and explore their home. Sassy sipped and noted that it was a solidly built stone house, capable of withstanding anything man or nature had to throw its way. She stepped through French doors onto the wide porch wrapped in golden twinkle lights, which complimented the flickering glow from the stone chimenea. She walked towards the inviting flames and glanced out at the charcoal darkness. In the distance, a ribbon of light studded with stars and a big full moon hung above an outlined mountain range. She wondered if the Cajun moon, disguised in pale yellow, had followed to spy on her—to make sure she was still unhappy.

Hypnotized by the chimenea's dancing flames, she closed her eyes and listened to the quiet night around her. As a city girl, she found the silence loud but soothing. The music from inside wafted out to her. Luther Vandross crooned "If Only For One Night" with crickets as backup singers.

"Hello." A male voice pierced the stillness.

Sassy jumped.

"I didn't mean to startle you," he said with an easy smile.

It was him. The dean's friend. What the hell was he doing at a party in Napa? Her heart began to beat wildly at the presence of him.

"Haven't we met?" he said.

"No." She nervously pulled her hair to her neck. "And that's a tired line," she said, trying to calm her palpitations and regain control.

"Aidan," he offered his hand in introduction. "You are?"

In one quick motion, she looked at his hand, then back at his face. His penetrating eyes waited for a response.

She blinked at him a couple times before taking his hand. "Sass—iere," she stuttered slightly, giving him her formal first name. She couldn't bear to hear another man call her "Sassy" right now.

"Sassiere," he repeated, rolling his "r" to perfection and ending with a flair of French affectation.

Sassy listened to her name coming from this stranger. With the exception of her mother, she hadn't heard her given name in years, and Maman never said it like this. From this man's lips, *Sassiere* sounded like a Gregorian chant. Like he was the priest renaming her at a baptism, christening her with a new beginning, anointing her with a rebirth of promise and possibilities. *Sassiere,* she replayed his voice in her mind.

"That's a beautiful name," he said.

She released her hand from his. *Especially coming from your lips,* she thought, but said, "And if you never call me 'Sassy' we'll get along just fine." She took a sip of wine and glanced beyond the porch's banister.

"I wouldn't dream of butchering such a lovely name, Sassiere."

Her name flowing from his lips cascaded over her body like a warm-water bath on a cold winter's night.

"Family name?"

"Belonged to my grandmother many moons ago." She looked away and wondered why his gaze was so unsettling to her. Why was this stranger having such an effect on her?

"You look bored, Sassiere." He put one hand into his pocket. "They have a beautiful garden. Would you like to take a walk? It's lit by these enchanting—"

"I don't know you, and I don't make a habit of going off with strange men."

He snapped his fingers and said, "Now, I remember. I saw you on campus. You were leaving, and I was going to meet the dean before the board meeting."

"You're on the board at Tulane?" She looked at him and he absorbed her with his eyes.

"Yes . . . and Xavier also. So, does that mean we aren't strangers?"

"You have a good memory, Mr.—?"

"Symonds. But please, just call me Aidan. May I freshen your drink for you?"

"No, thank you," she said, eyeing his well-cut sports jacket and bare left third finger, which, she'd learned, didn't really mean a damn thing.

"Do you know the Coleridges?" he asked to fill the silence.

"Not really. I just met Taylor and her husband at a gallery showing last night. And you?"

"I'm a business partner of sorts with Cody."

"And what business is that?"

"Investments, commodities, stocks, bonds, futures, hedge funds, that sort of thing. And you?" he volleyed back to her.

"I'm an art history teacher at Tulane," was all he needed to know.

"Oh, really? I have a few rare antiquities. A Louis the XIV commode, a vintage grandfather clock. When you get back to New Orleans you'll have to come and see them."

"Another tired old line," she said, needing to say something to counteract the magnetic pull he seemed to have over her. "Like asking someone to come up and see your etchings?"

"The weather isn't the only thing that's a little chilly out here," he quipped and continued, "The difference is my rarities are real, including two Fabergé eggs and Marie Antoinette's writing desk." When she didn't appear impressed, he said, "Well, nice chatting with you, Sassiere. Enjoy San Francisco."

He began to leave, and she looked at the way he moved, cool and confident.

He then turned and asked, "Is this your first trip?"

"Yes, it is."

"Would you permit me to show you around? I'm sure you're interested in all the touristy things."

Sassy stared at him for a few moments, blocking out his disciplined demeanor and asked, "Are you married?"

Taken aback by her candor, he finally said, "No." He held up his left hand and wiggled his third finger.

"Are you involved or committed to anyone here or in New Orleans—on the planet earth?"

"No." He chuckled. "Is there a written questionnaire and blood test too?" he asked playfully.

"Did Ivanhoe send you out here?"

"Who? I'm asking to show you around San Francisco, not walk down the aisle."

"Touché," she said with a demi-smile. "It's just that I just got out of a serious relationship and—"

"Whoa." He threw up his hands in surrender. "That's more info than I need. I just thought two displaced New Orleanians could break bread and enjoy the city. That's all."

"I'm sorry. I really—"

"No need to apologize," he interrupted. "I guess we did clear everything up."

"I guess we did," she said with an embarrassed smile. The golden glow of the inside party lights escaped through the window and cut across his features. He wasn't drop-dead gorgeous, but he was pleasant-looking on the verge of handsome, and appeared honest.

"So, where would you like to start? There's an art museum—"

"If you don't mind, this is a vacation of sorts. I don't need art."

"Okay. Well, there's Fisherman's Wharf, Ghirardelli Square, Sausalito, Pier 39, Alcatraz—"

"If we nix Pier 39, where I've been, and Alcatraz, where I don't want to go, you're on."

"Great. Where are you staying?"

"The Fairmont."

"I'm across the street at Mark Hopkins."

"Aidan? Where are you, man?" Cody was calling him from inside. "Aidan!"

"I'm being summoned by the birthday boy," he said as he coolly backed away. "So I'll meet you in your lobby at noon."

"Noon," Sassy repeated with a wide smile. *Finally,* she thought, a man who slept in, but said, "Fine."

"Wear comfortable shoes," he said, disappearing as easily as he had arrived.

As her heart returned to calm, Sassy stood on the porch for a few minutes and wondered what just happened. After twenty years, she had a date to go sightseeing in a strange town with a strange man who had rechristened her Sassiere. *Savvy Sassiere Crillon,* she thought. *Another adventure,* she mused, as she walked around to the side porch and into an open door.

Dead ahead—there it was. It stood at least six feet from the fireplace mantel to the ceiling. It had to be the portrait of Taylor's great-great-great grandparents. It was imposing. The man stood tall, straight, the color of a brown egg with a duster almost grazing the ground and a cigar perched between his lips. The woman stood in front of him dressed in finery, her skin black as a thousand midnights, accented by an upsweep of fine black hair, tendrils showering from their origins longer than the bejeweled earrings that matched her necklace. What an unlikely pair they seemed, but clearly solid, formidable, and in love.

Sassy went over to the plaque on the bottom, which read *Promise and Hecuba Quade.*

"Striking, isn't it?" Taylor said from behind her.

"Breathtaking," Sassy said without removing her eyes from the couple.

"I grew up with them watching over me. When I was a

child I thought they were huge and splendid and I was proud part of them lived in me."

"That must be wonderful, to know so much of your history." Sassy thought of herself, whose history and family basically ended with her and Maman. "They didn't pose for this?" Sassy asked.

"No, actually it was a gift from the Cultural Society for all they gave to the community. It was done from photos before Hecuba died in 1927."

"It is magnificent."

"I come from a long line of strong and loving folk. In the 1940s an upstart and visionary named Tom Coleridge convinced my great grandparents that they should devote half of their acreage to the future of Napa—wine. My great grands were content with their cattle ranch but Tom persisted and prevailed and took the land and my grandmother's heart in a brand new direction. In his honor, part of Kismet Cattle Ranch was renamed Coleridge Winery. My father, Quade Coleridge, built upon that success by introducing mechanized irrigation which increased production and boosted distribution. With the help of an excellent staff, Cody and I manage the day to day operation of the vineyard; maintaining the quality control, securing its reputation, protecting the brand, anticipating and exploring new trends. You know, keeping us viable in the industry."

"What about your parents?"

"They have a small vineyard in the Tuscany region of Italy where dad is trying to cultivate the international market for our wines. Supposedly." She chuckled. "At their age they are having lots of fun which is as it should be. They've worked hard and now it's our turn."

"Quite a legacy."

"That's true. Taylor, my mother's maiden name, and Coleridge are names I wear as proudly as Sykes."

Sassy was named after her grandmother and always admired how many religious, nationalities and aristocrats passed family names down through the generations. She hoped to do that one day.

"So hard work, tradition and romance run in your family as well," Sassy said with a smile.

"Never a divorce—yet. All are great DNA traits. But it started with the ex-slaves. Promise and Hecuba," Taylor said, looking up at their images again.

"It doesn't need restoring, maybe just a touch-up at best."

"Exactly. I just want the colors brightened. So will you consider it?"

"I'd love to, but I can't possibly commit to the week or two it would take to do the painting justice. My mother's ill—"

"Oh, I'm sorry to hear that."

"It's just not doable."

"I understand."

Sassy looked up at the couple again and said, "They are a powerful legacy."

"Yes." Taylor looked at the portrait and then back at Sassy and said, "And you are looking powerful in that copper dress, girl. Fabulous. It compliments your skin tone to perfection."

"Why, thank you."

"Pardon me, Mrs. Coleridge," the caterer interrupted.

"Excuse me, Sassy."

"Sure," she said, glancing at the couple in the portrait before returning to the party.

For the next forty-five minutes, she circulated through the roomy house as her eyes surreptitiously scanned each room, hoping to run into him again, but there was no Aidan. This was the second night in a row she'd looked for this man. At least this time she was sure she'd seen him.

"Who are you looking for now, chère?" Ivanhoe asked, popping in his head to block her view.

"No one. Ready to head back?"

"Yep. Let's say our thank-yous and good-byes."

Sassy rose at ten and showered. While waiting for room service, she wrapped the ring with masking tape and tried it on for size. It was big, but stunning, and filled the void left by her old engagement ring. The "S" sparkled and seemed to blink "Sassiere." She took that as a positive sign. After she ate, she dressed in a natural-colored pantsuit and a striking white blouse which show-cased her caramel-cinnamon skin. Her straw shoulder bag, knotted with a silk scarf, complimented her sandals, which revealed perfect feet and toes adorned with coral polish that matched her fingernails. She smiled at her-self appreciatively in the mirror.

At 12:05 exactly, she descended in the elevator, and when the door slid open, Aidan stood to face her. She watched him watch her approach. She might have been out of the game for a while but she could see the plea-sure of her reflected in his eyes. She liked the feeling.

"Good afternoon," he greeted with a wide smile. "Right on time."

"Good afternoon. Where to first?"

"Are you hungry?"

"I had a late breakfast. But if you're hungry—"

"No. But I'm up for chocolate. How about we start at Ghirardelli Square? "

"Lead the way." She sat in the passenger's seat and watched him close her door and walk around to the driver's side. Again, she was struck by the way he moved— half swagger, half sway, but all male.

They were at the famous chocolate confectioner's in no time.

"This is paradise, and it smells soooo good," Sassy said, as she eyeballed the chocolate possibilities safely secured under glass.

"Here's their famous dark chocolate."

"No nuts. What's the point of chocolate with no nuts? Now, pecan bark," she said, pointing a manicured nail against the glass with a quiet click. "That's a real accomplishment."

Then he noticed it. His ring on her finger. It made him happy that he hadn't lost it, and he smiled, that she was wearing it. It was like a cosmic endorsement from the ancestors before him that they agreed with his choice.

"That's an interesting ring. Family heirloom?"

"Not mine, but somebody's." She held her hand up and admired it again. "Isn't it stunning? I found it."

"Really? You should size it for a better fit," he tested, wondering if his heirloom was in jeopardy of being permanently altered.

"Oh, no. I wouldn't want to destroy the symmetry of the piece. It's definitely a man's ring. Maybe I'll have a jeweler put a ring guard on it and wear it on special occasions."

Aidan loved this woman. "I'm glad you think being with me is a 'special occasion.'"

Sassy felt flushed and answered him with a smile.

"Besides, it looks at home right where it is," he added.

"I'll take good care of it. Maybe pass it on to my son."

Our son, he longed to say, but replied, "From your lips to God's ears."

"What?"

"So have you decided what you want? Chocolate-wise?"

They bought enough chocolate to fortify them for a drive through Chinatown and a trip to see the famous Painted Ladies. Aidan parked and they strolled up to Alamo Square Park for the classic view of the often photographed Victorian houses which exemplified San Francisco. With her artist's eye, Sassy absorbed the intricate architecture of each house as Aidan reached over and pulled something from her hair. She jumped nervously at his almost touching her. He then showed her the piece of airborne lint that had lodged itself in her chestnut curls.

She felt stupid for her reaction and ran her fingers through her short-cropped hair. Each curl immediately sprang back into place. She wasn't ready for any of this, but she couldn't resist him, and the way he made her feel nervous and relaxed at the same time.

"Ready to cross the acclaimed Golden Gate Bridge and see Sausalito?" he asked evenly, not acknowledging her jitteriness.

"Sure." Jeeze, why was she so jumpy? She felt his hand gently cradle her waist as he guided her across the busy street and opened the car door for her. He was out of her league. She was out of her element, but not so much that she didn't find herself looking forward to seeing him round the hood of the car and sit behind the driver's seat next to her. *Relax,* she told herself.

As they drove, the gentle breeze blew in comfortable swirls around them and music played softly on the radio. They lunched at Gary's Seaside Restaurant where they both ordered and devoured lobster with relish. With him seated across from her sipping cognac, it was the first time Sassy had a chance to observe him without being obvious. As he spoke, she noticed the physicality of him; not only the neat natural framing of his lean, clean-shaved face, but his generous nose accented with a flat freckle on the left side. When he looked at her, his deep-set obsidian eyes seem to pierce right through her. He had a strong jaw line, and his lips—he had great lips—sculptured and full and, when he smiled, framed by parenthetical laugh lines created by his inner cheeks. He wasn't jaw-dropping gorgeous like Roux, but he was handsome—symmetrical—very pleasing to the eye. His easy laughter, precise speech, and intensity when he looked at her spoke to the refinement of him, as did his exquisitely cut navy blue cashmere jacket, which covered an expensive Italian knit. She observed the cuff of his jacket, which allowed intermittent glances of the understated, but expensive, gold watch. Aidan Symonds was a subtle but obvious testament to superb upbringing and good living. The breathing epitome of her Maman's old saying, "If you *really* have money, you never need to *say* a word."

She watched him express himself momentarily with the wave of a hand before it returned to the glass goblet; the nails clean, manicured without polish. The fingers long, tapered and sculpted like his lips. She imagined what they would feel like on her naked skin—

"I'm sorry. Am I boring you?" he asked. "I get a little carried away when I talk about investments."

"No. No, not at all," she stuttered. "It's all pretty fascinating and overwhelming." She took a sip of water, glad that his talents didn't include mind reading.

"You have to prepare for your future, Sassiere. A little of it comes every day."

"I have a few years."

"It's later than you think. Twenty, thirty years from now,

where will you be? Now is the time to think about your future." He sat back while the waiter removed their dishes.

Sassy had never thought of growing old. In thirty years, she'd be sixty-three. She'd certainly never thought of growing old alone. "What should I do? I have an annuity and Social Security through my job."

"Diversify. Invest. Whether it's single stocks or a mutual fund." He looked at her questioning eyes. "Let me show you. Waiter," he called. "Business section please." The waiter complied without hesitation and when he brought the paper, Aidan went on, "Now this is the Dow Jones and this is the NASDAQ." He then proceeded to break down stocks and demystify how to read them.

"Wow. Can you help me? I'll give you a commission or whatever."

"Can't," he said simply and sat back in his chair. "Conflict of interest."

"What? How?" she scoffed playfully.

"You see, I'm interested in you, Sassiere." His eyes penetrated hers and snatched the playfulness from them.

Sassy grew immediately uncomfortable and rubbed the back of her neck as her heart began pounding loudly, though her lips remained mute.

"That doesn't mean that I don't understand and respect your situation," he continued. "I just can't handle you professionally. I can refer you. I can suggest you start with real estate, owning your own home or condo. Renting is like flushing your money down the drain each month. Now," he said, clapping his hands once in anticipation. "Let's order dessert. Waiter. Dessert menu, please."

Sassy wondered how any man could be this cool, calm and collected. He was considerate and supremely confident without arrogance. He was relaxed and seemed to have all the time in the world and nothing to prove; certainly antithetical to Roux, who had an itchy soul that never sought peace and quiet. Roux had to be the center of attention while he burned both ends of the night. At the end of an evening out, Sassy often felt like the lucky groupie picked to go home with the star. But this was nice, just having a relaxing drive and a quiet lunch with a man who didn't want to be somewhere else.

Sassy inhaled a decadently sinful devil's food cake, and said, "Oh. I'm going to pay for that later."

"Do you work out?" Aidan took a little of the raspberry coulis up with the lemon chiffon cake, deciding not to go for the obvious line and keep the discussion above-board. "Play tennis or swim?"

"I swim quite well, 'cause I learned at the levee."

"You swam in the levee?" he asked with surprise.

"Sure and a few other little known pocket-inlets along the Pontchartrain."

"Wasn't that dangerous?"

"Swimming down by the docks was dangerous," Sassy said, thinking that only Roux did that crazy mess. "We didn't have swim clubs where I grew up," she offered sarcastically, not knowing why she wanted to antagonize Aidan when he'd been nothing but nice to her.

"I didn't have swim clubs either," he said evenly. "I had my own pool," he countered without apology, as if he knew her intent.

"We grew up in two different N'awlins. Two different sides of town; two completely different worlds," Sassy said.

"But we're together now. In this place—hopefully having a nice time. Aren't we?"

"Yes, we are," she admitted under his steady gaze and her heart fluttered.

Aidan called the waiter for the check. He peeled off

the cash and laid it on the tray. The waiter whisked it off, and Aidan sat back to finish his drink.

"What's your game?" Sassy asked with a smile-smirk.

"Game? No game. As you just pointed out, we grew up separately and unequally." He dabbed the corner of his mouth and said, "I'm just trying to bridge the gap; make up for the injustices of the world." He smiled. "Ready to head back?"

"Sure."

The valet brought the car, and Aidan turned it to-wards San Francisco.

"That was great," she said. "Thank you."

"My pleasure," he said with a glance and slow grin.

Sassy blushed and looked out the window.

He wanted to take her left hand with his ring on it. Seeing it there made him smile again. It was not only prophecy but a blessing—a blessing like she was.

"Oh, my daddy used to play this song to death," she said, as she reached over, turned up the radio's volume and began singing "When Sunny Gets Blue."

"Dakota Staton," Aidan recognized to an obviously impressed Sassiere.

"Yes!" Sassy laughed.

He began to sing, and Sassy entered into a duet with all of Dakota's inflections and clipped words, followed by deep, then soaring notes. They laughed together at the end.

"Wow, that was pretty retro."

"Are 'Cherokee' and 'Misty' on that album?" he asked.

"You know them too?"

"Our worlds aren't so different after all." He glanced over at her. "Are they?" He wanted to stroke her cheek tenderly with back of his fingers.

"No. I guess not," she admitted, then changed the subject. "But if you're talking "Misty," that's Sarah Vaughan."

"The best. I saw her a couple of times. She blew the audience away." He steered the car with controlled energy. "Sarah and Ella Fitzgerald—you can't get better than that," he said.

"So what's your all-time favorite song?"

"I can't do that," he said with a quick glance at her.

"Yes, you can," she teased.

"Ummm. Now, I'm doing this under duress," he qualified before his face broke into a big grin. "'Do Nothing Till You Hear From Me' by Ella."

"Yeah. Good one. Boy, her voice was so clear. So pure and clean."

"The girl could chirp. Whew. Now you."

"What?"

"You didn't think I was going give it up and expect nothing in return." He glanced and steered.

"That's easy."

"Oh, yeah?"

"Yeah."

"So stop stalling. What is it?" He grinned.

"'The Very Thought of You' by Johnny Hartman." A self-satisfied smile graced her lips

"Wow! How old did you say you were?"

"I didn't and I won't."

"Now *that* was a voice. Smooth, sexy and classy."

Like you, she thought but said, "The phrasing and the music."

"*The very thought of you,*" he began singing, and Sassy joined in. They sang, teased, and taunted the lyrics musically.

Sassy felt full of love, remembering her daddy and happy to be in the company of this man on this afternoon.

Laughter claimed them again. "I think we better quit while we're ahead," Sassy said.

"What do you mean? We sound good."

"Yeah, right." She chuckled and thought wistfully about her Daddy's record collection she hadn't played in years. Roux only liked instrumental jazz; he said lyrics just messed up perfectly good music.

Fearing he was losing her to internal thoughts, Aidan asked, "You like old movies too?"

"How'd you guess?" Sassy responded, happy for the interruption.

"Favorite old movie?"

"*Madame X, Backstreet, Magnificent Seven, Cooley High*—"

"Older than that. Black-and-white," he challenged playfully.

"*Mildred Pierce, Stella Dallas*—And you?"

"*Out of the Past.*"

"With Robert Mitchum and Gene Tierney."

He was flabbergasted. "Who would imagine that you were so deep. More than a pretty face."

"When I was a little girl, one of my favorite things to do on a rainy, gray N'awlins Sunday after church was for Dad and I to get an old movie on the tube and watch it until Maman called us to dinner," she mused.

"I know what you mean. When I go skiing, after a few days on the slopes when I've had my fill? I like settling in in front of the television to catch an old movie and doze on and off."

"Yeah," Sassy agreed.

"I mean, you have the snow—one of nature's best co-coons—and it's cold and gray and you get a fire going and a hot toddy, prop those pillows up and snuggle down and—wow. . . . heaven."

"Yeah," Sassy said, not knowing why she was disturbed

that the scene he described wasn't usually done by one. He snuggled down with some lucky someone.

He was losing her again. "So, you love good music so much you must play an instrument."

"Nope. Just my vocal cords in the shower. But I took dance. Boy, did I take dance. Forever it seems."

"That explains your excellent posture and graceful carriage." He smiled.

She shot him a sideways glance, and she asked "You play an instrument?"

"A little violin, piano, drums. But trumpet—that's my heart."

Which explains those gorgeous lips, she thought, but asked, "So who's the best?"

"Dizzy. Miles. Roy Eldridge," he answered quickly.

"Saw him a couple of times too, huh?" she teased and he smiled. She was beginning to like the way she could summon that parenthetical smile to surround those gorgeous lips.

"Yep. You like all music?" he asked.

"Everything except zydeco. I'm N'awlins born and bred but I just don't get it."

"You don't like Rosie Ledet?"

"You just like her miniskirts and long hair."

"No, she's very talented," he said seriously, then added, "And a little easy on the eye."

"Umm-humm."

They chuckled, then he said, "Well, you'll have to go to the symphony with me sometime."

"Symphony," she repeated quietly. On occasion, she liked the high-brow, bombastic stuff to clean house by, but the rest of it was a real snore to her. "That'd be— lovely," she hedged.

"You mentioned your dad. Are your parents still living?"

"He's been dead awhile, but my mother is living. Barely. At Willowbrook." She didn't want to get into all of that, and asked, "Can we stop back by Ghirardelli Square? I need reinforcements."

"You ate *all* that pecan bark?"

"Every morsel."

"Absolutely. I'll do that if you promise to have a drink with me at the Top of the Mark before we turn in."

"Before we turn in" had a delightfully naughty ring to it. "Sure. The least I can do after you've shown me around today." She wondered what it would be like to be enveloped in his powerful embrace and kissed. With those lips, she knew he'd be a good kisser.

They returned to Ghirardelli's, and as they left with the pecan bark, Sassy noticed an antique shop. "Was this here before?"

"Yeah. We parked on the other side."

"Can we go in?"

"Absolutely."

The small shop was cluttered with regional oddities. "Know what this is?" she tested him with the crystal box that had the hole in the center.

"A hair receiver," he identified.

"How'd you know that?" She was impressed.

He answered her with that classic, parenthetical smile and continued, "Victorian women would save their hair for hairpieces. Even make ornaments out of them."

"Well, you're more than a pretty face," she counter-complimented with a smile. Roux wouldn't have wanted to stop in the shop at all, and he wouldn't have known that, she thought. He had never taken any interest in her work; "old junk" he'd called it. She walked around the shop. "Oh! This is exquisite!" she exclaimed, removing an ornate, stone-encrusted needle from a cushion.

"Victorian hat pin," Aidan identified over his shoulder before she could ask.

"Isn't it gorgeous?" She rotated it so the light caught in the stones.

"Yes. You have a hat big enough to accommodate that thing?" he teased and she laughed. "Ready to head back?"

"Yeah. I'm hungry."

"What?" Aidan laughed.

"Do they serve food there?"

He smiled and said, "My, you have quite an appetite. That's refreshing." He opened the car door for her.

"Well, I'll go freshen up and meet you at the Terrace Bar at the Fairmont." She changed the location to the safety of her hotel.

"That'll be great." He steered the car into traffic, thinking he'd meet her on the moon if she asked. He hated letting her go even for a few minutes.

Forty-five minutes later, Sassy stepped from the elevator into the Terrace Bar and Aidan was there to greet her.

"Wow, Sassiere. You look wonderful," he said, as he offered her his arm. She smelled of fresh peaches. He loved fresh peaches.

"Just a little soap and water," she answered, relishing the sound of her name coming from him. The chiffon of her strapless dress billowed behind her.

"You've never think you spent all day sightseeing," he said to her, and then to the maître d', "Two by the window, please."

The couple followed the waiter to their table. "Oh, look at this city," Sassy said as all San Francisco twinkled before her like sparkling diamonds laid on black velvet. "It is beautiful."

Aidan hadn't removed his eyes from her and said, "No. You are."

Sassy blushed as the waiter opened and offered their menus. She ordered shrimp scampi to his filet mignon— rare. She sat back and once again noticed his polish and ease as he ordered their wine. She was becoming comfortable with his understated flair. He snapped the wine list closed, and she immediately began to look elsewhere.

"Oh, they have a band," she noticed.

"Yes. They're quite good," he said as the sommelier came and proceeded with the production of offering, opening, and having Aidan sample the wine before being authorized to pour the red nectar in her glass.

"To San Francisco and the Coleridge vineyards," he toasted.

"To San Francisco and Coleridge vineyards," she agreed, and they clinked glasses, and sipped. "Umm, that's good."

"Cody and Taylor will be happy to hear that," he said, and sipped before continuing, "You see, if we had more time, we could tour wine country, sampling its wares, and have what we like shipped back to N'awlins."

"We can do that next time." She didn't believe she said that, as she watched his face break into a parenthetical smile on either side of those sculptured lips.

"I like the sound of that," he said.

They both sat back into their plush seats as the waiter served their appetizers. He had her sample his escargot; she did not reciprocate with her smoked salmon. By mid-dinner, they were on their second bottle of Coleridge Cabernet and chatting like they were old friends. By the time his cherries jubilee had stopped flaming and her chocolate confection was devoured, he was swirling and sipping a brandy to her cappuccino.

"So tell me how you've managed to escape marriage all these years," Sassy asked playfully.

The question caught him off guard, but he covered with a smile. How he longed to tell her that she was the reason he had never married. If he couldn't have her, he didn't want anyone else. He only thought briefly about the women of his youth and of how none of them could compare with his then-fantasy—now reality—of Sassy. He answered with a smile, "The usual reasons—too busy building a career and refusing to settle—" He looked at her smiling at him and said simply, "Tell you what. When the time is right, I'll tell you the real reason."

"I bet," Sassy teased.

"Ah, listen," he directed. The band was playing "For All We Know." He stood gallantly and offered his hand. "May I have this dance?"

"No one's dancing."

"That'll change once we get on the floor." He led her to the dance floor and began singing quietly.

She giggled like a sixteen-year-old and hoped the cappuccino chaser would quiet her wine buzz.

"Is my singing that bad?" he teased her.

She blushed and said, "No. But folks are staring at us."

"No." He looked intently at her in the dimly lit room and said, "They're staring at you. You are beautiful, Sassiere."

With great effort, she struggled to breathe in and out. She hadn't felt this special in such a long, long time, and whether it was the wine or the attention, she didn't want it to stop. She was Sassiere. A woman on business in San Francisco with a handsome, old-fashioned gentleman with urbane manners she'd met at a party. She was miles from reality and hurts, dancing on a cloud atop the City of Lights to intoxicating old music which revved up nostalgic, loving memories of her Daddy and happier times. Aidan was mysteriously familiar and comforting as he held her close, boldly, possessively, with a dash of respect and caring. She could feel the warmth of his strong hands sear her skin through the silky chiffon; one at the small of her back and the other clasping her own inches from his massive shoulders. He put his cheek to hers, and his smooth-shaven skin caressed her like a loving kiss. The wonderful crescendo of violins and piano and the smokey, sexy sax masked her loudly beating heart and enveloped her like the welcoming embrace of an old lover. She closed her eyes and let his body guide her from side to side. He was graceful and in total control. The faint smell of his cologne, the soft texture of his cashmere jacket, the light starch of his collar—she thought she was in heaven. . . . until . . .

The vocalist approached the mike and began to croon, *"The very thought of you . . ."*

"Ah!" She reared back and looked into his playful dark eyes. "You did this!"

"What?" He feigned innocence and his sculptured lips broke into a satisfied smile. The kind you give someone you've just pleased.

If Ivanhoe did pay for this guy to romance her while she was in San Francisco—he was worth every penny, Sassy thought. This was not the place and time for reality. This entire day was pure fantasy, and Sassy reveled in it all.

Aidan swirled, spun and dipped her and they owned the dance floor. He danced her with a flair she didn't know she had. She couldn't remember when she had been so unabashedly, little-girl happy. She danced and danced and thought she would cry from sheer bliss.

This is what memories are made of, she thought. It was all
too perfect, like a movie, and she didn't know when she
would ever get a chance like this again. This would be a
night—a memory, she would savor for years to come.
There was no past and no future with this man, only the
present in the presence of this dapper, sophisticated,
worldly male being—this unbelievable man. She could
never have conjured up a man like this or scripted a
night like this, and as the lyrics said, *We may never meet
again.* In that moment as their bodies meshed in perfect
sync, Sassiere Crillon decided that if this man—Aidan
Symonds—had condoms, she would sleep with him.
Once. He was the healing elixir she needed to start her
on the road to recovery—toward forward movement.
She'd never slept with anyone but Roux, but Aidan
Symonds could be her entrée into the "big girl's world."
Into "womanhood." She'd sleep with him here in San
Francisco at the Fairmont Hotel so she could wipe the
stain of Roux away and wouldn't be thrown by the next
man to enter her bed. If he didn't have condoms, she'd
curse the night and tomorrow begin carrying her own,
like a high-schooler waiting for her next golden opportunity. As Sassy felt her cheek next to his and his maleness against her thigh, she knew in her bones that a
magical night like this was rare and she'd be a fool not
to take advantage of this gift.

Aidan dipped her at the song's end and brought her
slowly up to him. Their lips were inches from each other,
his gaze welcoming as he closed his eyes and kissed her.
Tenderly. The crowd roared. Sassy didn't even care. She
just relished feeling his lips on hers.

"It's been a long day. I think I better get you to bed,"
he said, huskily. "Excuse me." He left her.

As he tipped the band and paid the bill, Sassy couldn't

believe that a man she hardly knew and had dismissed at a party had metamorphosed into this remarkable man. *The Lord and Cabernet work in mysterious ways,* she thought. *Takes one man away and replaces him with an unbelievable substitute.* She must remember to thank Ivanhoe.

"Ready?" Aidan returned to her and extended his hand.

"Yes." She took his hand and the well-wishes of a few restaurant patrons, who complimented them on their dancing prowess.

"Newlyweds?" one man asked.

"No," Sassy said.

"Not yet," Aidan remarked, punctuated with a kiss as they climbed onto the elevator.

They were alone in the padded cubicle, and she turned into him. He slid his hands around her waist, and she reciprocated. She tasted his perfect lips, and he smiled. In mirrored reflection he returned the gesture, and then—they truly kissed, his tongue the wick that lit desires deep within her. As the elevator drifted effortlessly from floor to floor, Sassy and Aidan joined in a long, languid kiss. Their serpentine tongues explored the caverns of each other and their bodies meshed in symbiotic unison. They didn't notice when the elevator door chimed open and spectators cleared their throats.

"This is your floor," Aidan said as Sassy remained oblivious.

They sauntered arm-in-arm to her room. "Number 324. This is it." She handed him the key and watched as he opened the bas-relief molded door. She leaned against the doorjamb. "I had a really good time," she said as his parenthetical smile reappeared. Just the thought of him and her nude in that big bed started her juices flowing.

"It was my pleasure."

"We'll have to do it again sometime," she teased,

knowing at any minute he was going to ask to come in. She wondered how many times they'd make delicious love before they went their separate ways come morning light.

"Yes, we will. We'll get together once we get back to N'awlins. But right now, I have a plane to catch," he continued. "Before I go, may I have another kiss?"

He held her gently yet possessively as their bodies clung together in one gapless embrace. She smelled his skin, tasted his lips, felt his power and magnetism. He seemed to consume and transport her to a place she'd never been. She could kiss him forever. When he broke their embrace, her pulsating lips wanted more. She had to remind herself to breathe.

"I'd better go," he said. "I leave you reluctantly. Promise me you'll call when you get back home. I won't be back until about Wednesday but here's my number." He handed her a piece of paper. "Sorry. I'm out of cards. But we'll go horseback riding."

"Horseback riding?" She repeated and wondered what he was talking about. She was ready to ride him—right now.

"Have you ever been? I think you'd like it. Or we can do whatever you like."

What is he talking about? she thought. *What did I miss?*

Their expressions hadn't changed; him smiling and her dazed and confused.

"Well," he said, stepping in to kiss her quickly. "Safe trip, Sassiere. Call me Wednesday," he said as he backed down the hallway and into the elevator.

"Ah!" she sighed aloud. "What the hell just happened?" she asked herself as she walked into her room, flicked on the light, kicked off her shoes and spotted the bed with the turned-back sheets and chocolates on the pillows. "Well,

I'll just be damned. I'm supposed to be frolicking with a man and destroying that made-up bed right now." She turned around and looked at herself in the mirror. *I know I tasted desire on his lips.*

"Jeeze Sassy. You can't even give it away."

She plopped on the side of the bed. "How drunk am I?" She slid the top of her dress off. "Well, I'm not so drunk that I've got no self-respect. Mr. Aidan Symonds. You blew it. This night was your chance. This was perfection. I got enough problems waiting for me when I get back to New Orleans, and I'm not adding you to the mix." She took his number. "Oh, heeeeeeell no." She tore up the paper and threw it in the trash. "Not in this life." She crawled up across the bed, half clothed, and fell asleep.

Once outside, Aidan turned his collar against the chill of San Francisco's early-morning air and smiled, savoring the sweet taste of her on his lips. *Sassiere,* he thought and looked back at the Fairmont. Leaving her was the hardest testimony of his deep love for her, but Aidan was both selfish and patient. He wanted to be her Mr. Right—not Mr. Right Now. He wanted Sassy to love and need him and only him. He wanted to satisfy her mind, body, and soul. He wanted her to see the wonderful woman she was reflected in his loving eyes.

He crossed the street and walked toward his hotel. Knowing that it was all working out better than he expected put a bounce in his step, a glide in his stride, and he couldn't wait to get her back on home territory and work his magic. They'd hit it off just as he had dreamed, and that placed a grin on his face. He was sixteen and "in love" for the first time again. It was all just a matter of time before she would be his, and they could begin their life together. He began whistling that old standard, "Nice and Easy Does It" as the doorman opened the door. He ascended in the elevator, took his room key and went in to dream the dreams of conquerors and kings. His private jet sat in the San Francisco hangar awaiting his orders. He had no flight to catch.

Chapter IV

Roux's hazel eyes combed the knoll at Willowbrook for the familiar sight. Seeing her, he smiled and walked towards her. "There she is," he said, approaching her with an arm full of sunflowers.

Maman blushed as she watched him jog down the slope towards her.

He kissed her cheek and knelt in front her. "How are you, Maman?"

"I'm all right, son."

"You looking good," he said, flashing that classic Roux Robespierre smile.

"Psh, boy," she scoffed, but somehow, falling from Roux's lips, she believed the words. She touched his cheek with her frail, gnarled fingers. He kissed them as she asked, "How you doing, son?"

"I've been better, Maman."

The nurse interrupted and said, "I'll take these beautiful flowers, Madame Crillon." She batted her eyes at Roux who returned a perfunctory smile and looked past her. "They're so many. I'll put them in your room."

When neither Madame nor the handsome man responded, she walked away.

"I guess you heard about me and Sassy splitting. But I'm gonna get her back," he said, flashing his clear hazel eyes at her—half plea, half prayer. "I've got to, Maman. She is my life—I love her as deep as my heart goes."

"You not going to do anything foolish now, are you, son?"

"Oh no," he answered quietly. "Besides, I won't have to, because Sassy is mine. Always has been. Always will be," he said playfully, not liking the serious tone of this conversation.

Maman laughed.

"Let's go over here," he suggested and pushed her slowly to a bench. He sat beside her as if they were at an outdoor café. "Yeah, this is nice."

"She loved you long and powerful, Roux, but you stomped it out."

"I know I messed up. Big-time," he admitted quietly, turning the high-school ring around on his finger, the one Sassy had exchanged with him for the solitaire engagement ring.

"You looking for forgiveness?" she asked.

"More like absolution."

"Humph. I told her a good-looking, high-spirited man like you is bound to mess up from time to time."

"What'd she say?"

"Said it was one time too many."

"I just can't lose her for good, Maman. She's been a part of me for too long. She's the only woman I let *in,* Maman." He touched his heart. "She knows all my secrets, my feelings and fears—and she loves me anyway. Not for my money or my looks. She doesn't want anything in return. . . . but me."

"And your fidelity. Couldn't give her that."

"I can now. That well ran dry, and I now know the value of water, Maman. I'm a reformed man. There's nothing out there for me. I know. It's a hollow, superficial world full of freaks: high energy and low morals."

"Women got no self-respect these days," Maman said. "Will do anything to have a piece of somebody else's man in bed for a few hours than be by theirselves alone. They willing to take any leavings from Sassy's table. They know there's no future, 'cause it's always been you and Sassy."

"True that, Maman," he said. "I could never respect a woman who snuck around with married men. Sassy would never do that."

Knowing his history and sensitivity to it, Maman treaded lightly and remarked, "Now, Roux, your mother was a good woman who did the best she could by you."

He stood abruptly in a fit of controlled anger and raked his fingers through his curly hair. "Being a married man's whore and having a bastard son leaves a lot to be desired, Maman," he seethed.

"I won't have you speaking ill of the dead since I'm about to become one."

Roux bit back his comments.

"You grown now. When are you going to forgive your mother for doing the best she knew how?"

"Loving a married man?"

"One man, Roux. Who took care of you. Gave you-all a house, money—"

"Money isn't everything." He folded his arms against his chest as if protecting himself from the hurt of old memories. But they came anyway and Roux, in the safety and comfort of Maman, reluctantly gave them permission.

He gazed beyond the lake to the watery surface of the bayou and remembered. How his father had traveled a lot but when he came home, they had a great life until he was six years old and his father died on one of his trips. A car fire had burned him so badly there was no body to bury, or so he was told. Six years later, while he was downtown where he wasn't supposed to be, he saw a man that looked like his father. Not believing his eyes, he ran to the car where the man was standing with a woman and two children. The man *was* his father, and Roux was filled with jubilant happiness that his father wasn't dead. It had all been an awful mistake. Roux called to him and ran up behind him as his father opened the door of a fancy black car and ushered the woman and the girl into the backseat. Only his father and the boy stood on the sidewalk. "Papa! You're alive," Roux had said.

The adult Roux would *never* forget how the man's cold black eyes fixed, then bored into his innocent hazel ones. Instead of elation at the sight of Roux, his father's draw dropped and his lips formed an irritated slit of disgust on his angry face.

"Get in the car!" the man roared at the boy before he looked back at Roux like he was dog-do on the bottom of his shoe. "You must be mistaken, little boy. This is my *only* son," he spat, as he wrestled his son into the car before hurriedly following behind him, slamming and locking the car door.

Thinking about this childhood rejection still sent shivers up Roux's adult-male spine.

He'd run all the way home and it was dark when he arrived. He was so excited to share the news that when he called out to his mother, he hadn't noticed she'd been crying. His mother kept telling him that he was wrong and his father was dead and Roux must promise never to go near this man and his family ever again. Roux kept saying that his father was alive; he'd *seen* him with his own eyes. His mother grabbed his arm and squeezed it hard, and told him if he bothered that man again, they would lose their house, the car, and all the money.

Roux's twelve-year-old mind reeled, and he didn't understand right away. Slowly, he came to realize that his daddy didn't want him or his mother, and he would *pay* them to stay away from him.

Roux shifted his weight and Maman said softly, "He did take care of you, son."

"He threw money at her like a used-up whore," Roux said above a whisper.

Maman didn't protest. Only she and Sassy knew the deep scar carved into the psyche of this fine-looking, successful man with the hole in his soul. Any reference to his mother would cause his cool veneer to flash razor-hot. Sassy didn't know the details because the secret was kept by Maman and those of her Gert Town generation who knew the entire sordid story which was like a thousand others.

"I didn't get his name, Maman," Roux continued absently. "Didn't get his time—the traditional ring he promised me when I grew up—an 'R' in diamonds on a bed of black onyx. To pass on to my son."

Roux remembered his parents' betrayal and the whole charade of the neighbors coming to the pathetic memorial service when they all knew. They all knew that his mother was a married man's mistress and Roux was their bastard spawn. They all knew that the man had left them and gone back to his legitimate family. Everybody knew but Roux. It hurt then, like losing Sassy hurt now. He'd never thought he'd ever feel this abandoned again. He thought he was safe. Sassy made it safe.

During his thoughtful silence, Maman remembered

that this was about the time Roux started hanging around with Sassiere and missed so much school he stayed back.

"Chèr, all that's ancient history. A different time when women did what they had to do. Say what you want, but it was his money that got you that club."

"I made that club what it is today, Maman. Not him. Not any of them. Me . . . and Sassy made that club the success it is today."

"What did Sassiere do?"

"She's my inspiration—my *raison d'être.* I wanted to make sure she'd never have to worry about anything. That she'd always be taken care of."

"But you messed up," Maman reminded.

"I messed up."

"Well, admitting you done wrong is the first step to recovery, son. Can't talk right and walk left."

Roux wasn't comforted.

"It might be a blessing in disguise," Maman said.

"How?"

"Sassiere has never had any other boyfriend but you, Roux. You've had other women, so you know what you got in my Sassiere. Good, bad, or ugly, she doesn't know what she has in you. Not truly. Not in the practical sense. If she dates another man and finds out what she's missing in you, she'll hightail it back to you lickety-split."

"So, are you saying she's dating somebody else?"

"No. But let her well run dry too. Let her try another well and when she finds out it's worse. . . . she'll want you back, guaranteed."

"No. I can't picture Sassy with another man."

"I bet she never pictured you with another woman. You two got a lot in common."

"No. No way."

"Dying gives you a clarity not clouded by details and nonsense. You want her back at any price? This may be your price—your penance."

Roux sighed heavily but didn't speak.

"Right now, with her not seeing you—seems to me you got no choice. You know how stubborn she can be. Keep pushing her and I see a restraining order, not wedding vows, in your future. Let her realize what she had in you, and with your new redemption, you'll have a perfect reconciliation and live happily ever after with your children—who I'll never get to see."

The nurse came over to get Maman, and Roux began to push the wheelchair to the portico. When he didn't reply, she looked back at him and asked, "You thinking on what I'm saying, son?"

"Yeah. I don't know, Maman."

"It's a long, hard road back to love and trust again, Roux. Not gonna be easy."

Roux didn't want to think about it and changed the subject. "I'll see you next week, Maman." He bent to kiss her cheek. "Oh, yeah. I almost forgot." He knelt before her, looked right, then left, before he slipped a small brown package from his pocket and tucked it under her frail thigh.

She looked at him lovingly with a sparkle in her eye. She managed a weak smile and said, "Thank you."

Her pleasures were so few, and she relished the contraband he brought her as much as the visit. She'd dissolve bits of the sugary pralines on her tongue and add sweet joy to her bland diet. If Sassiere was unwilling to accept her imminent death, Roux did, and he wanted to make her last days happy ones.

"Thank you," she repeated and caressed his cheek. "I'm gonna miss you, son. Now, you remember if

Sassiere's too busy grieving, I want Sebastien Funeral Home to lay me out."

Roux's hazel eyes brewed red-hot anger.

"I know," she soothed and continued, "How you feel about them 'cause they couldn't bury your mother—"

"*Wouldn't,*" Roux spat.

"Wouldn't," she conceded, then added quickly, "I'm not going into all that now. I'm sorry about your past dealings but every respectable N'awlins family wants Sebastien. I saved for it all my life—not enough for a second line or the Golden Chalice, but they buried the Mister and made him look fine, and I'm going to need all the help I can get. They are the best in all of Louisiana and that's who I want."

Roux gritted his teeth, causing his jaw to flex and relax—flex and relax, trying to swallow the hate.

"I never know which of these visits will be my last, Roux. So promise me now." She forced his eyes to hers, before his hazel ones darted away again. "Roux? Promise me if you come to my funeral, you'll be dignified. That you won't use my last time on this earth to get back at the Sebastien family? It's the last thing I'll ever ask you to do. Promise me, Roux."

He cleared his throat and replied huskily, "I promise."

"Thank you, son." She embraced him until another nurse came to take her away.

"I love you, Maman."

"Love you too."

"See you next week."

"Lord willin' and the creek don't rise."

Back in New Orleans, Sassy worked at Rare Finds, trying to put Aidan behind her. Wednesday, the day she was to call Aidan, came and went and Sassy thought that was the end of her San Francisco adventure. On Thursday, Sassy worked at the shop as usual.

Mid-morning, the UPS man entered the shop and asked for "Sassiere Crillon?"

A puzzled Cyril shot her a glance.

"Yes, that's me," Sassy said, signing quickly for the small package before Ivanhoe caught wind of it. She knew it was from Aidan. Had she told him where she worked? What else had she and two bottles of Coleridge's California Cabernet told him?

She put the package inside her desk and continued working, trying to appear nonchalant about its arrival. When both Ivanhoe and Cyril were with customers, Sassy opened the card.

Thought you might need reinforcements by now, it read. Signed simply, *Aidan.*

She opened the brown paper and a Ghirardelli box jumped into view. The contents, pecan bark, made her laugh. Both Ivanhoe and Cyril glanced over at her and she stifled her glee with a cough. She swiped a piece of the chocolate confection from the box and resumed the inventory, thinking how Roux had always given her chocolate-covered cherries for every event—Valentine's Day, birthday, Mardi Gras—never understanding how much she *hated* chocolate-covered cherries. But Roux loved them and always got them by default. Here, this man had already recognized that she loved pecan bark and he had given her what *she* wanted.

She tapped her pencil absently on the ledger until she noticed Ivanhoe and Cyril looking at her. She then disappeared into the back room.

* * *

Later that afternoon, Cyril let the telephone receiver dangle from his manicured finger. "Sassiere," he lilted sarcastically. "It's for you."

Beneath knitted eyebrows, Ivanhoe looked from Sassy to Cyril and back to Sassy again as she went over and took the receiver from Cyril.

"What's that all about?" Ivanhoe asked Cyril.

"She has an admirer who calls her *Sassiere* and sends her gifts."

"Hello," Sassy said quietly into the phone.

"Hello."

She could hear him smile through the receiver.

"How are you?" Aidan asked.

"Fine," Sassy said nervously, eyeing Ivanhoe and Cyril across the room.

"Did you receive your reinforcements this morning?"

"Yes. Thank you. That was nice."

"You're welcome," he said, thinking that was an oddly reserved response. "Well," he continued because she didn't. "You must have been busy, or did you lose my number?"

"What?"

"I thought you were going to call me on Wednesday?"

"Oh. Yes. I don't have your number."

"Well, I didn't have yours but luckily I don't give up so easily."

There was silence.

"Did I call you at a bad time?" He asked.

"I am busy," she said looking dead into the eyes of the curious couple.

"Well, that's all right. It won't take long for you to accept my invitation this Saturday to the symphony."

"What?" She challenged Aidan, then looked at them looking at her.

"The symphony we discussed in Frisco. I'll pick you

up, we'll get dinner first, spy on Beethoven and his friends, then home for after-dinner drinks—"

"I have to work," she blurted out.

"Okay. We can do dinner some other time, but certainly the shop will be closed by eight. I can pick you up there—"

"No. I can meet you. Where?"

"That's hardly a proper—"

"Where?" she repeated in a take-it-or-leave-it fashion.

"At the Orpheum—"

"That's fine. At eight?"

"Seven forty-five would be better, but certainly we'll talk before then."

"Okay. Seven forty-five on Saturday," she whispered into the telephone. "Thanks. Bye." She hung up.

"What was that all about, chère?" Ivanhoe asked.

"Nothing important," she said and went to the bathroom.

Across town, Aidan still had the telephone in his hand, not believing the cryptic conversation he had just had with Sassiere. She was eons away from the way she appeared when he left her in the plush corridor of the Fairmont, and light-years away from where he planned for them to be Saturday night after the concert. What had happened? He wondered as he replaced the telephone into his receiver and swiveled his chair toward the mammoth window of his office. He ran his hand across the corners of his mouth and cradled his chin in deep thought.

"Aidan," the toffee-brown complexioned woman said, stepping into the office.

"Humm?"

"Your two o'clock appointment is here."

"I'll be with them in a minute," he said to her retreating back. He stood and snatched his French cuffs over his eighteen-carat, monogrammed cufflinks. As his Ferragamo shoes crossed the expanse of the Abusson carpet, he thought, *It's Thursday. Tomorrow's Friday.* He supposed he shouldn't bother her and should just expect to see her on Saturday. It was a day away. Then what would be her mood? Perhaps something was happening at the shop and she couldn't talk. He turned the eighteenth-century gold knob on the French door and thought, he'd never had to work so hard to get a woman before, but greeted, "Good afternoon. Please, come in—"

The bell of *Rare Finds* tinkled, and both Ivanhoe and Cyril looked up together.

"Well, this will surely improve her mood," Ivanhoe said sarcastically as he went to greet the customer.

"Roux. May I help you?"

"Is Sassy here?"

"Oh, you don't want to purchase any of our valuables?" Roux stared at him evenly.

"The both of you are in such good moods," he said just as Sassy came from the back.

"Ugh!" she sighed seeing Roux's face. "What do you want?"

"I want to talk to you."

"About what?"

"About us."

"There is no *us*."

"I don't think you're being fair."

"You dare stand there and talk to me about fairness!"

They both looked over at Ivanhoe and Cyril, who looked away.

"C'mon, Sass. Coffee at Serendipity."

Sassy shook her head in exasperation and said to Ivanhoe, "I'm going on break."

"Be careful," Ivanhoe said as she walked to the front door.

She walked ahead of Roux to the corner of Bienville and Royal.

"Sassy, Serendipity is this way."

"We're not going to Serendipity or anyplace else Roux. I just wanted to get out of the shop. It's not everybody's business."

"Well, everybody knows."

"Except you, Roux. You don't seem to know that you and me are over."

"I'm not letting you go, Sassy."

"Ha! You have no choice. Our past is my prologue, Roux. I'm moving on."

"I know I hurt you," he said, quietly. "A man can make a mistake, Sass."

"Try three that I know of—"

"They didn't mean nothing to me."

"But they meant something to me, Roux. Every time you turned from me toward another woman—" She walked towards him. "Every time you slid your penis between some other willing woman's thighs, with each thrust you stabbed a hole in our foundation. You chipped away at it so there's nothing left, Roux. But lessons and regrets. *You* killed my love for you, Roux."

"I'll never love any woman the way I love you—but sex is just sex." His hypnotic hazel eyes caressed hers.

"Oh, I see. So if you were to find me on my knees with some other man's—"

"Don't!!"

"You can't even bear to *hear* me say it. How do you think I felt *seeing* it, Roux? With my very own eyes?" She stopped, pinched at the bridge of her nose to ward off tears. She swore if she had a gun, she could have easily blown his brains out. Splatter red all over Royal and Bienville and feel nothing but pleasure and relief.

"Sassy. Everyone knows those women didn't mean nothing to me. They knew. I would never leave you. You are number one. They all know that."

She stared at him. "That's your defense? That I'm 'Number One' among of a bunch of lowlife women?"

"I always practiced safe sex."

She glared at him and thought, *I could just snap his neck with my bare hands.*

"I get it. I wasn't supposed to be having sex with any woman but you."

Sassy shook her head in utter disbelief. "How did we get so far apart?" she wondered aloud. "I thought we shared the same values. We aren't even on the same page—not even in the same book. All these years we were just intimate strangers."

"Sassy, you've got to give me one last chance."

"I don't 'got to' do nothing but stay black and die."

"Sassy, you can't throw away everything we had and meant to each other."

"I didn't, Roux. You did." She began to walk away. "There's no way back for us now. We just don't see eye to eye."

"What happened to 'together forever,' Sass?"

"We were children, Roux."

"It was last month, Sass."

Disgusted, she continued walking.

"What do I do with the tape? You know the one with the crooked heart etched into the black plastic."

Sassy stopped. "Well, that's rich, Roux. You didn't hear a word I said. You can take the tape of us making love—

no, correction, two people having sex, and sell them out of the trunk of your truck or put them on the friggin' Internet for all I care. Gee, does emotional blackmail usually work for you? Maybe on those lowlife women—"

"Sassy," he said, trying to draw her back before she bolted. He was thrown by her. He didn't know this Sassy. "There's nothing about you that doesn't do something for me—"

She aimed her eyes at him. "But all that wasn't enough for you was it, Roux?"

He stepped to her and asked, "What do you want, Sassy? Just name it." His sincere hazel eyes implored her.

She returned the stare and said, "I want you out of my life. Can you give me that? I want you to stay away from me. I'm tired of waiting for you to catch up and grow up. What I really want you can't give me—so it's time to stop fooling each other with this game-playing and just get on with it." In frustration, she raked her hands through her short cropped hair. "I want peace and not have to wonder what you're doing and with whom. I am not going to do that anymore. Our time is up and over. I wish you well," she said, abruptly turned and left him standing there.

"Sassy, I know how you Crillons are when you're finished with somebody. Don't throw me away like you did CoCo."

With the mention of her name, Sassy stopped but did not turn around.

When she resumed walking, Roux continued, "I don't want to be someone you used to love, Sassy. You'll realize how much I love you and when you're ready to come back to me—I'll be waiting." He watched her continue to walk down the street and, without a backward glance, throw up her hands in exasperation and reenter the shop.

"Serendipity's service must have improved. That was a

fast cup of coffee," Cyril said, and Ivanhoe scolded him
with his eyes as Sassy resumed taking inventory without
a word.

Take it, just another little piece of my heart now, she mentally recited Irma Franklin's old record as she rotely
added the numbers. She flipped the page and added the
next column, wondering how couples go from adoring
love to defiling one another. *We trust them with the deepest,
darkest secrets, and then they betray us with them later when we
are most vulnerable,* she thought. The tape; the one tape
she'd forgotten about. The tape done on a lark for laughs
when they were young and in love on their way to forever.
Now, years later, he'd turned that same tape into a cheap,
pornographic weapon and thrown it in her face.

But even more than the tape, Sassy's mind became in-
flamed with the mention of CoCo. She hadn't thought
about her sister in awhile. When her mother fell ill, Sassy
thought CoCo deserved some of the blame and most of
the responsibility. But unlike her mother, Sassy had for-
given her sister years ago. Her beautiful older sister with
the creamy skin, long dark hair and exotic almond-
shaped eyes whose body matured before her mind. At fifteen, she may not have known what to do with her
curves, but boys did, and Collette reveled in the attention: gifts and favors—things her parents couldn't give
them. She ran away three times, and three times her
Daddy dragged her back—locked her in her room. The
fourth time he let her go. By seventeen, she'd moved out
and in with Nitro, the black-Italian thug and pharmaceu-
tical kingpin. In four years he tired of her, so he turned
her on to his wares then turned her out. The stress and
strain of dealing with CoCo sent her father to an early
grave and drove her mother into ill health. When the in-
evitable news of her death came, they didn't know

whether it was an accidental overdose or suicide that finally removed CoCo from her private hell. She tore the family apart. No one could save her from herself, so they saved themselves. Maman didn't even attend CoCo's funeral. Sassy did. Roux was right; self-preservation was the first law of nature. Sassy couldn't save CoCo, and she couldn't save Roux. Sassy had to worry about Sassy.

Roux stood on the corner and watched Sassy turn into the shop, waiting for her to come to her senses, come back out and run to him.

"Hey, Roux!" women pouring out of a convertible yelled at him.

He flashed his smile and waved at them. Women had never been a problem to him or for him. There had always been plenty of them who readily admitted that, unlike Sassy, they understood his adventurous side and needs. But he didn't want a woman who'd let him roam. He needed an anchor, a woman who'd tame him and make him settle down, and Sassy was it. He was no angel; he *wanted* other women from time to time but he *needed* Sassy.

He began walking slowly toward his club, convinced that if she just married him, his player days would be over. He'd be married with children and no energy for anything else. He would never do what his father did or be what his father was. Once he married, that would be it for him. He'd be faithful to Sassy and a great father to their children.

He walked around his club, up the gallery stairs to his apartment—their apartment, and someone was playing Otis Redding's "I've Been Loving You Too Long." He added, "I can't stop now."

He looked around the apartment. Instead of getting

easier without her, each day grew harder and harder. Every day he felt further and further away from her. Disconnected. Other women had "heard" he was free and offered comfort, but he had no taste for any other woman right now. In the quiet of his own apartment, he finally admitted that he was lost and a little scared. He didn't know the woman who shouted at him in the street. But he knew he had to make serious changes for Sassy's sake—for their sake.

Absently, Roux chewed on his thumbnail.

"Damn!" he said aloud, then thought, *If only she didn't know now what she hadn't known then.*

Chapter V

"Aidan," Sassy said, approaching him from behind. "Sorry I'm late."

His heart soared at the sight of her. "Everything all right?" he asked, just glad she was here.

"Yes." She brushed her hand brusquely through her hair.

"You look marvelous," he said, noting the tasteful cocoa-brown attire, apparently her version of the "little black dress." "Let's go in," he suggested. He proudly took her arm.

Sassy walked into the cool cavernous hall with the ornate chandeliers dripping from the ceilings. She let the sumptuous red carpet cushion her feet and tried to remember if she'd ever been inside the Orpheum Theater. If she had, it wasn't for an opera or classical concert. "This is magnificent," she remarked, feeling his hand at the base of her spine.

"Yes, in your business, I'm sure you can really appreciate its beauty," he said as they followed the usher to their seats. He'd forgone the family box for tonight's performance and donated it in a charity auction.

"Third-row center," she said and thought, I'll have to stay awake. "Wonderful seats."

"You need to feel the music as well." He helped her remove her wrap. She smelled of fresh peaches again.

"Uh, huh," Sassy said as she settled in for what promised to be the most boring evening she'd ever spent. She hoped she wouldn't doze off.

At precisely 8:00 PM, the curtains parted, revealing the full orchestra in a sea of stark black and white. The crowd clapped politely. The conductor rushed assertively from stage left, did a curt bow, accepting the applause before he turned to face his orchestra, tapped his baton, and drew the first sound from the strings. The music filled the hall as it rallied, soothed, and inspired the enthralled patrons.

After the last movement of the Brahms' Piano Concerto no. 1, the lights came on, and Sassy was surprised at how fast the concert was going.

"Intermission already?" she noted as her eyes adjusted to the sudden light.

"You're enjoying it?" he asked, framing his lips with that parenthetical smile, wanting to hold her hand.

"Yes." She was enjoying the music and his smile.

"I noticed you're not wearing the ring?"

"I don't wear it to work. I can name at least five clients who'd pay big bucks if they saw it, and since it's not for sale, why tease them?"

"I was afraid you didn't think this occasion was 'special' enough."

He stole her breath with his sincere gaze. How could one man have such an affect on her without even touching her, she wondered.

"Let's stretch our legs," Aidan suggested.

She felt free enough to accompany Aidan to the lobby

for a flute of champagne and mingle. Certainly she wouldn't run into Roux or any of his friends who might cause an ugly scene which neither she nor Aidan needed. After a few moments, she excused herself and went to the ladies' room. As she washed her hands she looked at herself in the mirror and admired the happy-looking woman who smiled back at her.

When she returned to the lobby the smile froze on her face when she saw Aidan talking with a magnificently coiffed woman with flawless makeup and a spa body. Sassy felt like Cinderella without a ball gown, but when he left the woman to come to her, the frozen smile melted into genuine grin. She proudly took his offered arm just as the lights blinked signaling the end of Intermission.

Aidan reached for her hand during one movement and held it casually in his, as if it were the most natural gesture in the world. Roux hated tender displays of public affection, unless he was trying to French kiss her in front of his buddies. Aidan's hands were big and cool and looked as if they belonged over hers. It took most of her concentration to make sure hers didn't tremble and sweat.

At the concert's end, they filed out with the other patrons, who greeted him affably, although he didn't introduce her. Once they were on University Place in front of the Orpheum, he said, "I'm right around the corner," and they began to walk.

"So what did you think of the concert?" he asked, shoving his hands into his pockets, the only way he could keep from touching her.

"I must admit something to you," she said with a smile.

"What's that?"

She watched his eyes dance in the streetlights. "I *really* enjoyed it. I hadn't intended to, but I did. Until now, I thought Tchaikovsky was only for dancing ballet at

Christmas. Ah, and Beethoven's Piano Concert no. 5 'Emperor,' makes me want to take piano lessons."

"You should. As George Eliot said, 'It's never too late to be what you might have been.'"

"Ha. Well, I'd be torn between the piano and the French horn—I am in love with that sound!"

"Oh, really?"

"It sounds so strong and clear. So regal . . . I just want to say thank you."

"You are more than welcome. The pleasure was mine," he said, and thought, *There is so much more I want to show you and do with you. The world can be ours.*

"I'll have to reciprocate with an Earth, Wind & Fire concert when they come here."

"Earth, Wind & Fire? Great horn section."

"You expose me—I expose you."

He stopped and said, "I'd love to." His deep obsidian eyes seemed to shine in the night.

He gave her pause and she couldn't speak. His voice was soothing yet commanding. He could easily teach a class or be a hostage negotiator. She wondered how he would sound saying, "Now, remove your panties and come over here."

She blushed as they began strolling again. She wanted to be kissed by him and she sucked in her own lip.

He noticed that he'd lost her to that quiet place she would go to, so he asked, "Are you hungry?"

"Oh, it's too late to eat."

"Then a nightcap?"

"Where?" she asked, then silently self-admonished, not wanting him to say—at SASSY's, the hottest night spot in the Quarter.

"How about my place? I promised to show you my Marie Antoinette desk and Fabergé eggs," he smiled.

She didn't. Suddenly, she was conflicted again . . . antsy. Nervous and unsure.

"Oh. Uh," she stammered. "Actually, it's a little late and I have to get home. I'm going to see my mother tomorrow and it's an early start," she concluded, nervously. She didn't want to go to his place. She didn't want to see it or be alone with him. She wasn't in San Francisco anymore—she was home in New Orleans. Things were happening too fast, and she didn't have a handle on it.

"Oh. Would you like some company?"

"To go see my mother at Willowbrook?" she said. "You must be kidding, right?"

"No. We could drive out there and then get some dinner—"

"No. No, I don't think that's a good idea. She's not well, and meeting new people would be a strain—" her voiced trailed off.

"Okay." He didn't want to press her. "You were honest with me about the concert, and I want to be honest with you." He stopped at the corner, and she followed suit. "I just wanted to spend some time with you, Sassiere. I wasn't trying to invade your privacy."

"Okay. I respect that." She gave him a quick, insincere smile and began walking again. "So, are you going to put me in a cab, or take me home?"

"No after-concert drink?"

"No. Not tonight."

"Then, my chariot awaits." He opened the car door for her.

"Oh." She looked down at the two-seat BMW Roadster. "Thank you," she said as he opened the door and she sat in the front seat, waiting for him to round the hood of the car and claim the seat beside her like he'd done in

San Francisco. She wanted another magical night like that. This time she wanted to dance one third of the night, kiss for another third, and make love for the last third. That would be idyllic. But they were in New Orleans now, and the fantasy was over. So why was she here with him now? *Get a grip, girl,* she said to herself. What is wrong with you? *What is the protocol on home turf? You've only dated one man in your entire life, so cut yourself some slack.*

He put his car in gear and pulled away from the curb. "Christmas carols this early," he noted to break the silence, then changed the station to the soothing classical music they'd just heard.

"They don't even let you get through Halloween and All Souls' Day first. Of course, that's just God's signal that Sister Claire Regina will be calling me soon about the bazaar."

"For whom?"

"St. Gabriel's Church of the Scared Heart. I do the Christmas bazaar every year to help raise money."

"Beautiful, smart, and giving," he said as he downshifted. "Where do you live?"

"On Chartres and Clemenceau, just outside the Quarter. Know where that is?"

"Yes, I do." He made a U-turn. "So, what's your favorite Christmas carol?"

"'This Christmas' by Donny Hathaway. It's not Christmas until I hear that."

"The way you love the classics, you must have an old traditional favorite too."

"As a matter of fact I do. 'Have Yourself a Merry Little Christmas.'"

"From *Meet Me in St. Louis*—Judy Garland," he identified to her delight.

"That's right. I cry whenever I hear that song," she

said wistfully, thinking of how bleak her Christmas would be this year. "You are an old-movie buff?"

"Old movies are a lonely child's best playmate," he said without rancor.

He recalled his Christmases full of expensive presents but devoid of warmth and caring. After the tradition of watching him open his gifts, they sat for breakfast prepared by servants, and when his parents could no longer tolerate being in one another's company, they'd excused themselves from the table. Aidan had spent many holidays wishing he could go home with the help. His mother and father loved him, but not each other. As a result he had separate outings with them and few friends, so he excelled in boarding-school sports—swimming, soccer, tennis, golf—not the basketball he longed to play. With no siblings or close friends his trumpet was his passion and constant companion. Music, old movies and a longing for normalcy were his company.

Sassy noted his silence and, not wanting to get too personal or into him any deeper than she was, asked, "What about you? Your favorite Christmas carol?"

"I'm a traditionalist. Nat King Cole's 'Christmas Song.'"

"Certainly someone as avant-garde as you must have an untraditional favorite," she teased.

He smiled and she felt better.

"'What Are You Doing New Year's Eve?' By Lou Rawls," he answered.

She chuckled and said, "Always looking ahead?"

"Always." He glanced at her intently. "Planning is the only way to get what you want."

Sassy smile-smirked with a blush.

"We're here."

"Oh, we certainly are." She hadn't even noticed. She didn't want to go. She didn't want him to go.

"Nice house. Formidable gates."

"To keep Killer the Great Dane in. I only occupy the second floor," she said, hand on car handle, ready to bolt.

"I don't suppose you want me to walk you up?"

"No. I can manage." She opened the door, closed it and leaned in from the rider's side. "Thanks again, Aidan. I really did enjoy myself."

"We'll have to go horseback riding, and you still have to see Marie Antoinette's desk."

"I will," she smiled.

"Promise?"

"Yes." She wanted a kiss good night. No, she really didn't want it to stop there.

"That's good enough for me. I'll watch you walk up, if that's all right?"

"Yes. Good night."

"Good night, Sassiere."

She walked the few steps to the gate, unlocked it and shut it with a quiet clang. She glanced at Ivanhoe's apartment, then proceeded to unlock her door to the upstairs gallery. She waved at Aidan, who tooted lightly and pulled off.

What was she doing? She did want to be with him tonight, but she didn't. It was all so complicated for her, but Aidan was at such ease, like he was waiting for her to come to her senses. She wondered if she'd always be this indecisive. She needed time to heal before she jumped into a new relationship. But Aidan seemed so . . . right. Or was he just the male manifestation of her longing for a perfect man she could trust, or was she just horny? She kicked off her heels and went into the bathroom. As she washed her face, brushed her teeth and stripped to her camisole and vowed never to see him again—not until her fragile heart mended. She couldn't take another heartbreak on top of Roux's.

As she climbed into bed Sassy remembered the stunning woman at the symphony. Aidan was probably tired of those spa ladies and was slumming with her. Sassy knew she was different from anyone he'd ever dated—could ever date. He was curious, and she was too vulnerable to be someone's curiosity quencher; once he had his fill, he'd return to what he was used to.

She turned on her side, and the moon rays spilled across the window sill. Maybe when she got herself together she would be ready for him and all the wonderful things they could do together. But maybe by that time he would have moved on and it would be too late for her. She had to cut him loose for her own sake. He wasn't Prince Charming; he had foibles and weakness just like any other man, and she didn't have the time, strength, or inclination to learn them and trust a man again. Although she could use some lovin'—it was Saturday night.

The savvy Sassy sighed, closed her eyes and invited sleep. The emotional Sassy missed Aidan Symonds already.

Aidan drove home. There was nowhere else and no one else's company he wanted. His mind flitted across available possibilities. He'd had women on five continents and many in between: the island girl in Martinique for two summers of his youth, the Brit in the London flat, the agile Japanese girl who loved his black skin, the Italian contessa who wanted to follow him home to New Orleans, the dancer in Rio, and Michelle Micheaux who said she'd been in love with him since he escorted her older sister in the Cotillion. She wasn't one of the original five families of the Old Creole Guard, as the Micheaux wealth only

went back three generations, but she had the pedigree.
He'd dated her most consistently and she was the only
one he'd considered marrying. But she'd perpetuate the
home life he was trying to avoid—the money, fund-rasiers,
luncheons, boarding schools—and he refused to have his
children raised by nannies. Michelle, as with the others,
shared the same fate—he never led them on or hurt
them, and any of them would be glad to see him again.
But in the end, all of them, despite his youthful attempts
to the contrary, paled in comparison to Sassiere Crillon.
In his maturity, he finally decided he wouldn't settle. Five
years ago, Michelle had given him an ultimatum which he
graciously declined, but whenever he wanted, she was
there for him. Michelle loved him, he loved Sassy, and
Sassy . . . who'd loved Roux, was now free to love him. He
had to make it happen.

Aidan pulled in at the front of his house and used the
keys to open the door. It was relatively dark with just the
perpetual lamp burning to the rear of the staircase, casting an eerie patina to those who hadn't lived with the
welcoming glow all their lives.

The grandfather clock chimed as he threw his keys on
the tray with a jingle and opened the double doors to the
front parlor. He stepped to the bar, poured himself a short
brandy, and while it breathed, removed his jacket, undid
his tie, and sank into the Louis XIV chair. This sure wasn't
the night he'd envisioned, but he was fast learning that the
one thing that was predictable was the unpredictability of
an anticipated night with . . . Sassiere. He got up and
opened the French doors to the sticky breeze that waited
to envelop him. He picked up the brandy sniffer and
swished the amber liquid around a few times before he
let the golden nectar slide down his throat. It was satisfying
and familiar. He went over to his trumpet case, opened it

with a click, and pulled out the instrument. He put the mouthpiece to his supple lips and breathed life into the metal. The pure sound of "Moody's Mood" pierced the silence of the thick night air as it had always done when the Prince of N'awlins was restless. It's a good thing he was good or the neighbors would have called the cops as they did when the Dumas' boy played. But the years of melancholy practice had left his lips supple, his timing impeccable and his fingers agile as they danced effortlessly over the valves producing full, fluid, soulful notes which fell like sweet nectar of night jasmine. His music was magic.

"Been a long time since I heard you play," Simone said, stepping from the shadows into the parlor. "What ails you, boy?"

"Nothing. Did I disturb you?" He dropped the trumpet to his side.

"Not at all. Your daddy always said you had a natural gift with that horn. Could name your price at any New Orleans club. Thank goodness you opted for the family business." She chuckled.

"I may be bringing a young lady home for a visit soon."

"Oh? It's been years since you've done that. She must be special for you to bring her *here*."

"Yes. She is."

"How special?"

"Only time will tell," he said, returning his trumpet to its case. "I'm going to turn in now. Good night." He bent and kissed her toffee-brown cheek, which was warmed by the golden glow of the hall light.

"Good night, son."

"Hello, Maman," Sassy kissed her mother. Sassy noted how terrible her coloring looked, her skin ashen and tight. Her mother only grunted in response, so Sassy continued, "Nice day." She inhaled deeply and looked down the knoll to the bayou. "How you feeling? The doctor called and said you had a rough couple of nights."

"Of course I did. I'm dying," she spat.

Okay, we're in one of those kinds of moods, Sassy thought.

"Roux came to see me," Maman said.

"Did he?" Sassy didn't care. She didn't want to talk about him.

"He's sorry, Sassiere."

"We're all sorry, Maman."

"I told him you needed time to heal and maybe another experience."

Sassy didn't want to argue with her mother.

Maman took her silence for interest and continued, "I told him you need another boyfriend so you'll know how good you have it with him."

Sassy bit her tongue to hold the words she wanted to hurl at her prying mother. She breathed deeply and let it go. "The last thing I need is another 'experience.' It's all said and done."

"He really has changed, chou-chou."

"Maman—" Sassy warned and cut her eyes in exasperation.

They fell silent. Mother and daughter feigned interest in the sway of the dripping moss on the warm bayou breeze.

"I'm sorry, Sassiere," Maman said quietly.

"For what?"

"For not providing for you better."

"Maman, I'm fine. I'm grown with a career that I not only like but I'm good at."

"But if I hadn't gotten sick and lost the shop you could have gone straight through college like Yvette—"

"It's okay, Maman. I took a little detour but I finished. And now, all I have to do is finish my thesis and I'll have a master's in art history. Besides, you did more than most mothers."

"Yes, but this all should have been set years ago. That's why I'm so anxious to see you settle down with Roux, have some babies. And you'll never have to worry about money—that boy's set for life."

Sassy refused to escalate, perpetuate, or retaliate, so she gritted her teeth and remained silent. Maman was going to have her say, regardless, and they'd best be done with it.

"Sometime a man just needs a good woman, Sassiere, to save him from himself."

"I'm no one's life preserver or rescuer."

"Is there someone else?" Maman asked cagily.

The question caught Sassy off guard. "What?"

"You're too calm and collected, usually the signs that there's someone better waiting in the wings."

"I've been through this with Roux a few times. I'm tired of it and him. It has nothing to do with anyone else. It has to do with me and how I expect and intend to be treated. Right now, I'm concentrating on me and getting to be the best me I can be. You, Maman, should concentrate on getting better as well."

Maman thought her daughter's words were sincere but impotent.

The rain fell steadily and heavy, shaking loose some of the blossoms so that the fragrance of the night jasmine perfumed the air.

Saturday night, Sassy thought, the loneliest night in the week. Her Saturday nights for fifteen years had always been spoken for and now they were up for grabs—or were they? Aidan had called Wednesday, and the practical Sassy had declined. Soon, she would alienate him to the point that he would no longer try, and then where would she be? Here, sitting on the windowsill instead of correcting those research papers, watching the rain and the way the moon danced silver on the part of the yard that wasn't concealed by the cistern. The emotional Sassy thought about Aidan constantly, but the practical Sassy always countered with—it was too soon and she wasn't ready to deal with him or a relationship. Sassy wished she smoked; this would be the perfect time for a cigarette, or to talk to Yvette. They'd talked six times since she and Roux broke up and Sassy didn't have the courage to tell her best friend. And why not? Was it because deep down inside, she knew she and Roux would eventually get back together, and she didn't want to waste a long-distance call on something that would in time rectify itself? Or was it that she knew it was over but she didn't want to hear Yvette go on ad nauseam about how fine Roux was, what a good catch he was, and that no man was perfect? Her precious Gardner Reynolds was pert-near, although Sassy would never forgive him for keeping Yvette in New York City. Sassy was sure that her best friend, then a twenty-seven-year-old CPA at Price Waterhouse, was sick of the city and on her way back to New Orleans when she met Gardner. They dated for a year, and all of the sudden, according to Yvette, New York was the most fascinating place on the face of the earth! The next year, she and Roux stood as Yvette and Gardner were married at St. Gabriel's, then the newlyweds returned to New York where he was a lawyer who specialized in securities arbitration. Sassy had read about the experienced investor lawyer in *Black Enterprise*, *Forbes*, *and Kiplinger's,* all of which reported in varying degrees, that he worked on contingency for thirty to forty percent of the awards and refused cases that would net him less than $100,000. Sassy knew Yvette wasn't coming back to New Orleans.

"Chère! C'mon down," Ivanhoe called up to her.

The "no thanks" was stuck in her throat, so Ivanhoe appeared at the threshold of her bedroom, honoring her space. "Did you hear me call you? We're having a soirée."

"I heard you. I didn't want to answer or come."

Gauging her mood, he said, "Look at this room." He sauntered in and over to her windowsill seat. "What is it? Your sixth Roux-less Saturday night and your resolve is melting fast?"

Sassy sucked her teeth defiantly.

"I got it!" Ivanhoe exclaimed. "It's not Roux at all, is it, chère? It's the one who calls you . . . Sassiere," he said with an air of drama that made her chuckle.

"Do you and Cyril discuss everything?"

"That's what lovers do, chère." He bumped up against her shoulder playfully. "You been out with him?"

Sassy fiddled with the shutter pull and answered, "Yes," with a girlish blush.

"Aw! And you didn't tell Ivanhoe? The Fairy Godmother of all mothers?"

"Because it's nothing."

"Don't piss on my shoes and tell me it's raining. I know you, chère."

Sassy shook her head without speaking.

"What?" Ivanhoe prompted.

"He's a nice guy. He deserves better."

"You are better, chère."

"I mean, he deserves someone who isn't lugging

around twenty years of old baggage. Someone who isn't on the rebound."

"Who is? Not you. You've moved on. You told me so." He chuckled then said, "Look. As long as you live, Roulon Robespierre is going to be your first love—just as the older married gentleman was mine. There's no way around that fact. This guy also had a first love—everybody's got to start someplace. But there are second and third loves too, chère. You just don't want so many you lose count. Then they'll have another word for you, *n'est-ce pas*? But you know that. So! What's really eating at your old Creole heart?"

"He's different and a little sad."

"Women give him the runaround?"

"Hardly. Old sad—childhood sad. Like despite everything he's had and done, he feels he's missed out on the most important things."

"Well, he must think you can make him happy."

"I wouldn't go that far."

"Good different or bad different?"

"We had fun in San Francisco—"

"San Francisco!?" Ivanhoe bellowed.

"I met him in San Francisco, but he lives here."

"*Mon dieu*! You went all the way to the coast to meet somebody who lives right here in N'awlins? Now that's destiny. Kismet—"

"In fact, that's where I met him—at Kismet—the party at Taylor's ranch in Napa."

"Oh, this is too spooky, chère. You have to have Madame Foquette read—"

"Oh, Ivanhoe!" she scoffed and chuckled, knowing he was intentionally being funny. She didn't believe in all that mumbo jumbo.

"But seriously, chère. I mean, case closed. This is some kind of divine intervention. Did you know him before?"

"No. He looked vaguely, remotely familiar when I saw him on campus—"

"Campus?"

"Yes, apparently he is on the board at Tulane and Xavier."

"Well, ain't we living high off the hog?" He slapped his thighs. "So tell me how is soon-to-be lover number two coming?"

"Tsk. I can't tell whether I'm really attracted to him per se or whether it's the lack of continual fantastic sex."

"Well all right, Roux."

"The man does have skills. But that don't mean diddley now."

"That was indelicate of me, to bring that up when you ain't gettin' any, but what's wrong with killing two birds with one stone? Tell me about him?"

Sassy smiled. "Like I said, he's different. He's confident, settled, mature, sophisticated, solid—"

"Everything Roux isn't."

"Everything Roux isn't," she repeated quietly. "We've been to the symphony—"

"Highbrow. Who *is* this man?"

"I don't want to say and jinx it just in case."

"Ah-ha, see, chère, you do believe it's possible."

"He's not like anyone I've ever met."

"Is he black?"

"Of course he's black," she snapped and continued with a smile, "He's articulate, cultured, well traveled, and not at all arrogant. And his clothes are classic and expensive. He had on a pair of those twelve-hundred-dollar Ferragamo loafers you've been drooling over for two years."

"If I've said it once I've said it a thousand times, it is obscene to wear that much money on your feet."

"But money is never discussed. It's just there in the way he is treated and expects to be treated. The way he wears those clothes. He discussed stock and bonds some—but that was more career-related than about actual money."

"So, he's a N'awlins stock-money-person?" Ivanhoe searched his mental Rolodex for who this man could be. "Who is this Black Blueblood? I'm clueless."

"You don't know everybody in New Orleans."

"Who says? I know everybody black with money in N'awlins. I devoutly read the society pages. Besides it's my business to know the high rollers."

"Let's just say he didn't travel in our circles. The private schools, the studying abroad; he speaks five languages and he knows antiques."

"Really? That's the reason I don't know him, because probably he hasn't been around here much," Ivanhoe said to justify his ignorance. "One thing for sure, chère. He is not a man to be toyed with."

"I know. But I don't think he wants to rush me."

"Smart man. But he also sounds like a man who's used to getting what he wants."

"I'm sure of it."

"Tell me, just how far have you two gone?"

"Why, sir," she drawled. "That is none of your affair." Her face split into a wide grin. "The brother can kiss. Umph! Those lips."

"Okay. Be like that, chère. But if you are *truly* over Roux and attracted to this guy—then what's the problem?"

"I'm just not ready to start a new relationship and won't be for some time. At least that's the way I feel until he puts his hand around my waist when we cross the street. Or holds me when we dance. He can move," she mused. "Or sends me pecan bark from Ghirardelli Square for no reason at all."

"So, what are you going to do?"

"I need to get away. To distance myself. Cool me down. Slow it down."

"I can send you to Paris."

"Oh great. One of the most romantic cities in the world and I'd be there solo?"

"Then go to New York for me. Nigel Fitzwilliams is there."

"The noted Egyptologist?"

"He's giving a lecture series at the Metropolitan."

"Since when are you interested in Egypt?"

"And since when do you look a gift horse in the mouth and get a chance to *see* instead of just talking to Yvette?" He struck a pose. "Have you told her about Roux yet?"

"Nope. She's very preoccupied and pregnant."

"Ain't that grand!"

"Yep. You're looking at the godmother of all godmothers. She said she wanted Roux to be the godfather if we tie the knot before the baby's born."

"Humph. Even she doesn't want to take a long-range chance on Roux."

"I accept," Sassy said with a smile. "It will be good to see her and Gardner, but I want to stay in a hotel."

"Demanding little bitch, aren't you?"

"I like staying in hotels."

"The Stanhope is right across the street. I love it there. You know Yvette is gonna have a cow when you tell her you aren't staying with them."

"I know. I can handle it."

"I know you can, chère. I'll have Cyril register you for Fitzwilliams and make all the arrangements. You can leave the Friday after Thanksgiving. The conference doesn't start until Monday, so you'll have the weekend with Yvette."

"My girl. From the womb to the tomb."

He rose to go, Sassy caught his hand and said, "Thanks, Ivanhoe. You always know what to do."

"No problem, chère. That's what Fairy Godmothers are for." He kissed the top of her curly locks. "Gotta get back to my party. I know they miss me!" He flitted from the room and down the stairs.

Sassy accepted the delivery from the UPS man and, with care, opened the long slender box from San Francisco addressed to SASSIERE. She knew who it was from, but only imagined what it could be. She pushed past the hot-pink tissue paper, and her suspicions were confirmed. The lovely Victorian hat pin she had admired at Heirlooms in San Francisco lay on a bed of cotton. The card read simply: *Thought you might like this. Aidan.*

She smiled. He was slowly penetrating her practical reserve.

"Oh, how exquisite," Ivanhoe said over her shoulder. "This man has taste in artifacts and women. He's a keeper, chère."

"Sassiere," Cyril called, dangling the phone from his long, coffee-colored finger.

"Hello," she said smiling into the phone.

"Hello," Aidan chimed back.

"Thank you. It's just arrived."

"You're more than welcome. I was back there on business last week and thought I'd send it to you."

"It was very thoughtful of you."

"'The Very Thought of You' made me do it."

She blushed and turned her back to Ivanhoe. "You really get around."

"That's my business. So, how about horseback riding?"

"What's up with you and horseback riding? You must be exceptionally good and just want to show me up."

"No, I just want to spend some time with you and I think that is as un-intimate as we can get," he teased, and she laughed. "But seriously, do you think you can get away?"

"Not anytime soon. I know that's at least a half-day trip and I haven't got that kind of time yet."

"All right. Plan B—it's more intimate. Spend Thanksgiving Day with me?"

"Sorry. I'm spending that with my mother, then I'm off to New York," she said, loving the cosmopolitan sound of that.

"Ah! This is amazing. I'm going to be in New York that week as well," he enthused.

Sassy hedged, not believing him. "That's none too smooth, Aidan."

"No. Really, a financier always has business in New York. You're not at Marriott at the Park are you?"

"No. The Stanhope."

"Good little hotel. Your business must have something to do with the Met."

"Yes, it does."

"Then we'll have to get together while we're there. Have you ever been to New York at Christmastime?"

I've never been to New York at any time, Sassy thought, but said, "No."

"It's amazing. Magical."

"I'll be there on business and to see some old friends. I just don't think I'll have time to—"

"Don't shut me out, Sassiere," he interrupted with a tender urgency.

Sassy was quiet. His words masked that sadness she felt was there.

Sassiere—that's who she was. A self-confident, urbane career woman who was going to "happen to be" in New York City the same time as a man she'd met in San Francisco. Sassy liked this image. A clean slate with no past; to Aidan, she was not Roux's lifetime girlfriend, just a woman who'd ended a long relationship that had left her fragile-hearted and cautious. And Sassiere's future? Was up for grabs.

"That would be nice," Sassy finally answered.

"Great. If I can't get you horseback riding, maybe I'll get you on ice skates at Rockefeller Center."

"I did take years of dance, you know," she chuckled.

"Well, I'm back to the Coast for a couple of days, so I'll say 'Happy Thanksgiving' now and plan to see you in New York."

"Happy Thanksgiving to you as well."

"Dress warmly. New York can be frigid in more ways than one," he said.

"Thanks for the warning."

"Bye, Sassiere."

"Bye, Aidan, and thanks again for the Victorian hat pin."

"My pleasure."

Sassy held the receiver with a half-smile gracing her lips.

"Well, this is new," Ivanhoe said. "Usually after talking to a man you're ready to spit fire." He laid absentee-bid forms on her desk.

"I told you, this man's a little different," she admitted with a wide grin of happiness.

"Well, here's something guaranteed to wipe the smile from your face and force your fingers to form a crucifix." He handed her the message from line two. "Sister Claire Regina from St. Gabriel's Church of the Sacred Heart."

"It's bazaar time," Sassy said. "Can I count on you?"

"Always, chère. The only surefire way I'll ever get to heaven."

"Will I ever get out of this? My penance for graduating from there in the eighth grade, I suppose. I need some new ideas."

"It couldn't hurt. The last few years have been so bo-ring."

"How do you spice up an Annual Catholic Christmas Bazaar?"

"Don't know, chère. Don't want to find out, either. My life is not that pathetic."

Chapter VI

Sassy boarded the plane and sat in first class for the second time within weeks. As the plane taxied, she smiled at Yvette's mock indignation at Sassy's staying in a hotel instead of with her and Gardner. As the plane took off, Sassy scowled, remembering her chat with Sister Claire Regina about Roux.

"So sorry he can't join us for the bazaar this year since he'll be in the Bahamas for the month, but we'll put his usual generous donation to good use. I don't suppose he'll ever forgive us for keeping him back a year in the fifth grade," the nun had said with her characteristic warped sense of humor. She was right. Roux had passed all the tests but he would never forgive them for keeping him back for something as trite as attendance. His mother was a staunch Catholic who believed everything the nuns and priests said was "good for her son." In the absence of a father in the home to speak up for him, Roux repeated a grade and graduated with Sassy.

As the plane reached cruising altitude, Sassy wondered what, or rather who, Roux was doing in the Bahamas for the month. She couldn't get him to go anywhere when she'd asked for a simple beach vacation, and now he was off to the Caribbean with some low-self-esteem-having woman. As the seat-belt light chimed off, with a jolt of reality, Sassy realized that she didn't really care what Roux was up to, or with whom; It was both funny and sad at the same time.

She blushed as she thought of Aidan, taking his wardrobe tips and packing "heavy" for New York's hawk. She reluctantly admitted that she was looking forward to seeing him more than Dr. Fitzwilliams and his Egyptian artifacts.

Sassy arrived at midday and took a cab to the Stanhope, which she remembered from the old television show, *Lifestyles of the Rich and Famous*. She unpacked and relaxed before she had the doorman call her a cab, which deposited her with another doorman, who opened the cab and then the plate-glass door to the vaulted lobby of Yvette's Central Park West condo. When Sassy stepped off the elevator on the sixteenth floor, Yvette was already standing with her doorway flung wide open and the two old friends shrieked and screeched down the hallway until they were locked in each other's arms.

They rocked one another, and it didn't matter that one went straight through college then earned a master's and the other hadn't, or that one made three times as much as the other. Or that one was happily married and expecting a baby and the other wasn't. That one's life seemed perfect and the other one was crap. All that mattered was the bond of friendship that endured, unaltered. The faint scar on each of their wrists where they cut themselves and mixed their blood as sisters "forever and a day" when they were nine years old in that garage off the alley of Ms. Foquette's was proof positive.

"I can't believe Roux let you leave N'awlins, girl,"

Yvette said, still holding Sassy's hand as she led her best friend into the spacious apartment.

"Got-Damn!" Sassy exclaimed as the sumptuous condo took shape before her. "Your pictures don't do this place justice. Yvette, this is gorgeous!" Sassy shed her coat and walked to the windows. New York stretched out before her, a mesmerizing labyrinth of glowing lights. "Look at this place!" Sassy flopped down on the couch and pillows tumbled upon her. "You didn't decorate this yourself, did you?"

"So what you tryin' to say?" Yvette posed her hands on her hips. "All my taste is in my mouth? Huh?"

"Honey, I remember some combinations—"

"Okay, Sassy. You don't have to go there."

"Oh God, it's good to *see* you," Sassy said, jumping up for a hug again. "Oh, I'm not squeezing my godchild too tightly am I?"

"He can take it."

"You know it's a boy?"

"No. I'm just humoring Gardner."

"Where is that lucky man?"

"It's only six. He's still working. He's got to keep working 'cause I'm fittin' to stop once this baby's born."

They laughed at her intentional colloquial slip.

"From what I read in *Black Enterprise* and *Forbes,* he could have stopped working five years ago and still have money to last until the next millennium."

"Girl, you can't believe everything you read. But we ain't hurtin'." They slapped five. "God, Sass. I've missed you, girl. How's that fine-as-wine Roux?"

"Excuse me, Mrs. Reynolds," the cook interrupted. "The food is ready when you are. I'll go now."

"Fine, Isabella. Thank you," Yvette said as the maid put on her coat. "We'll see you tomorrow."

Once Isabella cleared the threshold and closed the door, Sassy said, "Excuse the hell outta me!"

"Ooh, girl. If they could see us now!"

"That ole gang of mine," Sassy chimed in and they sang a few bars from *Sweet Charity*. They crumbled into laughter, and Sassy said, "That's the real reason Gardner didn't come home yet. Gimme time with my girl! You hungry? You're always hungry. C'mon." Yvette padded to the kitchen and Sassy followed. "He knows you're here on business and all, but he wants his time with you too, so he wants you to come to dinner next Friday. He had to actually plan to be home at a reasonable hour, so if you don't come you'll break his heart."

"I'll come."

"Great." She grabbed one plate and Sassy followed suit and they went into the dining room where the table was already set and a chilled bottle of wine stood in an iced bucket.

"I know you're not drinking that?" Sassy eyed the white wine and noted it was a Coleridge Chardonnay. She smiled, but said nothing.

"Hell no. I'm not doing nothing to jeopardize this baby. That's for you."

"You trying to say I'm an alkyholic?" They died laughing at the familiar mispronunciation.

Sassy poured herself a glass of wine and grape juice for Yvette, who used the remote to cut on background music.

"I'm scared of you," Sassy said as she twirled a forkful of shrimp-stuffed pasta before placing it in her mouth. She started beating the table with her free hand. "Oh, my God! Nectar of the gods."

"Can't Isabella burn?"

"I'm surprised you don't weigh a ton."

"Why do you think I got pregnant? Camouflage." They

laughed before she continued, "And you just wait until you see dessert."

"To our 'forever friendship,'" Yvette raised her glass and toasted.

"Womb to tomb," Sassy countered as the crystal clinked signaling that the two old friends were off and running.

An hour later, they sat on the couch with their shoes off, finishing up dessert and planning a Saturday shopping spree.

"So, you think you'll ever get Roux out of N'awlins?"

"He already is. According to Sister Claire Regina, he's in the Bahamas."

"That old bat. How does she know the boy's in the Bahamas?"

"She's always had a crush on him."

"Like everybody else. The horny heiffer threatened to put you back in the third grade because you asked a simple question. 'Which is right, the Adam and Eve thing, or the evolution thing?'"

"Old prune sent me to Father Lewis. I was on my way to being expelled for blasphemy."

"Whoa. Wait a minute. You said Roux was in the Bahamas . . . and you're here. What's up, Sass?"

"Nothing's up. Except maybe Roux's huge, horny—"

"So why are you here and not there with him?"

"Roux and I are no longer," she said casually.

"What!?" Yvette choked.

Sassy watched her friend try to wrap her mind around the incomprehensible content of what was just said.

"Isn't that humanly impossible, for you two to break up? Doesn't that defy the laws of nature? Destroy the order of the universe?"

"We have split, and the world still spins on its axis," Sassy said, reaching for another hunk of chocolate cake.

"What happened to 'It's easier to take the wet from water' than to pull you two apart?'"

Sassy looked at Yvette with mock-dagger eyes for quoting Roux's familiar words.

"I just can't believe it." Yvette let the fork drop in her plate and placed it all on the coffee table. "I mean, why? Will you be getting back together?"

"Caught him receiving oral sex in the hallway of his club. So that would be a 'no.'"

"No! That disgusting dog."

"Let's not denigrate dogs. A dog would have gone to the alley."

"Now, you know that girl don't mean nothing to him."

"Maxine Dupree meant something to me. And my quarrel is not with the slut-woman but with the dog-Roux, 'allowing' her to perform her act on his person."

"Well, you seemed to have taken this very well."

"Is there anything sadder than an old man at the club or a married Casanova? And if that's the best I could hope for with Roux, I don't need it or him. I deserve more, or at least I deserve the option. I opted out."

"Good for you, Sassy." She patted her hand in support. "When did this happen?"

"A few weeks ago."

"And you didn't tell me?"

"I couldn't. I didn't want to tell you over the phone. Then Ivanhoe sent me on this little trip."

"Bless his little gay heart. How's he doing?"

"He's been a real friend. And confidant."

"I'm so sorry I wasn't there for you, Sass."

"It's okay. Really, the worst is over. I don't even care who he took to the Bahamas."

"Maybe he went alone. To reflect on his life, to

cleanse his body and be celibate—so sex doesn't confuse the issue."

They both eyed each other at the sheer lunacy of it and burst out laughing.

"If he's breathin', he's lovin' on somebody. But let's just say he may have *gone* alone. You best be believin' that he's not alone now."

"Yeah, the old sand to the beach theory."

"Right up Roux's alley."

"That's too bad, Sass. Jeeze, I feel like I've just experienced a death in the family."

"That relationship's been circling the drain for a lot of years. I just didn't know it." For the first time, her eyes watered. "But it'll be all right."

"You keeping my wife up?" Gardner said, entering the living room. "Hey, sweetie." He bent to kiss Yvette and then kissed Sassy on the cheek. "Hello, sweetie," he teased.

"Hey! I don't play that," Yvette teased back. "What time is it?"

"Midnight," Gardner answered.

"Oh. I better get going if we're going shopping tomorrow."

"You mean later on today," Gardner corrected. "You might as well spend the night in the guest room."

"Yeah, Sassy," Yvette agreed.

"No. I'll meet you at noon."

"At Saks, there is this bad black velvet dress made for her," Yvette told Gardner.

"You just take care of her and the heir apparent to the Reynolds throne," Gardner told Sassy as he gazed lovingly into his wife's eyes.

"Will do," Sassy said feeling like the third wheel, and for the first time that she could remember, she envied what her friend had. To have a man look at her the way Gardner did Yvette would be heaven.

The couple walked Sassy to their door and, as Gardner helped her with her coat, he asked "I'm not chasing you out, am I?"

"No. We've been at it since six," Sassy said. "I think we're all caught up now."

"You look great. You cut your hair," Gardner noticed.

"Yep, wash-and-wear hair. Good night." She kissed him on the cheek, then Yvette.

"Let me tell the doorman to hail you a cab," he said and went to the phone to call downstairs.

"Get some sleep, kiddo," Sassy said, embracing her friend again.

"I love you, Sass. Everything's going to be fine."

"It already is. Later. Bye, Gardner."

"See you this Sunday and next Friday, right?"

"She doesn't want to come on Sunday," Yvette chimed in. "Hell, I don't want to come Sunday."

"Be nice," Gardner admonished. "I have some friends—"

"Clients, colleagues and business associates—it's a gather, grip, and grin affair," Yvette corrected with a disgusted smirk. "Sassy is a *friend* with whom we'll be spending some quality one-on-one time with on Friday."

"She can come Sunday if she wants to. Might class up the joint some."

"This is her first time to New York," Yvette said. "Why would she want to spend it with a bunch of boring strangers?"

"Who provide you a good lifestyle," Gardner interjected.

"No, sweetie," Yvette softened and said to him, "You do that for me." She kissed his cheek.

"Thank you, baby. Let's let Sassy decide for herself."

"If you come, Sassy, I'll have someone of substance to talk to," Yvette switched sides.

What did she have planned for Sunday, Sassy thought. *Not a blasted thing, especially if Aidan doesn't show.* "Okay. I'll be happy to come, but I'll have to get something to wear."

"That's what later on today is for," Yvette said with a laugh.

"See you then. Bye. Thanks."

As the cab meandered through the still heavily trafficked streets, Sassy noticed how dressed up for Christmas New York already was. *The city that never sleeps,* Sassy thought, feeling alone and lonely in a city teeming with folks. She then reflected on how happy Yvette and Gardner were. She wanted a solid, death-do-you-part kind of love, and wondered if she'd ever have it. She thought she had, but she was so wrong.

"Messages for 324 please," Sassy asked at the desk.

At the elevator, she rifled through two; an earlier one from Yvette and one from Ivanhoe. None from Aidan. She opened her door and the winking red glow from the answering service greeted her before she flicked on the light. She smiled, shed her coat and kicked off her shoes as she checked the message. It was the concierge checking to see if all was to her liking and offering his services for theater tickets, restaurant reservations or limo service. Nothing from Aidan.

She opened the entertainment center and clicked on the television for noise. She looked at the turned down bed for one and the lone foil-wrapped chocolate. She prepared for bed then opened the heavy drapes which revealed another view of New York and The Metropolitan Museum. Suppose he doesn't call? Suppose, after all the brush offs or less than enthusiastic responses he's decided that she's not worth it. That nothing was going to happen and he's moved on. Certainly a man of his *joie de vivre* had many women he could call upon at any given time in any given port, be it San Francisco or New York. Suppose he thought, as Roux's friends used to say of women, "She's just too much work when others are so willing and able."

She picked up the receiver. "Yes, I'd like a wake-up call for eleven o'clock, please."

"Eleven AM. Suite 324. Good night," the efficient voice verified and dismissed.

"Good night."

Sassy thought she slept fretfully until the telephone blasted her awake.

"Good morning. Eleven AM. Have a nice day."

"Thank you."

She called room service, showered, ate breakfast when it arrived, dressed and was in the cab, directing, "Saks, please."

She tipped the cabbie and headed up in the elevator to the lingerie department. She was looking at a leopard-print teddy when Yvette snuck up behind her and asked, "Who is that for?"

"Hey, girl," Sassy replied with an air kiss to her friend's cheeks.

"In fact who are all these for?" Yvette flipped her fingers through an assortment of hot pink, lemon yellow, and poppy orange matching bra and panties sets. "Not Roux."

"You got that right. In fact, if you never mention his name again I won't be mad at ya."

"You got it, girlfriend. So who?" Yvette followed her girlfriend to the saleslady.

"We'll talk over lunch."

"Sassy," Yvette said, turning her girlfriend around and

intently looking in her eyes. "Are you serious? There really is somebody else?"

"I'm not sure but like a girl scout, baby—I'm prepared."

"Oh, Sassy. I hope so." Yvette had kept Gardner up for a hour and a half after Sassy left talking about the breakup of her friend and Roux. About how devastating it must be after all those years and how Sassy needed all their support, how she deserved a good man and they may have to find her one. "So tell me about him," Yvette said as Sassy accepted her change from the saleslady.

"Not now. Over lunch."

"I'm hungry now. You hungry?"

"No. Let me see this bad velvet dress."

They headed for the formal wear department where Yvette gave Sassy the dress and thrust her though the louver doors to try it on. Sassy stepped from the dressing room and stopped everyone in their tracks. The sweetheart neckline demurely showcased the rise of her breasts while the slinky black velvet clung to her curves. The short, slightly weighted train dragged dramatically along the rug as she walked to the tri-mirror.

"Oh, Sassy! Was I right? This is you. Sexy and innocent."

"Oh, madam. It is perfection," the saleswoman said as she was joined by two others. "Are you a model?"

"She should be," Yvette said. "Look at the way your skin tone sets off that dress and—I think it's the short hair. Nobody's looking at all that long stuff, they're looking at you wear that dress, girl. I have the perfect gold choker and just some little drop earrings to match."

The saleswomen clapped and agreed with Yvette's assessment. "And strappy black poult-de soie heels," one of them added.

"Oh, and I have an opera cape with either a hot pink or a gold lining," Yvette was offering.

"Try on the red one," a saleslady suggested.

"Red?" Sassy objected.

"Oh, it's an elegant rich red, Sass. Not that bama-red," Yvette said. "Get it for her."

Sassy obliged and lit from the dressing room to more folk with the same reaction.

"I do look great don't I?" Sassy teased, as she pirouetted in front of the three-way mirror.

"Drop-dead gorgeous," Yvette agreed.

"Which one?" Sassy asked, looking at the sales tag.

"Both," Yvette and her chorus of saleswomen chimed in.

Sassy looked at the astronomical price, and said, "Shi—I can't afford either of them."

"Sassy. C'mon. This dress was made for you. You buy one and I'll buy the other."

"Yvette, I cannot let you do that."

"Why?"

"It's too much," Sassy said, walking back to the dressing room with Yvette in tow.

"It's only money, Sass," Yvette said, unzipping her.

"Too much money. For a dress? Negro, puleeze."

"Sassy I want to do this for you. I can, so let me. I promise I won't go hungry behind giving you this dress for Christmas."

Sassy pulled the sweater over her head, and Yvette watched Sassy's curls pop individually through the wool yarn, and waited for a sign of weakening in her friend's eyes. "Please, Sassy. Remember when we were little girls and we'd pretend we had all these fabulous clothes and houses and men? I can't give you nothing but the dress, honey. Please take it. Remember our pact? We always said whoever 'made it' first would share with the other one. It's just a dress, Sass."

Sassy sat on the cushioned bench and pulled on her pants with a sigh.

"C'mon. Who knows what you might be doing New Year's Eve," Yvette smiled.

Sassy blushed, thinking of Aidan's favorite Christmas song and said, "Okay."

"Yeah. Lord, I never worked so hard to spend my money before. We'll take them both," Yvette said to the saleswoman. "Oooh!" Yvette exclaimed. "Sassy! The baby just moved. Shush. Shush." The two women stayed still and quiet while Yvette took Sassy's hand and laid it on her stomach. They waited for what seemed like an eternity, and the fluttering returned.

"Is that it?" Sassy asked.

"Does your stomach flutter like that? Yes, that's it."

"Wow. That's pretty amazing."

"See he or she thinks you should have those dresses too. Must be a girl with our impeccable taste."

"Wait until Gardner feels this."

"Ready to go?" Yvette asked.

"We just started, girl. Grab your bags."

The pair shopped, living the dream they had as young girls when they couldn't afford a designer dress between them. They settled into a booth at Scassi's in Little Italy, juggling and arranging all their merchandise booty. The waiter came and took their orders, flashing his pretty teeth and flirting outrageously.

"You know Italian men love black women," Yvette confided, batting her lashes playfully.

"And when I run out of black men, they got next. Fine specimens."

"Yes, the are."

"Cabernet Sauvignon," he identified, setting the drink

in front of Sassy. "And lemonade." He served the frosty glass to Yvette.

"So tell me about Mr. Cabernet Sauvignon."

"What?"

"C'mon, Sassy. You don't really drink and neither did . . . you-know-who who owns a bar. So somebody's corrupting your body and turning you on to Cabernet, and I don't think it's Ivanhoe. You ordered it with a gleam in your eye."

"You," Sassy said with a chuckle, "should have been a detective."

"I'm a married woman. One and the same. Tell me."

Sassy reached for a calamari ring from the antipasti plate and said, "Well, I met him in San Francisco."

"San Francisco? He lives in San Francisco?"

"Are you going to shut up and let me continue or not?"

Yvette made the motion of zipping her lips and throwing away the key.

"I met him in San Francisco, but he lives in New Orleans. In Frisco we did the touristy things—"

Yvette watched her friend become more and more animated as she spoke of this man and the things they did. *My friend's falling in love again,* she thought. *How wonderful!* The luxury of "new love" was always easy—all hormones and hopes. It was the staying in love that was the ultimate accomplishment. Sassy could have been hurt by Roux for as many years as they had been together, but Sassy was too smart to let Roux ruin it for other men, and she was miraculously moving on. She was scared, curious, and cautious, but this man sounded great for her. *Oh, please God, let this work out for her,* Yvette prayed. She was such a good person. If this man hurt her, she might not be able to come back from the pain ever again.

"Do we know him?" Yvette asked after Sassy finished.

"No. He's from the other side of the tracks. He grew up attending private boarding schools all over the world."

"He sounds nice, Sassy. I mean sending you the hat pin and the chocolates."

"And that's what I like about him. He must have as much money as you," Sassy teased before continuing, "But he isn't wowing me with a bunch of expensive flowers and other ostentatious crap. He's giving me what I like, which means he's taking his time to get to know me. *Me.* Sassiere Crillon."

"A real plus. Do I have to come to N'awlins to meet him? I'm willing, now."

"Well, he supposed to be coming to New York on business—"

"Ohmigod. Are you kiddin' me?"

"But he hasn't shown up yet. Or called me."

"Well, he might just be getting here tomorrow. You know, business folk only come in on the actual day of the business and usually go back to wherever they come from the same day. New York ain't for everybody. Oh wow, Sassy." Yvette thought she would cry.

"C'mon, Yvette. It might be nothing. It might come to nothing."

"But he might be The One. The reason what's-his-face had to get out of the way for someone like him. You're going to play it out?"

"Yep, my mama didn't raise no fool. That is if I haven't turned him completely off yet."

"Honey, if he kisses and dances the way you say . . . and didn't jump your bones in San Francisco, he's already a keeper. Or at least you have to see where it goes."

"I know. I'm sacred to, and I'm scared not to." She fiddled with the napkin edge. "But if I don't, I'm afraid I will have really missed out on something special."

"Well, all right, now."

"I don't know much about him. But what I do know about him, I like . . . and want to get to know better. He's older."

"Well, how much?"

"Maybe four or five years."

"Jeeze, Sassy, everybody doesn't date folks the same age like you and . . . which-a-mi-callit. Gardner is five years older than I am. That's nice, 'cause I'll always look good and be a fine young thing to him. You stop trying to pick this man apart before you get to know him. Don't sabotage yourself out of the possible relationship of a lifetime. I'm with Ivanhoe—it sounds like destiny to me."

"There's something else," Sassy said ominously.

"What? He's married? He's bi? He's four feet four tall and cockeyed?"

"He drives a BMW."

"Awww, damn!" They laughed uproariously, both re-calling their joke: How can you tell a porcupine from a man with a BMW?

"In a porcupine—the pricks are on outside!" they chimed in together and convulsed in laughter until tears ran down their cheeks. "It's a two-seat Roadster, so I think he's exempt," Sassy finally said.

"Oh well. Nobody's perfect." They laughed.

They finished up their private conversation talking about her mother at Willowbook and how Sassy'd pawned her three-carat engagement ring to pay for a few more months of care. When the cab stopped in front of the Stanhope, Sassy got out and Yvette rolled down the window and said, "Promise if —no, *when*—he does come in, you'll bring him tomorrow. Please. Believe me once you get there solo, you'll wish you had. Okay, Sassy? Bring him. Talk to you later."

Sassy took her gowns and other packages to the front desk to check on messages. None. When she entered the room, there was no blinking light. *Don't panic,* she told herself as she hung up her gowns and smoothed out the bottom trains. "I sure hope I have somewhere to wear you," she told the expensive garments. "If not, I'll look stunning hanging around at the old apartment."

The next day Sassy rose late, went to the gym to work out, returned, read the Sunday paper and reviewed the lecture series brochures over brunch in her room. She thought of calling Yvette, but figured even with caterers, florists and the like, her friend would be busy with finishing touches for tonight. Sassy showered and dressed and walked across the street to the museum.

She admired the immensity of the museum searched and found the Temple of Dendur, dedicated to the goddess Isis, where the seminar would begin tomorrow. Once she got her bearings, she toured some of the other exhibitions. "Pharaoh's Gifts: Stone Vessels from Ancient Egypt" and "Nefertiti and the Royal Women" captivated her most and kept her enthralled until the museum closed.

When she returned to the room, the telephone was ringing.

"Hello?"

"Hello," the distinctive, mellow voice belonging to Aidan replied.

"Well, how are you?" She sat on the bed and tried not to grin like an ingenue who'd just been called by the captain of the football team.

"I'm fine. Just got in about an hour ago and wanted to catch you and ask if you had plans this evening."

"As a matter of fact I do."

"You do?" he asked, somewhat surprised. "A reception or something to do with your lecture series tomorrow?"

"No."

"You going to make me sweat this out, huh?"

She chuckled and said, "No. Actually, you're invited."

"I accept."

"Don't you want to know to what?"

"If I'll be with you, the 'what' and the 'where' doesn't matter."

"So you won't mind attending the fertility rite passage ceremony of the Uwicki Tribe in the Hall of Dedun?"

"Sounds like I get to see you either nude or in a bathing suit. That's a win-win situation," he said and they both laughed. "What time?"

"Six. They're friends from New Orleans."

"Oh? A couple?"

"Actually, she's my best friend from New Orleans, and Gardner is originally from Maryland. He came to New York after graduating from U Penn. You two should have a lot in common."

"Great. I'll pick you up in the lobby at six. I know you don't want to be there when they put out the dip."

Sassy laughed. "Six'll be fine. See you then."

Sassy hung up the phone and went directly for her new lingerie. Then she rifled through her new purchases for the appropriate outfit. She stopped in the middle of the floor and said, "Get a grip, girl. Shower first."

She went over to the phone and dialed Yvette. She heard her say "Hello."

"I just wanted you to throw another shrimp on the barbee. I will be coming to your soiree' escorted this evening," she said with a practiced flair.

"He came!"

"Well, not yet," Sassy said naughtily, unable to contain her glee.

"Oh, girrrrrl!"

"Oh, one thing. Will you and Gardner call me 'Sassiere?'"

"Why?"

"Besides it being my given name—that's who I am to him. I introduced myself as Sassiere. Girl, you should hear the way he says it!!"

"I can hardly wait. I like this little mysterious Mata Hari vibe. You don't know him a lot and he thinks you're somebody else. This is the prelude to some good stuff— ah, Sassiere."

"Thanks. Tell Gardner."

"Will do. See you around six-ish."

Upon arrival, Aidan called up to her room. "I'm here."

"Great. I'll be right down."

When the elevator door dinged opened, Sassy stepped into the lobby sporting a winter white sweaterdress which superbly complemented her skin tone and curves.

Aidan stood in greeting. "You do know how to make an entrance," he said as she slowly walked toward him.

"Hi," she said to him, and watched him bend to kiss her gently on the lips. The sensation was electric.

"Hi," he repeated, tensing and releasing his jaw trying to contain himself at seeing her.

His smoldering eyes turned her insides to jelly.

"Ready?" He asked, crooking his arm. She took hold of it as the doorman opened the glass doors and whistled for a cab.

Aidan followed her into the cab, gave the address then

settled back beside her. Sassy tried to remember when she had ever felt so good just being in a man's presence.

"So, how do you like the Big Apple so far?" he asked.

"It's cold."

"That it is. What did you do today?"

They spoke casually until they reached the Reynolds' door.

"Sassiere!" Yvette greeted with a big bear hug.

"Aidan Symonds," Sassy introduced, "this is my best girl, Yvette."

"And company." Yvette rubbed her belly. "Welcome Aidan. C'mon in. Gardner!" she called to her husband as Isabella took their coats.

"Hey . . . Sassiere," Gardner hesitated and kissed her on the cheek.

"This is Aidan Symonds."

"Welcome to mi casa. What's your pleasure, Aidan?" Gardner said, steering his newest guest from the foyer toward the living room.

"Sassiere," Aidan stopped the procession and fell back. "What can I get you?"

"We have Cabernet Sauvignon," Yvette piped up with a glint to her eye.

"That'd be fine," Sassy told Aidan, who noticed the exchange of looks in the women's eyes.

"I think I've been discussed," Aidan said to Gardner.

"To death, man. Just go with the flow," Gardner said as they inched away. "With those two, 'discussing' is better than no honorable mention. Take my word for it. Let me introduce you around."

"I like him," Yvette whispered to Sassy as they followed the men down the hall.

"You don't even know him. All he said was hello."

"He had me at 'hello.'" Yvette fluttered her eyelashes. "He looks familiar."

"Yeah, he did to me too, but I can't place it. He used to play trumpet in some of the clubs in the Quarter, but I was afraid to pursue that line of conversation because SASSY's could have been one of them."

"Good point," Yvette agreed, smiling as Aidan approached with Sassy's drink.

"Thank you." Sassy accepted the red wine and took a sip. "Humm. Good."

"Coleridge Cabernet," Yvette instigated with a grin.

"Hey, Aidan, man," Gardner called him. "Here's somebody I want you to meet. He's in stocks and bonds," he said to the guys in the group.

"Do you mind?" Aidan asked Sassy.

"No. It's a party. We're supposed to mingle," she said while Yvette continued grinning.

"I think Gardner has a new best friend," Yvette said, as they watched Aidan swagger away with insouciant self-confidence and suavity. "Oh, Sassy. The boy can rag, girl. And he is so-so—" She searched for the exact word.

"Smooth," Sassy offered.

"Yesss. I can see what you said about him not being drop-dead gorgeous like—what's-his-face—but Sass. He's got it going on, girl."

"Yes, he do," Sassy teased. "The way he moves."

"And we're not the only ones who think so. Look at that skank over there coming on to him."

"I'm not pressed. Let's check out the buffet table," Sassy said, leaving Yvette to watch Aidan politely include the woman in the conversation then leave her to join Sassy at the table.

"They say salmon is an aphrodisiac," Aidan said to Sassy from behind.

She smiled at the sound of his voice and the brush of his breath on her ear.

"I thought that was oysters," she said, turning toward him trying, but failing, to suppress a smile that had sprung to her lips.

"For some people an aphrodisiac can be toothpaste. It all depends." His obsidian eyes danced and his beautiful lips stretched into a sexy smile. She fed him a salmon canapé.

Sassy and Aidan mingled with folks who approached them, although they preferred to talk quietly and survey the decor, the CD collection, and art artifacts around the apartment. Occasionally, Gardner would look for him and entice him over for a brief conversation, but he would only return to Sassy's side in a matter of moments.

On one such occasion, Aidan was across the room from Sassy as she talked with Yvette and two other women. He sipped his brandy and soaked in her image. She was just perfect. As perfect as he thought she'd be. There was always a danger that the reality won't live up to the fantasy, but Sassy had exceeded even his wildest dreams. She was as gorgeous on the outside as she was on the in. Smart, intelligent, with strong values and morals, almost a throwback to the way women used to be when they sang all his favorite old standards; "Embraceable You," "It Had to Be You," "The Best Is Yet to Come." When romance, not sex, was king, and the journey was just as important as the destination. He watched her unconsciously tug at her hair, and her hand fell on her neck—right by that freckle that used to be exposed when her hair was braided or in a ponytail, back in the day. It'd been covered by all her luxurious hair, and now, it was exposed again, just as she was, vulnerable, available and destined to be his.

Sassy glanced over toward the window and Aidan's image stopped her. She smiled, and with one hand thrust into his pocket, he toasted her with the glass of wine he held in the other.

Smooth, she thought. *Mr. Cool.* Her breath quickened, her body flushed like a menopausal woman's and juices began to flow from places she'd tried to forget she had. The way he walked, talked, held her, and made her feel without even touching her, awakened her spirit in ways she hadn't known. Unlike Roux, whose skin seemed to chafe his soul at times, Aidan always seemed in control.

Sassy and Aidan were the last to leave.

"Now you come back with her on Friday," Gardner instructed Aidan. "It'll only be the four of us, so we can really talk."

"That's if I'm invited," Aidan said to Sassy.

"If you're a good boy," Sassy said, and the four of them laughed.

"Thanks for the hospitality, man." Aidan shook Gardner's hand heartily. "I had a great time."

"I really like him," Yvette whispered to Sassy.

"Yes, I know," Sassy whispered back as Aidan turned his gaze to Yvette.

"And thank you and the little one," Aidan said to Yvette.

"It was my pleasure. Any friend of Sassiere's is a friend of mine. I hope you're good so you can come back."

"I'll do my best," Aidan said, his eyes never leaving Sassy's. He straightened out her coat collar. "Let me get her back. She's got a big day tomorrow. Good night."

"Bye," Sassy said as she held Aidan's hand.

He held her close in the cab, and, as ribbons of light flickered across her features, he rubbed his lips across hers and, with the sweetest pressure, eased his probing tongue in to taste hers.

She tingled and turned into him and the kissing became intense and urgent as she melted into his body. "Haven't you ever heard of the Taxicab Confessions?"

"We're not Taxicab Confession people are we?" he admonished playfully.

"If you say so," she teased and kissed him again.

They kissed with urgency like two teenagers whose impatient parents were waiting on the other side of the door. Again, she was swept away by his kiss. She was ninety-nine-point-nine percent sure she had never been here before, and she savored the destination to which only he had the key. His taste, his scent and his hands searing her back with a hot touch made her moan. He smiled, and they were forehead to forehead, nose to nose, as they smiled into each other.

"Here you go," the cab driver interrupted with a flick of the meter.

Sassy laid her head on his shoulder as Aidan paid the man and asked him to wait.

"What?"

"I'll walk you up," Aidan said.

You're not staying, she thought but said, "Don't bother." This is the second time he pulled this "tease" crap. She blew hot, knowing why, but not liking herself for it. She bolted through the hotel's glass doors.

"Sassiere." He ran after her, catching her by the hand. "I want to come up. I've thought of nothing else but not tonight."

Sassy stared at him, through him.

"I'm a little jet-lagged, you've got to get up early tomorrow. There's no rush for us—we have a lifetime."

His soulful eyes stilled hers and his words fell on her like gentle comforting rain.

"We will. I will—when we come," he let the double entendre sink in and cause a blush to rise in her cheeks. "I want to stay." He moved into to her and kissed her tenderly. "The morning after, I don't want you to have to rush from my arms to be with Fitzwilliams or any other man."

He rocked her in his arms as folks walked around them.

"Smooth," she said with a shameful grin. "All right Mr. Symonds. You win."

"By waiting, we'll both win. I'm good." They laughed.

"You are unbelievingly arrogant."

"No brag—just fact." They chuckled again. "I expect to see you every day this week. What time to you get off tomorrow?"

"The seminar is over at three."

"Humm. I won't be finished until about six but I'll pick you up and we'll have dinner and see a little of New York. How's that?"

"It's a consolation prize."

"Is that a no?" he teased, rocking himself into her.

"Don't start nothing you can't finish anytime soon." She pushed him away playfully.

"I'll call you tomorrow," he said, as she sashayed to the elevator.

"Doesn't matter. I'm saving myself for my husband."

"Will you marry me?" he teased playfully as the elevator closed her off from him.

A horny and disappointed Sassy opened the hotel room door and saw the neatly turned-down bed with the foil-wrapped chocolate on the pillow. She unsheathed the mint, popped it into her mouth as she shed her coat and clothes and made her nightly call to Willowbrook to see how her mother's day went. After verifying that they had her cell and hotel numbers, she hung up and prepared for bed. She slid her warm, taut body between the cool sheets and picked up a magazine. When she realized she hadn't turned the page in twenty minutes, she threw it aside and sighed loudly.

She looked over at the door and imagined that there was a knock. She envisioned herself going to the door and opening it on Aidan's smiling face and lips which said, "I changed my mind." He'd kiss her from the door over to the bed, removing what little she wore, and they'd tear up that neatly made bed with their torrid lovemaking.

Sassy chuckled, turned off the light and watched the moonlight funnel across the ceiling of the dark room. She turned over on her side and rubbed her hand across the place where Aidan should be. Again, she imagined him there, facing her in the darkness. She imagined him saying, "Sassiere—" rolling the "R" with the tongue that still tasted of the love they'd made. "You have a busy day tomorrow. You better get some sleep." She imagined him drawing her into his arms and her feeling so secure, safe and content there. She imagined thinking, "Heaven must be like this." She smiled, closed her eyes and began drifting, drifting, drifting into a delicious sleep.

Five hours later her wake-up call came. She showered, dressed, walked across the street and showed her special pass to enter the museum, which was closed to the public on Mondays. Her heels clicked down the hallowed halls to the Temple of Dendur where she took one of the packets and a seat just in time for Dr. Anwar from the Council of Antiquities in Cairo to introduce Dr. Fitzwilliams.

With great relish she listened to Dr. Fitzwilliams discuss the Eighteenth Dynasty and its star players: Akhenaten, who was married to Nefertiti and to Kiya, with whom he sired Tutankhamun, the boy king. Sassy was enthralled with the auditory history, punctuated by slides of site footage, artifacts, jewelry, and a detailed explanation of the significance of the solar disc. There was an astonishing film on the two infant mummies buried with King Tut, followed by a lecture from the physical anthropologist who was called in to determine their age and sex, and any diseases which could pinpoint the cause of their death.

The time flew, and Dr. Fitzwilliams, with his clipped British accent, closed with "Tomorrow we will begin with the next in line from King Tut, the rule of Rameses I."

Sassy couldn't believe how totally absorbed she was in the subject matter—or so she thought. When she looked down at her notes, written there, like a schoolgirl with a crush, was *Aidan and Sassiere Symonds, Sassiere Symonds, Mr. and Mrs. Aidan Symonds, Sassiere Crillon Symonds.*

She closed her notebook and laughed out loud. Was this a note from her subconscious? She wondered as she graciously declined an invite to join others for dinner and remembered that old saying, "Sometimes the heart can see what is invisible to the mind."

Chapter VII

Sassy stepped into the biting cold and scurried from the Metropolitan Museum across the street to her hotel room. She showered and dressed in a thick, nubby, oatmeal-colored sweater with slacks and met Aidan in the lobby, as he had instructed.

As she sauntered towards him she watched the parenthetical smile claim his handsome face. She loved the way the sheer vision of her summoned such smoldering but controlled admiration in his eyes. They exchanged greetings and quick kisses on the cheeks and walked through the hotel doors.

"Your chariot awaits," he said, bowing graciously in front of the hansom cab as the horse bayed.

"Oh, Aidan!" Sassy giggled with delight as he helped her up into the horse-drawn carriage and then arranged the blanket around her legs.

"Tavern on the Green," Aidan commanded the driver, and the horse began with a click-clack cadence of hoof on asphalt. "Take the long way."

"Oh, wow. This is amazing. I've only dreamed about these."

"I'm the dream merchant. Here to make them all come true." He nuzzled near her. "Warm enough?"

"Yes." She laid her head on his shoulder.

At the restaurant, they ate and talked, sharing stories, philosophies, and dreams and fed each other crème brûlée.

"Yes, I want marriage and children eventually," she answered his question as the sophisticated Sassiere; the career woman she'd become a few weeks ago. "But it's so hard out there. To find the right man."

He answered her with the most quizzical expression on his face, as if he knew she was lying, or was it her guilt about doing so. The third glass of wine birthed more uncorroborated nonsense she'd read in a woman's magazine. "I mean, the more you date, the more elusive the prospect of finding Mr. Right seems," she concluded and held her head.

"Time to get you some fresh air," he finally said and motioned for the check from the waiter.

"Good idea."

As he hailed a cab, he decreed, "Tomorrow Sylvia's in Harlem. Every self-respecting black person in the United Sates must visit Harlem when in New York." He opened the cab door for her. "But right now . . . Rockefeller Center," he told the cabbie.

"What's happening there?"

"You'll see," he said with a kiss to her cheek.

The cab dismissed, the couple absorbed the sight of the gorgeously lit Christmas tree.

"Nothing says Christmas in New York like this tree at Rockefeller Center," he said.

"It is beautiful."

"And look at the ice skaters. Let's give it a try," Aidan suggested.

"Oh no," Sassy said as she turned to go.

He turned her back and said, "Oh yes. No horseback riding, but we do have ice skating to work that meal off."

"I'll freeze down there," she protested, knowing the three glasses of wine wasn't enough antifreeze against the frigid, New York temperature.

From his cashmere coat pocket he pulled out two skullcaps.

She giggled. "You are kidding me?"

"Which color do you want?"

"They're both navy."

"No. Here, you take the black. You don't like navy."

"How do you know that?"

"C'mon, stop stalling." He ushered her down the steps.

He left her marveling at the majesty of the decorated landmark and returned with skates.

"I can't skate in stockings," she protested.

"True. Voilà." He pulled out a pair of socks with the flare of a magician pulling a rabbit from a hat. "Sit and put them on. The sooner you get started, the sooner we're finished. And just think—you might like it."

She put her socks on and, ready to object to small-sized skates, asked, "What size did you get?" She looked at the imprint. "Ten. How did you know that?"

"I don't trust little-footed women. C'mon." He bounced up and skated around her once.

"Umph. I think I prefer horses to cold," she grumped, struggling up to balance her weight on the thin blades.

"I know Sassiere Crillon is up for new challenges and experiences."

Sassy smiled. He was right, Sassiere was interested.

"Now, hold on to me and glide. Glide."

"This is a cheap stunt to get close to me."

"I don't think I'd have to go this far do I?" he teased, and as she smiled, she took her first spill.

"Ouch!" She sat sprawled on the cold ice.

"Oh, how unladylike." He helped her up and they began again.

Two hours and four hot spiced apple ciders later, Sassy got the hang of it. They glided across the slippery white surface in front of the picture-perfect Christmas tree. "Like Whitney and Denzel in *The Preacher's Wife*," she commented as the colorful glow of the Christmas lights framed his face like a halo.

The next four days flew by. Monday night, the couple dined at Sylvia's and toured Harlem. Tuesday night found them ensconced at the City Center being dazzled by the superb performance of the Alvin Ailey Dance Theater. Wednesday, they strolled through the campy boutiques of SoHo, where Sassy fell in love with a "too expensive," one-of-a-kind, designer hand-beaded skirt. She ran her hand over the rich garnet silk and the mesh overlay with the embellished velvet floral flocked detail and beautiful beadwork.

"Oh, Lawd," she fretted at the hefty price tag for the short, straight skirt.

"Allow me," Aidan offered, reaching for his inside pocket.

"Oh no," Sassy protested as a confused saleslady looked on. "If I want it—I buy it."

"It will look fantastic against your toasted-pecan skin," Aidan said softly in her ear.

Sassy grew weak in the knees. "Toasted-pecan skin. Ooooh," she repeated, liking the sound of that almost as much as him saying "Sassiere." "You know, hanging with you and Yvette is going to wipe out my bank account."

"We think you only deserve the best."

"I'll take it," Sassy decided, cautioning herself that she had neither Yvette's nor Aidan's financial resources, and this would be her last New York City purchase.

Sassy's skirt in hand, they'd strolled intertwined across and up through Greenwich Village, stopping at Balzac's where they dined and caught the jazz stylings of Wil Downey until the wee hours before summoning a cab home.

Thursday night they braved the cold atop the Empire State Building where they recited alternating Deborah Kerr and Cary Grant dialogue from *An Affair to Remember*. As they descended the one hundred and two floors, they amused themselves by quizzing one another.

"Best western?" she asked.

"*Shane*," he answered hurriedly.

"Aw. Wuss," she scoffed.

"Yours?"

"*Last Train from Gun Hill*."

"Kirk Douglas, Anthony Quinn, and Carolyn Jones. Yes. Favorite line?"

"When the cowpoke tells Carolyn 'get me a drink.' And she says 'Here. You can have mine,' and throws it in his face."

"Oooo. Somehow I knew you'd pick that. Best Kirk Douglas movie?"

"You first."

"*The Champion*. Great film noire."

"Excellent choice," she agreed.

"Yours?"

"*Spartacus*. I still cry when I think of the ending. Jean Simmons holding up his son to him while he's on the cross."

"They had the best kissing scene in all cinema."

"Oh, yeah they did. That tumbling, rolling across the grass."

"We can't tumble and roll, but how about a kiss?"

She obliged his warm and welcoming kiss as intoxicating as this last week with him in New York. When the elevator reached the first floor and opened to a sea of folks, they interlocked arms and laughed onto the sidewalk. They ate in Chinatown, so lost in each other's conversation that they slept on their tickets to Radio City's Christmas show. They braved the cold and strolled back to her hotel, ending with the usual nightcap kiss at the door. On Friday, her seminar ended at noon and she had the rest of the day to relax and dress for their dinner at Yvette and Gardner's. In all this time, he'd never questioned her "saving herself for marriage" creed. *He's such a good boy, he should be rewarded,* she thought with wicked smile.

Sassy selected her attire carefully, beginning with the salmon-colored teddy concealed beneath a handmade hooded sweater over a pair of matching pants. As she waited for his call, she dropped her purse, as she had the soap in the shower and the watch from her wrist. Now that her time with Aidan was coming to an end and she had decided to sleep with him, she was a bundle of nerves. Supposed he was into the chase, and once the "deed was done" lost interest in her? Suppose with only one man under her belt she wasn't any good in bed? She wanted him, pure and simple. At least just once.

The phone jangled.

"I'm in the lobby," Aidan's voice crooned.

"I'll be right down."

Yvette liked him and said she thought the sexual delay was all "kinda cute, and oh, so romantic. In a day when guys just want to jump your bones and leave, you have a man who wants to *romance* you, girl. He's saying nothing will happen unless you want it to."

Tonight Sassy wanted to. Sassy was going to. Sassy was prepared to.

The elevator door slid open. There he was, as fine as you please, dressed down in his cashmere coat, looking like the first delicious course of an elegant eight- course meal. And she was hungry for him.

"I wore pants in case we go ice skating again," she said.

"Ice skating is not on tonight's agenda." He took her hand and kissed it.

"Well, we can dine with the Reynolds or go ice skating."

"It would be rude not to show. We were both raised better than that." He arched his eyebrow quizzically. "Besides, I don't want to alienate the matron of honor in our wedding."

"You're a little sure of yourself aren't you?"

"Absolutely."

Maybe he wouldn't ditch her after tonight. Maybe there was a future for them. From ice skating he knew she was a quick learner, so he could teach her how to please him and vice versa. Hell, she knew he knew how to please her—just by getting naked. She'd be halfway there at the sight of him.

At dinner the two couples discussed everything from politics to films, from wines to travel to music and Sassy marveled at the way the two men got on as they discussed business, hedge funds, interest rates, 401(k)s, stocks, bonds, and NASDAQ. Roux and Gardner never got on this way, Sassy thought. When Gardner and Yvette visited New Orleans, Roux was always ready to leave to go somewhere else were the action was hotter, livelier. Aidan was charming, dynamic, funny, and so cool. He let her frosted-red toes slide up and down his calf and he didn't even flinch. Aidan was always in his element—smooth and confident; Roux had an itchy soul which always craved action . . . and he relished being its center.

"I like him, Sass," Yvette whispered to her friend as they got the dessert from the kitchen. "And I like him for you."

Sassy threw her girlfriend a big cheesy grin.

"He is so not Roux."

"Roux is Sugar Hill Gang and Aidan is . . . Donny Hathaway singing 'A Song to You.'"

"Oh, girl!!" They slapped five. "You ain't never lied! Oooh—I believe I'll give Gardner some tonight!"

The evening ended with Aidan giving Sassy a deep dip to Johnny Hartman's "The Very Thought of You." "Smooth, man. Really, smooth," Gardner said.

Sassy and Yvette laughed at Gardner's defining Aidan just as they had.

"Listen," Aidan said. "We only have two more nights here and I was going to take Sassiere to the Rainbow Room tomorrow. Join us? My treat. Dinner, dancing."

"The Rainbow Room? Ooh, classy," Yvette and Gardner said together.

"In fact, since we probably won't be together New Year's why not go all out? Dress to the nines."

"I like that," Yvette said. "'Cause I'll probably look like I swallowed a watermelon by New Year's. And Sassiere has just the dress for it. Let me get the choker and the coat." Yvette disappeared and reappeared in a flash.

"Doesn't seem we can pass up a chance as good as this," Gardner said to his wife.

"Great idea," Yvette piped up. "What makes a young hip cat like you want to hear this old music?"

"It's timeless," Aidan said. "And Sassiere likes it." He looked down at her standing beside him. "Ready to go?"

"Yes."

"So tomorrow at seven-thirty? Meet you at the top of New York City?" Aidan said.

"We've never been to the Rainbow Room. Why don't you think like that?" Yvette teased her husband.

"I got you and a bun in the oven. I don't have to work that hard anymore," Garner said as he closed the door. "See you two tomorrow night."

"So, your place or mine?" Sassy asked.

"Have you ever been to the Marriot at the Park?"

"No."

"The Marriot Central Park it is. Taxi!"

Sassy paid no attention to the Marriot's opulent lobby, the cushioned elevator or hallway antiques. She stood before the intricately carved door and watched Aidan slide his key in and push it open. He then swooped her up and carried her over the threshold. She laughed with delight.

"Just practicing," he said as he turned on the light with his free hand.

"You're a little anxious aren't you?" she teased him.

"Hey, neither of us are spring chickens." He side-stepped the end and cocktail tables and dumped her on the bed.

"Speak for yourself."

She was still laughing as he yanked up the telephone and ordered champagne and chocolate covered strawberries. As he spoke, he pulled off his scarf and shed his coat.

Sassy watched him with keen interest.

He danced over to the stereo and flicked it on.

"You're not all flash, dash, and no substance are you?" she asked, dangling her shoe from her toe.

"I'll let you be the judge of that. Why don't you make yourself more comfortable." He swaggered to her from across the room and took all the playfulness from her. "Let me have your coat." He tossed her coat on the chair by the fireplace, came up behind her and kissed the chocolate freckle on the back of her neck. The freckle he'd watched all those years.

And you can have anything else you want, she thought as his sweet, warm breath blew on her shoulders.

His hands slid slowly around her waist and she backed into him, feeling his love muscle rise against her right buttock. They swayed to the music until Sassy couldn't take his tonguing her neck any longer and turned into him. Her entire body trembled with anticipation as his perfect lips found her imperfect ones and escorted them on a journey of delicious tasting, probing and exploring.

God, he can kiss, was her only thought as every pore of her body expanded and opened, readying for the pleasure they had so long been denied. His tongue became the wick that sent a tingle then a blaze from the top of her head to the tip of her frosted-red big toe. Luther Vandross's "So Amazing" played softly in the background. From half-slit eyes she could see the backdrop of the New York City skyline splayed before her like twinkly diamonds crowned by a full, transplanted Cajun moon, which rounded out the satisfaction of her senses. It was all a fantasy, a dream; and she didn't want to wake up. The kissing gave way to moans as Aidan's long slender fingers ran across her back in an artful embrace, then down to cup her round behind. She pressed him to her and rubbed her pulsating cavity against his throbbing passion. She thought she would explode, but then Aidan ceased and pulled her toward the sofa where he leaned against its back and his hands disappeared under the silken-wool where he grabbed hold and pulled her sweater over her head. Sassy watched his perfect lips leave hers to kiss her collarbone, then carve a trail down to her brown mounds which he expertly released from their silk confines. Seeing the sight of her engorged nipples, preening for him in the moonlight was exhilarating and embarrassing until he drew them into his hot mouth and warmed each with the moist, rough-smooth texture of his serpentine tongue.

"Ooooo," she moaned as he treated each to his tongued expertise. His hands drifted down to unleash her pants, which he gladly sent to form a puddle around her ankles. He let his deft brown finger slide to the apex of her hairy triangle where he released the snap of her salmon-colored teddy so that he could explore her moist treasure unencumbered.

It was he who moaned at the slick feel of the warm, juicy coating of her swollen bud. He who played with it until it blossomed into a flower before he sank to taste its nectar with the perfect lips she so admired—in a place she thought they'd never be. She was about to burst when Aidan ceased again, rolling her over on the sofa—somehow in that balletic movement he managed to release his love muscle. She looked up, and it stood strong and powerful, chiseled against the city's skylight. Intuitively and without saying a word he leaned against the club chair and Sassy came to him. She stroked his manliness, held it as she flicked the tip and, ever so gently, moved into position to ride his projectile. She impaled herself on his rigid, throbbing muscle and slid into paradise; melted into him like butter on a biscuit, baby. Her feet left the carpet, and he caught her by the full ripe melons of her derrière, holding her in his hot hands as she exacted perfection from all he had to give. His look was so intense, yet tender. She attempted to kiss those perfect lips but he wanted to watch his stroke

of electricity enter her valley. He wanted to see the pleasure he was giving reflected in her every movement,
every quiver, every shake, every gasp of breath. As the
crescendo of their movement peaked, he thrust her to
the floor and they entered nirvana in perfect, rhythmic
syncopation.

In the surreal, mythical, entanglement Sassy was feeling something she hadn't felt in such a long, long
time—trust of a man. She'd done something she hadn't
done in such a long time, surrendered completely—the
kind of giving of yourself you can only do when you
desire and trust your partner. Then she heard something she'd never heard before—

"Sassiere, SassiereSassiereSassiere," he breathed into
her ear: part mantra, part litany, and she realized for the
first time in her life—it was Love calling her name.

"Oh wow," Sassy finally said when her breathe caught
up with her feelings.

"Is that good 'wow' or a bad 'wow'?" he asked, their
bodies still intertwined, slick, wet and pulsating. "'Cause
I'm willing to go again until we get it right."

She laughed and turned toward the side without his
fullness leaving her secret garden. "I was supposed to
'wow' you and you beat me to the punch."

"Is that a bad thing?" He smiled as she touched his lips
with her finger and he kissed it.

"No. Not at all but next time let's try the bed. I hear
they are very popular."

She began to move.

"Don't," he said seriously. "I don't want to leave you yet."

Sassy felt his quasi-hardness in her still-throbbing ori-
fice. "I don't want you to go yet either." She kissed him
softly and they lay nuzzled in each other's arms, reveling
in the love they just made.

Caught in the swell of emotion, Aidan wanted to tell her now. He wanted to say he loved her. He had always loved her. But now was not the time. He didn't want to scare her. Didn't want to blow it—blow them—now. She had to *feel* the love he had for her first, that it was unmistakable, undeniable, and forever.

The doorbell rang.

"I believe that's our room service. I hate to leave you." He withdrew slowly and Sassy sighed at the titillating extraction. He covered her with the sofa's afghan. "But I shall return," he decreed with a kiss to her nose and threw on a robe.

She chuckled as she watched him walk to the door. She didn't remember when he removed his shirt or donned that condom.

"Smooth," she said, propping herself up on one elbow as she watched him sign for the goodies.

Leaving the cart in the foyer, he dove to be beside her again and poised a chocolate-dipped strawberry near her lips. She licked at the chocolate before devouring the round fruit.

He relished watching her lips suckle the red berry.

"Humm. That's good," she said as he licked the pink juice from the sides of her mouth.

"Mercy," he said. "We got more lovin' to do."

"Yes, we have. The bed next time."

"I don't think there is enough furniture in here for all the times we're going to make love."

"And remember I have a suite across town. We can christen that too."

"Let's get started." He rose and extended his hands for her and they walked to the bed. "You see those berries were supposed to come before we did—so to speak."

"Who can count on room service?"

"Who can count on two horny people who have no self-control?" He flung back the comforter for her.

"Guilty," she said as she dropped the afghan and climbed in. He followed. She snuggled near him and rested her head against his heartbeat. She looked at the big, bright moon peeking in on them and wondered again if it was that Cajun moon in disguise—this time making all her dreams come true.

"Oh, Aidan."

"Hummm," he said, playing with the flat freckle on her neck; his own private trophy of accomplishment.

She looked up and asked, "Do you remember that old movie with Bill Cosby and Sidney Poitier?"

"*Let's Do It Again?*"

"Exactly." She raised up and over him and kissed him on the lips. And they did it again.

Aidan blinked in the darkness as his eyes adjusted to the moonlight streaming through the window, caressing the face of his dream come true. *Ah, yes,* he thought as he felt the warmth of her body nestled in his embrace. He smelled her earthy fragrance and listened to the rise and fall of her breathing. Inner happiness forced a smile on his face, and he kissed her lemon-scented hair. She stirred, moving into him like it was the most natural thing to do . . . like they'd slept intertwined in the spoon position all their lives. He let his hands glide down her side, over the curve of her hips, down her thigh, then between them. She moaned, half sleep, half awake. "Aidan," she whispered, as she parted her legs.

"I'm here. Don't move."

He let his hand fill with the softness of her derrière before slipping around to the front of her curly triangle, pulling her closer to his rock-hard manliness. As he slid it to where his hand had been, she began to move with him, riding him, and the physical rhythm matched the auditory one.

As he eased into her, she sucked in air through her teeth and rode against him with pleasure. "Don't stop—don't stop, don't stop, ooo—that's my spot, don't stop, don't stop," she exhaled in a stream of ecstasy.

Simultaneously, indescribable pleasure seized them both and they let it flow as their bodies shuddered and quivered with undulating pulsating until it finally ebbed. She reached back and stroked his head and shoulders as he squeezed her still-engorged nipples, waiting for the final throbbing to subside. "Am I dreaming?" she asked. "If I am I don't want to ever wake up."

He kissed her neck by that flat freckle, stroked her tenderly, and whispered, "Go back to sleep."

Sassy drifted, drifted and drifted off again.

The morning light cut across their faces and he awakened first. He looked at her, not believing that she was really here with him. He must have been very good during his lifetime to be rewarded with his dream walking.

Sassy woke next and looked at him looking at her.

"Hi."

"Hi."

"What are you doing here?" she asked.

"It's my suite."

Sassy gasped not realizing she'd asked him out loud. They were lying on their sides, face to face. She just stared at him. "No one was supposed to be here with me like this for . . . a long time. I have such stuff to get straight—"

"Can I help?"

"You already have."

"You want to talk about it?"

"No. Not just yet."

He was relieved. He didn't want to talk about it, or Roux. He didn't even care why; all he wanted was to be with her, here now . . . happy. He never wanted to cause her one moment of grief or worry. He'd never press her for any information about her past. He knew that her heart had grown incredibly sore that the touch of memory could hurt. He'd never hurt her. Not now—not ever.

"Don't ever lie to me," she said.

Her edict took him by surprise—like she knew. "Like those shoes don't go with that dress?" He tried levity, and she chuckled. "Right now we are in New York City at Christmas! Just you and me. No 'stuff.' No 'ghosts of relationships past.' It's just us, Sassiere."

She snuggled into him. "Besides, you'll never have to tell me that. I always match."

His heart was beating faster now, and not just because of the nearness of her. A nearness he'd never have if it wasn't for his "secret." It wasn't a lie, although in her black and white Catholic world she'd probably see it that way. He had a secret, not a lie, and it was too soon to tell her now, just like it was too soon to tell her he loved her. He didn't want her to bolt from his arms and cut him out of her life like she had Roux. He wouldn't risk losing her now but he had to tell her soon—and it had to come from him. Not today, not on this trip. He felt her hands slide down and stroke his manhood, which responded immediately to her touch. They made late-morning love in bed, which led to wet soapy love in the shower, barely leaving enough time for her to go and dress for the Rainbow Room.

"Stay," he asked as she gathered her things.

"I don't want to wear out my welcome."

"Why not just move out of your hotel for the night and stay here?"

"I'm a girl used to having her own place, thank-you-very-much."

"Sister Claire Regina would be proud of you."

"Oh, no she wouldn't. Envious, maybe. Bye." She kissed his nose, accepted his help with her coat and opened the door.

"I'm right behind you."

"You were right behind me this morning too," she sassed, kissed him quickly and left him and his paren-thetical smile at the door.

"Bye." He watched her strut onto the elevator.

The doorman opened the plate-glass entrance to the Stanhope for the dapper gentleman. On this night, Aidan stood directly in front of the elevator, not wanting to miss one glimpse of her in this dynamite dress he'd heard so much about. The doors parted and she stepped from the crowded cubicle. She did not disappoint. The rich, red, tastefully slinky dress clung to her curves. The sweetheart neckline reveled a hint of toasted-pecan cleavage as the opera cape billowed open, setting boundaries for her as she sashayed toward him.

He let out a long, appreciative whistle and Sassy smiled at the sight of him, handsome and resplendent in his tux.

"Not so bad yourself, Symonds." She twirled for him and the train seductively flicked itself around her shapely angles. She kissed him hello, and the crowd watched the elegant black couple stroll out and disappear into a waiting cab.

"Symonds," Aidan told the maître'd' atop the Rainbow Room as he led them to their table for four.

"Oh, Aidan, this is exquisite. I feel like I'm *in* a 1940s movie," she said, eying the expansive well-appointed and decorated room. The sparkling backdrop of the city's twinkling lights commingled with the chandeliers and the small, covered, '40s period shade lights on each table creating an Art Deco effect. "I feel like it's our last night before you ship out to World War II." She looked at the band; the smoky sax was playing "Unforgettable."

"Hardly. This is where our happy ending begins." He reached for her hand and kissed it before they had to separate to take their seats. He ordered an aperitif and a Cabernet Sauvignon.

"They're playing our song. Let's dance," he suggested. As he lead her to the dance floor, he appreciated her curves seductively moving beneath the fabric once again and remarked, "That dress is . . . scandalous."

"Why, thank you," she demurred as he held her close. "I can't make out the song," Sassy said as she melted into his arms.

"It doesn't matter. Tonight, they are all our songs." He kissed her temple and guided her across the polished floor.

After four songs they returned to their table and the Reynolds were there.

"I thought you'd forgotten you invited us," Yvette said, accepting a hello kiss from Sassy and then Aidan.

"You've got some catching up to do," Aidan slapped a handshake in Gardner's hand in greeting.

"I don't know, man. You looked pretty smooth out there. I'm just an old married man with a baby on the way."

"You braggin' or complainin'?" Aidan challenged.

"Oh my, Yvette. Did I just see your husband blush?" Sassy asked.

They all shared a laugh and ordered drinks and the foursome talked, danced and joked as if they'd been lifetime friends.

Three hours and eight courses later, Yvette and Gardner approached Aidan and Sassy on the dance floor.

"Excuse us, Fred and Ginger, but since it doesn't seem like you're ever coming off any time soon . . . me and my old wife—"

"Hey, watch it," Yvette smacked her husband playfully.

"—came to say good night. Got to get the ball and chain home, but thanks, man. We really had a great time."

"My pleasure," Aidan said.

"I know you're leaving tomorrow. When you-all coming back this way?"

"It's your turn to come to N'awlins," Sassy said.

"No offense, but there ain't a lot of security takeovers in New Orleans," Gardner said.

"You don't come to N'awlins to work. You come to play," Aidan said.

"When I get three days back-to-back, I might just do that, man. Take me out on your boat?"

"Boat?" Sassy said to Aidan.

"Plane, too," Gardner offered.

"Oh, really?" Sassy asked.

"Yeah, I have one," he said to Sassy, then to Gardner he continued, "It's a date, man."

"Cool."

"Thanks, Aidan," Yvette kissed his cheek. "For the evening but mostly for getting my husband out to relax with normal folk. We really had a great time." She kissed

Sassy's cheek. "I'll expect us to resume our weekly chats once you get back."

"Will do," Sassy said.

"You take good care of my friend," Yvette warned Aidan.

"That's my sole mission in life," Aidan said.

"Have a safe flight," Gardner said as they left the ballroom.

"I like them," Aidan said.

"And they like you. I have *never* seen Gardner so relaxed and normal."

"He's got a high-pressure job. But you know what I think?" He held her tighter and she giggled.

"What?"

"I think it was being with the two most beautiful, exciting N'awlins women in all the world."

"I think it was your boat and plane. What else don't I know about you?"

"Oh, I don't know. Not much left. The reason I never married—but I'm saving that one."

"It must be a real doozy." She smiled and laid her head on his shoulder. "I really don't want to go back tomorrow."

"Then don't. We can—"

"No, *we* can't." She looked up at him. "I have responsibilities." She recalled the doctor saying that Maman had had a really bad night.

"Ouch. That word should never be used when we're having such a good time." He twirled around then brought her close to him again. "I guess I'll just have to use my influence. I have great connections, you know."

"I wouldn't doubt it for a minute." Her smiled returned.

When Sassy returned from the powder room the dance floor was practically empty. A few couples speaking in hushed tones were the only audibles until the band began softly playing "The Very Thought of You."

Aidan met her halfway and bowed gracefully, "May I have this dance?"

"Absolutely," she borrowed his familiar word.

They gazed intently into each other's eyes, hearing nothing but the song, seeing nothing but one another. Sassy looked at him and those sculptured lips that had perfectly pleasured hers. She felt the heat rise between them.

He bent and kissed her. When the musical refrain reached its crescendo, the lovers of old movies felt like they were in the middle of one. He spun her around the dance floor as the spotlight's glow followed their expert moves. The train of her dress seductively wrapped around her ankles then unwrapped elegantly with all the timing of Ginger Rogers. The smoky beam of the spotlight commingled with the twinkling lights of Manhattan a thousand of stories below, and they felt as if they were dancing on a cloud. *It was all so perfect,* Sassy thought as the music ended and Aidan bent her back into a sweet dip. They didn't hear the few couples applaud.

As if by magic, they were back in his hotel room dancing to the stereo in their stocking feet. Her gown seemingly disintegrated from her body, just as his shirt evaporated, Aidan rolled the black lace teddy down her toasted-pecan skin and licked, sucked, kissed, and tasted the skin that was exposed as it fell. Her breasts sprung to attention and he returned to her engorged, taut nipples.

Oh Aidan, AidanAidanAidan," the mantra began deep in her well of desire and escaped through her lips as he seared his hot tongue all over her moist flesh. They tumbled onto the bed and she rose to kiss his nipples as he shed his trousers and deftly wrapped the source of her indescribable pleasure in its latex covering. He bent her back and entered her immediately, urgently, as if, if he didn't, he would explode and cease to exist just from the pure want of her.

She felt her moist center accept, then close around him, and massaged him to ecstasy. She held onto the muscled café au lait buttocks as he rode her across the finish line into pure unadulterated bliss. They became one—they came as one.

They lay in each others' arms and slept soundly in a deep, satisfying, dreamless sleep. The next morning, he awakened with a start, slightly disoriented, until he looked at the angel asleep in his arms. He smiled and reveled in watching her breathe. She was as beautiful now to him as she ever had been. With all he had done and all he had accomplished, this was his true prize—his true reward for living the exemplary life he had. He was no angel, but he never intentionally hurt a woman. A serial monogamist who'd admit to only one flaw . . . pretending that every woman he met was Sassiere Crillon. None of them could hold his interest for long, and they all fell short of his image of the original. The danger of building women up in your mind so intently was even they could not measure up to your contrived expectation of them. But Sassy was *everything* he had ever imagined her to be—and more. She was every love he ever had, every love he'd never had, everything he'd done, and everything he wanted to do again. She was as real as real could be, yet his complete fantasy. She was Heaven. Paradise. He couldn't ask for more. He couldn't chance losing her; he couldn't help who he was—it wasn't his doing. He held her hands and let her fingers drop individually, hoping that someday soon he could place a ring on this third left finger and make her his forever.

"Penny for your thoughts," Sassy said quietly.

"Good morning," he said, his face broke into a big smile. "I was thinking of what a fantastic time we've had here."

"You're not going home to the wife and kiddies are you?" she teased, then asked. "What time is it? It's awfully dark."

He stretched his right hand over to read the digital clock. "Eleven."

"Oh, shoot. I got a one o'clock flight." She rose and flew to the bathroom.

He went to the window to open the drapes. Then he laughed, and laughed. He lifted his hands in gleeful prayer and said, "Thank you, Jesus!"

She returned to the room in a fluffy white robe.

"You can slow your roll, as the kids say." He now stood by the window with just his trousers and socks on, no shirt.

"What? Why?"

"Come see." He held out his arm, and the sight of his bare chest was enough to get her to obey. "I told you I had connections. And baby, do I ever." He flung back the drapes.

"Ah!" Sassy let out a half-sigh, half-squeal. "Snow!" She pressed her hand on the cold window like a child. "I've never seen snow before."

"Not just snow. A blizzard! There's nothing flying out or in here today. I guarantee you."

"Oh, Aidan, really?"

"Look down at the street. Nothing's moving and it's still coming down."

"Isn't it beautiful?"

"Not as beautiful as you are. So now we've got one more thing to do in New York."

"What?" She asked skeptically.

"Build a snowman in Central Park."

"Aidan, I don't have a thing to wear."

"Well, I'll buy you whatever you need, and what we can't get, we'll improvise. We won't stay long. We'll run out and experience it, I'll run you a hot bath and have them build us a fire. We'll have brunch in front of it."

"Oh, Aidan." She hugged him. "I don't think I can take any more perfection."

"You deserve so much more. C'mon, let's see what we can outfit you in."

They waded through the frigid white, across the deserted street, and had a snowball fight, then tobogganed down a hill on a discarded piece of cardboard, and made snow angels and only half a snow man before Aidan thought it best to get her back inside.

He stood her in front of the roaring fire and said, "Look at you. You're shivering." He went to run her bath.

"I wasn't cold until I came into the warmth," she chattered. She began to peel off her wet clothes as he returned.

"C'mon in under the heat lamp in the bathroom," he ushered her toward the tub.

"Aidan, I can take care of myself," she protested weakly.

"I like to take care of you, Sassiere. It's your turn to be cared for for a change."

He was right, Sassy thought. It did feel good to have some one look after her—it seemed that as of late, all she did was look after Roux, her mother and her students.

"Bubbles!" she exclaimed, looking at the elegant clawfooted tub. "I'll get in on one condition. That you join me."

"You first."

Sassy dropped the fluffy white robe and let her nude body speak volumes.

Aidan smiled appreciatively.

She stepped into the tub, rotating her hairy garden so he could get a good look before she slowly lowered herself—inch by inch—into the pink bubbles. "Hummmm," she moaned as the hot water soothed and warmed every crevice of her being. "Now you," she enticed.

"Absolutely." He shed his clothes and struck a reciprocal pose so she could delight in his nakedness and the hard length of his desire that rose to please her.

"Bravo, Mr. Symonds." She grinned as he felt his magnificent body be consumed—inch by inch—into the hungry bubbles.

"Hummm."

"Isn't this exquisite?"

"Absolutely," he said. "Gimme those size tens."

Sassy hyperextended her leg perpendicular to the watery floor and executed a perfect ballet point before placing her foot in Aidan's waiting hand.

"You must do that again when there are no bubbles to block that view." He began to massage her foot.

"You are so bad."

"That's not what you've been telling me."

"That feels sooo good." Sassy closed her eyes to the sheer ecstasy, rotating her bottom on the slippery floor of the tub. "Where'd you learn to do this?"

"Can't tell you all my secrets." He began to knead each individual toe. "Just enjoy."

Had she ever had a foot massage before? she asked herself as Aidan worked on her size tens, and relaxed her entire body. Is this what her Maman meant by "Make sure you take care of your feet and your feet will take care of you?" The buoyancy of the water carried her, the aroma of the mango bubble bath soothed her, and the heat and the humidity of the bathroom produced a surrealism. At the end of the tub, the purveyor of this fantasy. Her eyes opened just a slit to view the intensity with which he was working those feet. *Is he an apparition? Is he real? Is he too good to be real?* She closed her eyes again and drifted—drifted on clouds. Stevie Wonder's "Overjoyed" spun in her head; she was suspended somewhere between real and ideal. Calm, quiet peacefulness and serenity claimed her in this Neverland. She wanted to stay here forever.

She jerked awake.

"Did I fall asleep?"

"Did you?" he asked playfully. "I wouldn't let you drown."

"This is as good as making love."

"Gee, thanks."

"You were at the root of them both."

"I like the way you think."

She reclaimed her foot and approached him on all fours; her rounded breasts hovered just above the bubbles. She kissed him on the nose, then nuzzled against his hairy chest and said, "Heaven."

They refilled the tub twice and, when they were both pruney, decided to leave their bubbly oasis.

"Allow me." He took the thirsty towel from the heated rack and let it wick the water from her wet skin.

She ruffled her wet hair with a face towel. "Ugh! I bet my hair is sticking out all over the place. I must look a mess." She swatted at him playfully.

"I like your short hair." He ran his fingers through the drying moistness.

"You've never seen my hair any other way," she said, noticing a glint in his eye. "Have you?"

"I just assumed that all properly brought up N'awlins girls had hair streaming down their backs at one time or another." He was talking too much.

"Now you." She took his towel and wiped off his muscled torso. When he turned around to face her, she gasped at the sight of his obvious readiness.

He delighted in the attention that his love member was receiving.

"You are insatiable." She tore her eyes away and said, "What do you think? Can we make it to the bed?

"Why bother?" He opened her robe and let it fall to the floor as he leaned her against the cool tile and they continued their snow-day lovemaking.

After showering off the sticky remnants of their latest tryst, the robe-clad pair went into the living room where the roaring fire performed for their delight. He ordered room service and let the maid in to make the bed while Sassy talked on the telephone.

"Yes, I'll call back in a few minutes," she said, hanging up and calling the airport, making arrangements to get out by two tomorrow. She then called Ivanhoe.

"Yes. I'm snowed in until tomorrow. I have a flight out at one-thirty. Oh, it's wonderful, my first snowfall," she said as the maid left and Aidan joined her on the sofa and began planting tiny kisses on her neck.

"Too bad you aren't snowed in with someone delicious, chère. You can't imagine how wonderful that would be," Ivanhoe said.

"I can imagine," Sassy said with a giggle. "Listen, they're getting Maman for me so I'm going to call her back now. When I come in tomorrow, I'm going straight to Willowbrook but I'll be home that night."

"Okay, chère. Give her my best."

She looked into Aidan's eyes and said, "And thanks, Ivanhoe. Thanks for everything," and hung up. They kissed, and she tore away. "I've got to call my Maman now. Go away," she said playfully, darting to the phone by the bed just as room service knocked.

"Yes, doctor," Sassy said and the next voice she heard was her mother's. "Hello, Maman."

"Girl, I'm talking to you more now than I do when you're in N'awlins."

"I just wanted you to know I won't be there today, I'm caught in a snowstorm and can't get out until tomorrow."

"All right. I'm not going anywhere. I'll be here when you get here. I got a postcard from Roux—he's in the Bahamas. Don't that beat all?"

"Yes, Maman," Sassy said wearily, realizing that she hadn't though about Roux at all. Aidan rejoined her on the bed and resumed his tickly kisses. She giggled.

"What are you doing, Sassiere?" Maman asked.

"It must be the connection. I'll see you tomorrow, Maman. Love you."

"Love you too."

"Stop that!" Sassy protested playfully as Aidan fell back on the pillows.

"You don't mean that," he teased.

"I certainly don't!" She hung up the phone and tackled him with kisses.

"When do I meet your maman?"

"What?" The question took her by surprise.

"I want to thank the woman who gave birth to you." He traced her lips then her collarbone down to the rise of her breasts and back up again. "We can go in together, rent a car at the airport and drive out to Willowbrook—"

"She's not really up to company, and new people just confuse her," Sassy said and thought, *Oh, the horror of me going to see Maman with anybody but her precious Roux*; she'd either ask a thousand questions or give them the silent treatment, and Sassy wasn't up to either. "Something smells good. What did you order for us?"

"An indoor picnic." He left the bed and sprang around

the couch to the front of the fireplace arriving the same time as she did.

"Oh, Aidan." She enthused as she saw how he'd laid out a blanket in front of the roaring fire, complete with ribs, chicken, potato salad, and champagne. "Perfection again."

She looked at the Oreo cookies and two hot chocolates, one sinking under marshmallows and the other without. He handed her the latter.

"How did you know I liked Oreos and my hot chocolate *sans* marshmallows?" she asked quizzically. "You're starting to spook me."

"Lucky guess," he deflected, "My lady, your feast awaits."

They feasted, the music played softly, and they napped in each other's arms until early evening. "You want to get dressed and go to the dining room to eat for a change of pace?" he asked quietly.

"No. I like the pace right here. You?" she asked as she climbed into his arms while he sat in the big chair in front of the fire.

"No place I'd rather be."

She fell asleep, and he watched her as the fire flickered on the face of his dream come true. Never in his wildest dreams had he ever imagined that he'd be holding her in New York City at Christmas. She filled his life as she filled his arms. He could smell the faint aroma of barbecue sauce, Oreos, and hot chocolate. He rubbed his chin gently back and forth across the top of her curly head, listening to the lullaby of her heart speaking to his. He was ecstatic and content and truly happy. He could stay like this forever—just holding her.

Early that next morning they made it through the snow to the Stanhope, where Aidan stayed until morning's light and later saw her safely into a cab. "I'm going to cook for you this weekend," she said. "After I see Maman, I'll go to the store and meet you at my house."

"First, we'll go to my house. Marie Antoinette's desk and the Fabergé eggs still want to meet you."

"Call me."

"That's a promise."

"I—" she hesitated, as he aimed his smoldering dark eyes at her. It was right on the tip of her tongue. *I love you, Aidan,* but she couldn't say it. Not yet. It was too soon. "You're the best time I ever had."

"I like being your best time." He kissed her and then closed the cab door. They waved to each other until they were out of one another's sight.

Chapter VIII

"So how's Maman?" Aidan asked as he shifted gears and his car sped under the canopy of trees on St. Charles Street, heading towards the Garden District.

"The same," Sassy replied, and breathed in the warm, sunshiny air. "Antiques, huh?" she said, changing the subject. She didn't know whether her mother really looked that bad or whether she always looked that bad, but being away caused her to look worse. "I think you're trying to take advantage of me, sir," she drawled in her best Blanche DuBois. "Antiques, indeed . . . ha!" She scoffed as Aidan laughed and turned left down a slender street. The homes were magnificent. After a few blocks, Aidan abruptly turned right and up a long driveway. "Where are you going?" she asked as the mansion grew nearer.

He answered with a wink and a smile.

"Okay, Aidan, a joke is a joke, but this isn't funny. I'm a respectable professor who can't afford to be arrested for trespassing."

"I live here," he said casually bringing the car to a halt under a stately covered portico.

"You do not," she said, refusing to budge.

"How do you know?" His sparkling, deep-set eyes asked.

"I'll wait in the car until you pick up whatever you're here to pick up."

"C'mon, Sassiere." He jangled his keys and opened his car door.

"I don't care how well you did with stocks. You couldn't have done Bill Gates well."

"Ye of little faith. Besides, I didn't do all this alone. I was born into the right family. Generations before me did this. All I had to do was keep it. And I have." He got out of the car, rounded to her side, and opened her door.

One side of the massive carved double doors to the house opened and a pleasant-faced, older woman in a French maid's uniform said, "Welcome home, Monsieur, Aidan."

"Ah, Lavinia," he greeted evenly. "I'd like you to meet a friend of mine, Sassiere—if she ever gets out of the car," he said with a smirk.

"Hello," Sassy said as she approached the woman at the door. "Who are you?" she asked Aidan as she passed him and walked into and was immediately dwarfed by the immensity of the grand hall. About fifty feet across from her was a Y staircase that led up to a spectacular open gallery. "A *Gone With the Wind* staircase. You didn't mention that."

"Welcome to the S—" Lavinia began.

Aidan cut her off and asked, "Is Ma—"

"Aidan. Welcome back," another woman, in turn, interrupted him. She appeared beneath the staircase and walked regally toward the couple. When she finally reached them, the dark-skinned woman with the olive undertones and keen features turned to Sassiere and introduced herself. "Hello, I am Simone. I've been with the family for years. You are?"

"Sassiere," Aidan spoke up, but Simone's eyes never left their guest.

"I'm sure she has a last name and a tongue of her own," Simone said with a wickedly frozen smile.

"Crillon. Sassiere Crillon. Pleased to meet you."

"Crillon? I'm not familiar with that name? Are you from New Orleans, chère?"

"Born and bred, but not from this side of town," she said without apology as she continued past the rude woman and asked, "Is this the vintage grandfather clock?"

"Yep," Aidan marveled at her knowledge of antiques and ability to put Simone in her place. "I still don't see Marie Antoinette's desk or the—"

"This way." He guided Sassy into the front parlor, eyeing Simone with a silent command to *behave*.

"Oh, Aidan," Sassiere commented as she entered the exquisitely appointed parlor with its antiquities tastefully showcased about the spacious room. "Here it is." She recognized it. "You weren't lying."

"Not if I don't have to." He crossed his hands over his chest and admired her appreciating the desk. "You'll notice two of the Fabergé' eggs to your right."

"Are you a connoisseur of fine things, Sassiere?" Simone asked, following them into the parlor.

"Yes. Antiques are my business. I'm an art history teacher at Tulane. But you-all *live* with these exquisite treasures. How fortunate you are."

"Yes," the steely Simone said, allowing a genuine half-smile graze her lips.

Sassy roamed through the room identifying *objets d'art* and exited through the door at other end of the room which led back to the grand hall behind the grand staircase. She looked out through the beveled glass windows to the garden. "Look at those flowers," she said almost to herself.

"You know flowers?" Simone's face lit up. "That's my area of expertise."

"You've done an excellent job. Orchids, jacaranda, gardenia, sweet olive, hibiscus, bougainvillea—"

"Come out and let me show you," Simone offered, as she guided the guest across the marble floor.

"Simone," Aidan began to object.

"I'm not going to hurt her, Aidan." She raised her left eyebrow. "I promise."

"Monsieur Aidan, telephone," Lavinia interrupted.

Aidan watched the pair disappear through the beveled French doors and enter the garden. He took the telephone into the parlor and kept his eyes on the two women. Simone never took to people in general or women in particular unless she was using them for sport and meant to eat them alive. But Sassy seemed to be holding her own and Simone's interest. Apparently, Sassy was identifying flora and fauna the way she had the antiquities, which seemed to delight Simone, who reveled in her thirty-year reputation as the eccentric town recluse who preferred flowers and oil painting to people.

As the women stood near the ornate Byzantine marble fountain, Aidan interrupted, "Simone, I wanted to show Sassiere the rest of the house before we get going again,"

"By all means," Simone demurred before she disappeared into an outer building beside the garden.

"Interesting woman," Sassy commented as Aidan escorted her back into the house.

"You don't know the half of it," he said. He escorted Sassy to the library, where over two thousand books were encased in rich, mahogany, floor-to-ceiling shelves.

"You read all of these?" she asked.

"Almost. I had a lot of time on my hands before you." He kissed her quickly and led her to the dining room, where the polished Louis XIV table, surrounded by twenty-four upholstered chairs, beckoned. Behind it and through pocket doors lay the gentleman's smoking room.

Sassy was too mesmerized to vocalize; even she didn't want to hear inane commentary on this spectacular abode. They ascended the staircase and Aidan noticed her glance through the open gallery balustrades to the three doors.

"The three bedrooms complete with bathrooms and fireplaces in their sitting rooms. My parents' room was on the front. The room in between was mainly for my cousin, who visited us from D.C. during the summers. She's married with children. My room is in the back. Care to see?" he said with a gleam in his eyes.

"And on this side?" Sassy teasingly, ignored him using the right staircase near a series of three French doors.

"The ballroom." Aidan flung open one side of the door and entered an immense long room with muted pastoral murals adorning the walls. At either end was a fireplace, and above, the ornate plaster ceiling was punctuated by three exquisite crystal chandeliers.

"You live in a museum. Talk to me, Aidan. You're not a very good guide," Sassy egged him on. "Who, what, when, why?"

"The house was built in 1840 by a sugar king who owned most of the land which is now the Garden District. Originally, in the plans of the 1800s each square was to house four 'villas,' which is what they called detached houses back then. This sugar king bought the entire parcel of land, all of which has remained part of the property; it's the largest in the District. My great-great-great grandfather, Xavier, bought it in the late 1850s. I'm told this ballroom, which accommodates one hundred and fifty to two hundred guests comfortably, and the smoking room downstairs constructed in 1845, were the selling points."

Sassy walked into the mouth of the fireplace and said, "A family of four could live in here."

"Only means of keeping the guests warm back then. Of course, the balcony overhead is where the orchestra played."

Sassy stepped out, turned around and looked up at the intricately carved marble cantilevered out over the dance floor. "Good God Almighty."

"When you aren't entertaining the masses, this also doubles as a music room. It's where I learned the trumpet, piano, and violin. You know, on this side. Away from the neighbors."

Sassy chuckled and looked at the faded but artfully rendered pastoral scenes painted on the walls. "Works of art." As she approached the window near the other fireplace, she looked down on that garden and saw Simone standing in front of a two-story stone building full of wicker furniture, mosquito netting, canvas, and oil paint. "That's quite a setup she has down there."

Aidan looked over. "She tends the garden and paints. That's her 'studio.' Originally, it was the kitchen when mansions like these were worried about fires so it was separate from the main house."

"Nicely decorated."

"Humm."

They walked back out into the grand hall. "What's on the third floor?"

"Originally, servants quarters now turned into storage mainly."

"You mean slave quarters don't you?"

"No. They had the separate building outside, next to the kitchen, over the stables. Later it was a workshop. The final incarnation is a guest house complete with three bedrooms and baths, a few plasma TV's, pool table, bar, game room. You know, can't have guests staying in here with us," he teased.

Sassy just looked at him as if seeing him for the first time. "You are funky, filthy rich," she realized. "I should have let you buy me that skirt in SoHo," she quipped and he laughed.

"C'mon. Last but not least. My room." He led her down the hall, across the upper stairs and through a fortress of a door.

She looked at the masculine interplay of butterscotch, mahogany, copper, and brown. "Oh, Aidan, you didn't decorate this, did you?"

"Why not? Did you notice the toasted-pecan motif?" He smiled mischievously.

"It's as big as my whole apartment!"

Sassy noted that to the left there was a sitting area complete with a couch and a chaise facing the fireplace with a mantle. She ventured down a hallway with series of closets on the left and bank of windows on the right; at its end was his bathroom, done in gleaming marble, and his weight set near a sauna.

"This is obscene," she said, returning to his bedroom. To the right of the main door, a magnificent half-tester antique bed perched catercornered between one immense window, through which a gorgeous magnolia tree stood sentry, and a pair of French doors which opened onto a small balcony overlooking the garden.

"That bed is unbelievable." Sassy let her fingers caress the rich mahogany. "You sleep in this—"

"All my life."

"With all this space, why is it right behind your bed-room door?"

"This was a mighty big room for a little boy. I wanted the bed near the main hallway. I just never changed it. Care to try it out?" He nuzzled near.

She laughed and, hearing the soothing water of the fountain, sauntered over to the French door and out on the recessed balcony. "This is great, but it needs a hammock."

"I spent a lot of time out here as a boy. It was one of the few things in this house made to scale for a little boy." He fell silent as if remembering his time here.

Sassy looked at him, realizing that we all have our own baggage. Anyone would have thought that a little boy who lived in this house on the hill like this had the best, most complete life possible. But he had felt alone, dwarfed and uncomfortable in his own home the way a lot of Gert Town kids felt cramped and overcrowded in theirs. It was all relative. Childhood was all a crapshoot. He was a victim of his parents' success just as they were victim of their parents' poverty. That was what Sister Claire Regina would call "ironic."

"What's over that wall?" She asked to bring him back, and pointed to the eight-foot stone wall beyond the garden in the distance.

"The pool."

"And this building to the left? Is this part of your property too?"

"The old *garçonniere*. Young boys were banished there in the old days to live outside the main house. So they wouldn't disturb civilized folk with their late-night comings and goings. Now it's just the garage on the bottom and Hughes' living quarters on the second floor. He's the driver who takes care of the cars."

"Cars?" She enunciated the plural.

Aidan shrugged in answer, realizing he might have misspoken. "His and mine and the house car for errands."

Sassy looked at him again and wondered how could a man who had all of this speak so casually of such opulent wealth. From her past experiences and by all measures, Aidan should be stuck up, arrogant, and snotty. But he was just Aidan, and despite herself, she was really falling for him. Not for what he had, but for who he was.

He sidled up behind her and enveloped her in his arms.

"I want to see the pool where you swam in safety while I risked my life in the levee."

"Your wish is my command."

From inside her sanctuary, Simone watched the pair stroll past her window down the middle of the garden, bypassing the guesthouse, through the walled gate to the pool. She wasn't sure about this girl who was interested but not impressed with all their family heirlooms.

Looking at the pool area, Sassy said, "Aidan. This is it!"

"It's what?" He looked quizzically from the striped cabanas and chaise lounge chairs that ringed the clear blue water to the diving board and barbecue pit, and back to her excited eyes.

"The *perfect* place for the St. Gabriel's Christmas bazaar. Remember I was telling you we needed something new and exciting. Well, we could have it here."

"Here?"

"Why not? The kids could swim in the pool while the bazaar part could be set up over there on the lawn and along the service driveway. We wouldn't have to bother or trample Simone's garden; in fact, she could showcase it. Oh, please say yes. It's just one day, for charity."

He looked at her and she was a young girl—the way he remembered her when he first laid eyes on her.

"C'mon. To whom much is given, much is expected. One day out of your life," she plead. "It would mean so much to St. Gabriel's."

Aidan was less concerned with the wear and tear on his home than he was the possibly of her finding out who he really was. There would be flyers with the mansion's name on it; in N'awlins society this address was as well known as the White House at 1600 Pennsylvania Avenue was in Washington, D.C. How could he do this for her and keep himself a secret until she was so in love with him his identity wouldn't matter?

"Aidan?"

"I'm just thinking. Haven't the flyers and publicity already gone out for this? It's in a couple of weeks."

"Are you kidding? The vendors would love to come here instead of the auditorium and school grounds of St. Gabriel's."

"Maybe next year we can plan it out—"

"It can be an annual event starting with this year. Simone could sell some of her paintings—if she wanted to. And Lavinia can bake something delicious. Who else lives here?"

"Only Hughes, who could conduct the pony rides for the kids in the outer yard."

She jumped up and kissed him in her excitement. "Yes! Yes! Oh, Aidan, I love you!"

He stared at her and the way the sunlight played with her skin. He wanted this exact moment frozen in time.

She realized what she had said. "Oh, I'm sorry. I didn't mean—"

"Don't apologize." His eyes gazed lovingly into hers. "I think out of everything I've ever heard in my entire lifetime—nothing has meant more to me than hearing you say that."

"I wanted to tell you—later, in a private way. In a quiet moment—"

"It was perfect." He kissed her. "That won't be the last time I'll be hearing it, will it?"

"Not if you're good." She loved the way he made her feel, as if she were perfect and could do no wrong.

"'Cause I could listen to you say that over and over and over again, twenty-four-seven."

She laughed at his use of slang and deflected, "Right now, let's just plan a bazaar."

He would give her anything at this point. "Since parking in this area is limited and traffic in and out of here nil—and since it's such short notice—I'll have buses pick up the folks at St. Gabe's and transport them here."

"You will?!"

"That way we don't have to do any flyers or phone trees—"

"That's brilliant. Won't Sister Claire Regina be surprised? If she agrees."

"Let me handle her."

"You know her?"

"I know Catholics and fund-raising. Besides, we have a history of giving to St. Gabe's. They'll be fine with it."

"What I don't know about you Aidan Symonds, could fill the Pontchartrain."

"But isn't the getting-to-know-you the fun part?" He

nuzzled near her, hating to keep anything from her, wanting to tell her the one secret that could tear them apart. *Soon,* he told himself. Soon she'd know it all, and it wouldn't matter because she loved him.

"It has been fun—fantastic" She stopped, smiled then said, "Oh, this is sooo exciting. Let's talk about it over dinner. It's grocery-shopping time." She pulled him toward the service driveway.

"Why don't I just have Lavinia fix us something here, and we can eat in the garden?"

"You just don't want to go grocery shopping do you? Have you ever been grocery shopping? Do you know where a grocery store is?"

"Okay. It's not top on my list of fun things to do but Lavinia is used to—"

"Uh-uh. I want to cook for you. I want you at my place tonight and with me tomorrow morning when we wake up."

His parenthetical smile split his face in two. But he still had to avoid being seen in public with her and risking someone greeting him with his real name. The symphony was one thing, but grocery shopping in broad daylight was quite another.

Sassy moved into him and kissed him, tasted him.

He enjoyed the deliciousness of her. "Humm. Okay. We'll compromise. You shop, I'll pay for it; you can take my car and pick me up after you finish."

"And what will you be doing?"

"I'm going to get the ball rolling here, make a few calls. We've got a bazaar here in a few weeks." He kissed her.

"Yes, we do. Okay. Gimme your keys, but the groceries are my treat."

"They're in my left pocket."

She exacted them from him, her hand lingering

against his maleness, before she kissed him good-bye. "See you in a hour, tops."

"I love an independent woman," he said as she left.

He watched her sashay down the driveway and caught a glimpse of her in his car as she sped up the street. He'd give it to her as an engagement gift. He wanted her in his life to live here and make this house a home again. As he returned to the house he decided that he would tell her who he was the night after the bazaar. It would be a smashing success, she'd be excited and nothing could come between them. He sat behind his desk and smiled. She loved him. Sassiere Crillon loved him. That's all he needed. He'd confess his love for her, and, in that state of mind, she could handle the truth and they could get on with their lives. They had plans and babies to make. Had he ever been happier in his life? The prospect of being the husband of a woman he'd only dreamed about caused him to clap his hands and laugh aloud.

"Aidan," Simone said, entering the parlor.

"Yes," he said tightly, slightly irritated by the interruption of his fantasy.

"Where has she gone? To get all her friends and bring them over here for a pool party?" she asked sarcastically.

"Does she seem like a gold digger to you, Maman?" He rose from his seat. "Seems to me she didn't care one whit about all this." He gestured grandly and touched her nose playfully with his index finer.

"Tsk. You're not fooled by her, are you? Where she go then?"

"She went to buy food, Maman. Seems after I offered Lavinia's service of cooking a meal, she wants to cook for me. Simone . . . she went grocery shopping—"

"Lavinia will have her hide if she messes up her kitchen," Simone scoffed.

"Well, first off, it's not Lavinia's kitchen—it's mine. And second of all, we're going to her place."

"Ah. The lure. Where she live? In a hovel someplace?"

"Wherever she lives, I'm sure it's clean. Wherever she lives—it's where I plan to spend as much time as I can." He started to leave the room. "Don't wait up, Maman. Oh!" He snapped his fingers, stopped and turned, "By the way, you remember St. Gabriel's of the Sacred Heart?"

Simone's eyes narrowed angrily, and her lips curled closed upon themselves so she couldn't speak.

"We're having a bazaar for them. Here, in two weeks."

"What!" The words dripped from her lips like venom. "*Mon dieu!*"

"Rather poetic isn't, Maman? You can be here—you can visit elsewhere—you can close yourself off and up in that living tomb if you like, but Sassiere invited you and thought maybe you'd like to sell some of your paintings—"

"She's touched!"

"Ah, ah. Let's not talk that way about the mother of your future grandchildren." He decided to remain in his office, returned to his desk, yanked up the telephone and began making his calls.

Two hours later, Aidan pulled up to Sassiere's iron gates, his car stopping short of contact and blocking the sidewalk. Sassy jumped out and unlocked the gate, and Aidan pulled his car to a halt in the driveway.

As they each reached for a bag of groceries, Sassy said, "I can't believe Sister Claire Regina caved so easily. That old girl used to be a hard nut to crack."

"Charm. That's all it is. And the chance to make more money."

"If this is an annual event—"

He eased up behind her and said, "I like the sound of that. It has a certain ring of permanency to it. Longevity."

By this time next year, she would know who he was, and they'd be married and perhaps about to give Gardner and Yvette's little son or daughter a playmate.

"You nut," she threw over her shoulder as she started up the gallery stairs to her apartment.

"About you . . . yeah."

Their laughter roused Ivanhoe, who sprang to the door and around to Sassy's steps. From behind them, he said in Betty Davis-ese, "So. Is this someone I should meet?" He watched them turn around slowly to face him.

"Yes," Sassy introduced, "Ivanhoe this is Aidan, Aidan Symonds this is Ivanhoe Fauchon—my friend, confidant, landlord, boss, and the man responsible for our meeting."

Ivanhoe froze at the sight of him.

The spark of recognition from Ivanhoe registered in Aidan's eyes, but he managed, "Fauchon. Like the famous Paris deli." Aidan offered his free hand and forced a smile—half-threat, half-plea, that Ivanhoe not give up his identity.

"You two know each other?" Sassy chronicled the interplay of stares as she juggled her bag of groceries, before continuing, "Oh, and Ivanhoe. Aidan offered his house for the bazaar! Isn't that fantastic?" She turned to finish her assent upstairs. "We're making gumbo. Come on up in a few hours and join us when it smells right."

"Good to meet you," Aidan said, letting his hand drop when Ivanhoe was too stunned to shake it. "I've heard a lot of good things about you." He backed away from Ivanhoe, their eyes still locked, and walked up two steps before he turned to follow Sassiere.

Ivanhoe just stared at the couple until they disappeared. Then he finally blinked, sank against the nearest wall and said, "Well, I'll be damned."

This explains everything, Ivanhoe thought. Aidan was the mystery guy, the man who brought her home in the limo that night she broke off with Roux. The one Sassy had no memory of. It explained the clothes, the money, the boarding schools and travel. Ivanhoe had racked his brain trying to figure out who this native son was, the descendant of the *gens de couleur libre*; his wealth derived from years of his family being free long before Lincoln's emancipation in 1861. Ivanhoe had ruled out all the N'awlins' Old Guard, the richest five families, including his. After all, this man was driving the tacky two-seater BMW and not Aidan's signature slate-gray Ferrari 360 Spider, which would have been a dead giveaway. Yes, Ivanhoe had ruled him out, yet there he stood, big as day.

Ivanhoe could hear Sassy laughing overhead in a way he hadn't heard her laugh since Roux. Would she still be laughing if she knew his last name wasn't Symonds? Would she be amused at all if she knew he was Aidan Maximillien Sebastien? A member of a family she was taught and groomed to hate all these years without knowing or caring for the real reason why? Programmed to do so by Roux—the only man she had ever loved and trusted. And now . . . she was falling for the enemy.

Ivanhoe dashed to his bar and poured a stiff bourbon, drank it down, and poured another short one. From the front courtyard he heard them romp and play overhead before they put on Sarah Vaughan's "I'm Glad There's You" obviously dancing, wrapped up in each other's arms.

"Damn!" he said as he swallowed the amber liquid again. Should he tell her who that was? Heir apparent to the Sebastien Funeral Home dynasty? The richest Creole family west of the Mississippi?

"Damn, damn, damn," he exclaimed again, and Killer looked at him lazily. No. No he wouldn't tell. To what end? But she said he was offering his house up for the bazaar. Was it the Sebastien mansion, or was it some other house he'd bought somewhere to go with the BMW? Did she know? No, she couldn't know. She wouldn't have given him the time of day.

From the way Aidan looked at her, he seemed genuinely to care for her—enough to disguise himself and invent this elaborate masquerade. Ivanhoe searched his brain for what he had read about Aidan Sebastien in the society pages. Not much. He was very low-key, avoided the press, and wasn't given to sleeping around or flaunting his wealth, which made him even more appealing to women and a target for every mother-daughter combination from here to California. Besides Sassy, was a beautiful girl inside *and* out, that's why he'd fallen for her. She didn't know him or care about his money. To test her motives on his wealth, he showed her the house. What he got as a reaction was his Sassy's thought that the house was a perfect vehicle for charity, a Christmas bazaar, not casting herself as Queen of the Manor, as most women surely had. Aidan had to admire her retro, innocence and unpretentiousness; in Aidan's circle of friends, that had to be a rare, almost nonexistent commodity. Sassy must be particularly appealing to a man like Aidan Sebastien, who'd been everywhere, done and seen it all.

"This is a disaster," he said, pouring another drink then setting it aside. "After all these years, how did they meet? Where on earth could their paths have crossed?" he asked a disinterested Killer.

As long as Aidan wasn't out to hurt his Sassy, Ivanhoe decided to retract his claws. "Truth is stranger than fiction," he toasted Killer with the last of the bourbon. *But jeeze,* he thought, and said, "Of all the gin joints in the world he had to walk into hers."

He put the empty glass back on the bar, made the sign of the cross four times and concluded he would let them have their fun and happiness now, because when Roux found out—he would kill them both. Ivanhoe crossed himself again then held his head. "I need to go make a novena or something—"

Two hours and several albums later, Aidan dipped Sassy at the end as Nat King Cole's and Ella's voices collided in perfect harmony.

"Your dad had some collection," Aidan said.

"I pulled them out after I met this wonderful man in San Francisco," she said.

"Tell me about him." Aidan's deep set eyes sparkled.

"Can't. I don't want to jinx it. Besides, it's time for you to chop." She walked to the kitchen. "Gumbo is almost ready, and we need salad. You know what one of these is?" She held up a knife.

"Gimme." He snatched and yelled.

"Oh, Aidan, did you cut yourself? Are you bleeding?"

When she came near, he grabbed her, buried her in kisses, and her laughter lilted down Clemenceau Street like springtime.

At dusk, they devoured the gumbo and the chocolate cake. She lay in her bed with him beside her. The brick wall was their backboard and the open French doors their ventilation. Too excited to sleep, she eased out of bed to the open window and sat on its sill. She drew her legs up to her chest. Beyond the cistern, the Cajun moon rose high and Sassy thought how different things were this lunar rising. Dinah Washington sang it best in "What a Difference a Day Makes," and absently, Sassy hummed a few bars.

She wondered if there were some definitive point in time when your past reconciles with your future and you are at peace. When you let go of your dreams and face reality—of becoming a prima ballerina, or the best basketball star, or marrying Roux and living happily ever after. A point when you realize that some things are just beyond your reach, and that realization forces you to reassess, and redefine who you are, where you are and where you want to be. She recognized that she had unresolved feelings for Roux, but she couldn't come to grips with them because whenever she thought of him only the hurt, pain and betrayal stabbed at her tender heart. She wanted to put him completely behind her, but things were just too good between her and Aidan to think about all that ugliness now. She had to keep the two apart as long as possible. Roux could be unbearable when he didn't get his way, and Aidan didn't deserve that just because of who he was dating.

Tell me who you love and I'll tell you who you are, she recalled an old Creole proverb. What did her loving Roux all those years tell Aidan about her? That she was young and foolish and dated a likeable rogue? That she didn't have enough good sense to see beneath his charming-doggish veneer?

Loving Roux seemed—a lifetime ago when she was young and trusting and wide-eyed—when she was "Sassy." But she was forced to evolve into a self-reliant woman who trusted her own instincts, not another person's. A woman who did things based on what she wanted and decided was right, not on Roux's direction or reaction. She was savvy "Sassiere," the mature woman who had and could articulate her own feelings, direction, and abilities, and with every fiber of her being, she wanted a future with Aidan Symonds.

Roux had been razzle-dazzle. Like a dress in a fine
shop that caught your eye and interest because it was different and outlandish, made a statement, a garment that
everyone would remember and you'd look fantastic in.
Sure—you'd have to worry about the strap slipping off
your shoulder, or get two-sided tape to make sure your
boobs didn't pop out, and keep pulling the shirt when it
would ride up—but it was worth it. But in that same shop
was a classic solid dress suit that could take you any
where. It wasn't flashy, but you could wear it comfortably as you gave a lecture or attended a business meeting;
this suit could carry you from work to play and never let
you down. It was reliable and would always look good.
That was Aidan. After twenty years of flash, Sassiere
wanted solid.

She glanced over at him in her bed and smiled. It was
as if Aidan knew how fickle the heart could be, and he
bypassed it and went straight for her soul; grabbed it and
wouldn't let go. She had love and sex with Aidan, but he
also gave her something she had never had . . . intimacy.
An interconnectedness, an organic, muscular feeling of
familiarity and security she didn't know existed. She ab-
horred the word "soulmate," thinking it a contrived
term, made up for the card industry's benefit. But for
the first time, she understood the meaning of the over-
used sobriquet. For the first time she *felt* the significance
of it. Through thick and thin—good and bad, Aidan
Symonds would be there. That was love.

She turned back to face the Cajun moon and thought,
I suppose I have you to thank for this. It was the lunar
red-orange-golden ball that had spun all this in the universe several weeks ago. How different everything was
now. She supposed, while she was in a grateful mood,
she ought to thank Maxine Dupree, too, for being the

lowlife woman who appealed to Roux's inability to "be a man and say no." Aidan would never have fallen for a Maxine Dupree and would undoubtedly be repulsed by the proposition.

Aidan came up behind her and slid his strong arms around her. "Can't sleep?" He grazed her temple with his perfect lips.

"Just enjoying nature's perfume." She leaned into his chest.

"Mmm. It is nice. Full moon."

"Nothing as spectacular as your view, with the fountain and the garden."

"Better. Your being here makes it so." He couldn't share with her how many sleepless nights he'd wished for her in his bed, wrapped in all the colors designed from her skin's hue. How many times he'd imagined her beside him. How he would have given it all up to hold her here—like this.

"I don't want this to end, Aidan," she admitted quietly.

"It doesn't have to." He squeezed her.

A single tear slid down her right cheek and glistened in the moonlight.

"You crying?" he asked.

"It's just so perfect, Aidan. It can't last."

"Who says?"

"In your world, everything always works out. But my reality is a little different."

He turned her around to face him and gently lifted her chin with his hand. "Sassiere, I'll do anything in my power to make all your dreams come true. We are two hearts with one dream—marriage, children, and forever after. It can happen. It will happen. I love you."

Emotion caught in her throat and she inhaled deeply without speaking.

"We have time, Sassiere. Lots of it. And I want to spend it all with you."

"Oh, Aidan." She collapsed in his arms and he kissed her fervently.

"We're magic remember? Destiny is ours—from San Francisco, Napa, and New York, and N'awlins. It's kismet. We were meant to be."

"I love you, Aidan."

"I hope you never stop."

The next morning a fully dressed Aidan kissed a sleeping Sassiere. She rolled over to him.

"Leaving so early?" she said, ending her feline stretch with him in her noose. He kissed her again.

"It's not early, but you go on back to sleep," he said. "My empire awaits. I left coffee brewing for you and French toast warming in the oven."

"You did that for me? Thanks," she said sleepily.

"Go back to sleep." He kissed her again and watched her obey as she rolled over and was fast asleep again. He backed away from her, turned and jogged down the steps by twos, humming "The Very Thought of You."

Ivanhoe was on the verandah watering his window boxes when he heard the footsteps on the steps. He steeled himself to ignore Aidan Sebastien.

Seeing Ivanhoe wiped the gleeful smile from Aidan's face. He fixed the collar of his jacket as he approached the man. "Good morning."

"Is it," Ivanhoe said without looking at him.

"I'm going out on a limb here," Aidan said, thrusting his hands into his pockets. "But I think you know my last name is not Symonds."

"I know very well who you are."

"How do you know?" Aidan was curious. He realized he had inherited the name, but he guarded his personal life fiercely.

"Don't you worry about how I know," Ivanhoe snapped. "The question is why doesn't Sassy know? I don't know what kind of games you are playing with my Sassy—"

"I love her," Aidan admitted simply.

The admission stunned Ivanhoe quiet. *How?* Ivanhoe's eyes asked what his lips could not.

"I've loved her for a long time. If you know me, then you know of my family. You know how folks love to drive by the Sebastien mansion and imagine how wonderful it must have been to be a Sebastien . . . but it wasn't all sunshine and flowers. Truth is, while folks drove by my house I was driving past theirs—envying them the love, affection, caring, and connection the families had to one another. Mine was a lonely existence . . . my father's profession provided very well for us materially but I didn't really have him—what I did have were the taunts from other school children because of him—'Dr. Death's son.' 'Do you live with dead people?' Not even the curious kids came over to visit. Fear can cause children to be cruel. So I spent as little time at home as I could. I went in search of normalcy and I found Roux—and Sassy." He grinned unabashedly and remembered. "Running for the ice-cream truck. Tutoring schoolchildren, jumping Double Dutch, volunteering at the soup kitchen."

Aidan looked back at Ivanhoe, and the man was crying. Aidan didn't know what to make of Ivanhoe's reaction. "It wasn't a bad life," Aidan said, attempting to console Ivanhoe. "But Sassy and I can have a different life—together."

Ivanhoe brought a tissue out from beneath his sleeve and blew his nose.

"I plan to tell her very soon. After the bazaar." Aidan implored, "Will you let *me* do that? Will you let me be the one to tell her? "

Aidan words pierced Ivanhoe's heart, but he stood straight, dabbed his eyes and thought about Sassy—that was his one concern. Ivanhoe hadn't seen Sassy this happy for a lot of years.

"All right," Ivanhoe said finally. "She won't hear it from me. But if you hurt her in any way—"

"I assure you that is not my intention," Aidan interrupted him.

"When Roux finds out he will kill you."

"I'll take my chances." Aidan smiled and simply said, "I love her." He grinned at Ivanhoe and walked away.

"Saints preserve us," Ivanhoe said as he made the sign of the cross. "A Sebastien in love with his Sassy and she doesn't even know it." He put the watering can down and crossed himself again. "Heaven help her, Lord. Help him—them. Oh, Lord!! Heaven help us all!"

Chapter IX

Bouquets of colorful balloons marked the iron gates of the mansion and punctuated the driveway every six feet, alternating with the ten buses which transported St. Gabriel's parishioners to the "Surprise Bazaar." The air was N'awlins thick and hot, but none of the participants noticed as they frolicked on the green carpet of the estate's grounds.

From his office inside the mansion, Aidan spoke into the telephone. He looked out at the tranquility of the flowers, the Byzantine fountain, and Simone's closed door. Resenting the objectifying of her place and property, Simone had retreated into her studio early that morning, refusing to participate in the festivities beyond the garden wall.

"You are certain he is still in the Bahamas?" Aidan asked into the phone.

"Yes, sir. The contact saw him there during the last hour," the man informed.

"All right. Thanks." Aidan hung up. A smile claimed his face as he shoved his hands in his pockets, delighted that he could now surprise Sassiere with his presence at the bazaar.

He turned to go when he caught a glimpse of two people opening the back black-iron gate. *Simone will have a fit if folks violate her sanctum sanctorum,* he thought. Just as the pair grew closer and crossed by the guesthouse, he saw it was Sassiere and a young girl of about ten, bearing plates of food. He watched them knock on Simone's door and wait patiently. When there was no response, Sassiere and the girl set the plates of food on a nearby table and left. As the girl followed Sassiere back out the way they had come in, she glanced back at the door apparently hoping that someone would answer.

Moments after the clang of the gate, Aidan focused on the studio door. He knew this woman and, on cue, Simone opened her door, peeked out then picked up the first plate, inspected it and savored the aroma of the barbecue and other delectable treats from beyond the stone wall. To Aidan, the second plate looked as if they were desserts. Simone's eyes combed her quiet inner courtyard before she returned inside, this time leaving her door slightly ajar.

"That's my mama," Aidan said. "Her bark is bigger than her bite." He went out the front door to circle the service driveway and enter as did his guests.

Sassy smiled as she watched the children cool their hot bodies in the pool, play games at the decorated booths, or wait for their turn on a pony ride—all compliments of Aidan Symonds' generosity. She was sorry he couldn't be here to see the results of his good deed, but he had an emergency business trip to San Francisco this morning. She supposed wealth ranked its own priorities.

She watched Sister Claire Regina try the ring toss. She then caught a glimpse of Aidan walking around by the pony line to the pool. She rushed to meet Aidan halfway. "You're here!" They embraced quickly.

"Yes, my business finished up early and I couldn't think of any place I'd rather be." His deep penetrating eyes roamed her body, causing her cheeks to scorch in a blush. "You look great. That gold compliments your toasted praline-pecan skin."

"Thank you." She nervously tried pulling her hair down on her neck to deflect the heat he was igniting in her. "Let me introduce you to Sister—"

"I don't want to meet her. I want to take you upstairs and make love to you all night long," he said evenly, with the most causal look on his face, as if they were discussing how the bazaar sales were going.

Sassy laughed throatily and said, "Smooth."

"As your skin next to mine."

"So you like me in gold?" she asked to bring the conversation to a less sexy topic.

"I *love* you in that gold. But I'd love it even more if it were in a pile by my bed."

"Aidan Symonds," she whispered in an exaggerated Southern drawl. "I believe you're trying to corrupt me, sir." She added batting her eyelashes.

"Every chance I get. How am I doing?" he teased as his parenthetical smile graced his sculptured lips.

"Well, since everyone is staring at us, why don't we join in the reindeer games?"

"Lead the way."

They circumnavigated the bazaar twice, eating cotton candy and playing an occasional game. Aidan won Sassiere a teddy bear after dunking five balls sequentially.

"I wouldn't have ever pegged you for a basketball player," she said.

"I got skills," he teased.

"Yes, you do. What else don't I know about you?" She smiled.

The question only reminded him of the one secret between them. He stared at her, then looked out at crowd. He'd decided to tell here tonight after the bazaar or at first morning's light. This time tomorrow they would have no secrets. This time tomorrow would mark the true beginning of their lives together, when they could live and love freely.

"Penny for your thoughts?" she asked.

"It's just nice seeing so many people enjoying themselves here. It's been a long time since this place has been—alive." He then aimed his obsidian eyes at her and said, "I have you to thank for that. Making this place alive again."

"It's a beautiful place, Aidan, and it should be used."

"I agree, but my mother—"

"Mother?" Sassy interrupted.

"Simone is my mother."

"What? But I thought she was—"

"Which is what she wanted you to think. She thinks you can tell a lot about a person from how they treat 'the help.' She's a bored recluse. She makes up her own games to amuse herself. This was just one of them."

"Well, I wonder how I'm doing?" Sassy asked sarcastically.

"Hey." He grabbed her hand, raised it to his lips and kissed it. "I'm the only one you have to worry about. And I think you're doing just fine."

She was lost in the sincerity of his soulful eyes.

"Lot of commotion out here," Simone commented from behind to announce her presence.

"Welcome, Simone," Aidan said.

"Hello, Mrs. Symonds," Sassy said, now noting her familiar resemblance to Aidan in the stark sunshine.

Simone let a beguiling smile rest in her features. "So you think you know everything, eh?" she asked. She could feel her son's objection without looking at him and continued, "Thank you for the food. It was good . . . and thoughtful."

"I'm glad you enjoyed it. I had a little girl, Monique, with me who wanted to meet you. She is interested in art, and I told her a famous artist lived in that studio."

"Oh, really?" Simone said casually, feigning disinterest.

"May I introduce her to you?"

"I suppose," Simone said noncommittally.

"Excuse us, will you?" Sassy said to Aidan as she and Simone went to look for the little girl.

Aidan watched the two most important women in his life saunter over the hallowed grounds of this estate. He couldn't remember the last time his mother had been beyond the garden wall, and there she was—walking with the love of his life. Sassiere was a godsend to them both. Bringing them from darkness into the light like a modern day prophet—delivering Simone from her reclusiveness and him from his work. He watched Sassiere introduce his mother to the people they met as they searched for the girl and, once finding her, introducing the pair. He followed Sassiere with his eyes as a nun called her to another part of the yard for some sort of troubleshooting. She was graceful and in charge and apparently respected by those she met. How could any man take this extraordinary woman for granted? Roux's loss was his gain, he thought, and it was his intention that no one would ever hurt Sassiere again.

Ivanhoe left the barbecue stand and walked slowly towards the stone wall. He tried to muster enough nerve to approach the forbidden garden gate. He reached the jungle of green plants, took a deep breath and peeked through the rod-iron bars. He drank in the sumptuous tropical lushness of the flowers and fountain but his eyes fixed on the buildings: the main house, the old kitchen, the guesthouse, and the *garconniere*. He wanted to leave, but his fingers wrapped themselves securely around the cold iron spokes, pulling him like a magnet. He clung to the stoic fence like a starving waif in a Dickens novel eyeing a feast just beyond his grasp. His gaze rested on the guesthouse; the sight of it burned tears into his eyes.

Aidan, noticing Ivanhoe peering into the garden, went over and offered, "Would you like to go in?"

Ivanhoe jumped at the intrusion.

"Sorry, I didn't mean to startle you," Aidan apologized.

Ivanhoe turned toward Aidan, his eyes wet and swollen, black mascara seeping into the crepey folds of his skin. "Pollen. You know," Ivanhoe defended. "How many flowers and trees are in there?" he asked in a shrill voice.

"Quite a few," a perplexed Aidan said. "I wanted to thank you for not telling Sassiere—"

"No need," Ivanhoe interrupted as he withdrew a handkerchief from his sleeve and began to dab at his eyes. "Just—don't you hurt her. I must look a sight! I need to blow my nose. Excuse me." He rushed off.

What was that all about? Aidan wondered; it was the second conversation they'd had and the second time Ivanhoe had ended up crying. He sure was a hypersensitive man, Aidan thought. Then Sassiere waved at him from across the pool, and suddenly trying to figure out Ivanhoe's crying jags were the last thing on Aidan's mind.

Six hours later, the last bus pulled off, with the balloons that the children had confiscated on their way out billowing from the windows. Within the next hour, the cleanup committee had left the grounds in pristine shape.

One hand in his pocket, Aidan threw his other arm around Sassiere's neck and kissed her on the cheek as she waved at the last to leave. It was like they had given a picnic and were bidding farewell to the lasts of their guests. Aidan relished the feeling.

"That was fun, wasn't it?" She turned into him for a full hug, and he obliged.

"Yes, it was. Let's go in."

"Why don't you come to my place?"

"Tonight, I want to pretend this is your place—*our* place," he said with a gentle kiss.

"It's too big."

"What is? You had no problem handling it before," he teased wickedly.

She play-pushed his side, relishing how the mere mention of their lovemaking made her moist and ready. "I was speaking of the house," she clarified.

"I promise you'll always be only a touch away." He kissed her again.

"Aidan, I can't come in there. Your mother—"

"Oh, please," he dismissed. "She doesn't care. She lives in that studio. Even if she did come in, we'd never know." He kissed her forehead. "One of the good things about being in a big house."

"How about you just drape me over the pool table in the guesthouse and ravish me there?"

"Okay."

"Oh, Aidan. Your mother would see us fooling around for sure."

"She *never* goes in the guesthouse. Never."

"Never?" Sassy asked with a gleam in her eye.

"Something about the dead spirits of slaves, bad juju or something."

Sassy accepted his warm embrace and kisses, then brushed her lips across his.

"Don't you want to stay?" he asked.

"For a little while."

He kissed her, and arm and arm they walked up the driveway to the house.

They stole upstairs like two teenagers trying to get into a bedroom before the chaperones discovered them missing. Once inside, Sassy was again amazed—by the beauty of this room, massive, masculine, and perfectly appointed.

"You live like this day in and day out." She walked toward the middle of the room as he locked his door. "And this heirloom that doubles as your bed." She peeked under its canopy.

He tackled her onto it and said, "A bed is a bed." She rolled over and lay on top of him. "And I've wanted you in it as long as I can remember."

Sassy couldn't think of a sassy thing to say. Aidan had a way of disarming her and just letting the purity of the moment speak for itself. She never thought of herself as weepy or sentimental, but he just seemed to conjure up all those wonderful emotions in her. She'd never felt this way before. That she could love and trust a man all at the same time. She now knew what the old songs meant and how her dad must have felt about her mom and all the other songs written for other people. But Aidan made them seem for her. She never thought this kind of love was possible. The sheer freedom and happiness of it. The shared intimacy—the linear, sustained connection that kept them in tune with each other, knowing what one another thought and felt without speaking a word.

"I love you, Sassiere."

"I love you, too," caught her throat and showed in her eyes and they kissed. His scent filled her, his taste overwhelmed her, and they rode the rhythm of their love to its finality. They lay in each others arms, exhausted, satisfied, and content, as magnolia blossoms perfumed the air and the trickle from the fountain soothed them to sleep.

Aidan awoke in the middle of the night as he often did—out of habit and necessity; to relieve himself, to make an overseas call, to get a glass of water. Only this time, he had everything he ever wanted. He could have slept straight through the night with Sassiere here, but he wanted to chronicle this coup. The first night she spent in *his bed*. He was now holding what his heart only dreamed of in this very bed. How many years had he wished and hoped and never believed this would ever happen? He would have given up his fortune if he thought it would bring her to him.

The moonlight caressed her face, streamed down the full length of her nude body, a body he now knew so well, which always excited and never disappointed. He smiled as he watched her breathe.

Am I dreaming? he thought. *After all these years, am I just imagining that she was here with me?* She stirred and snuggled closer to him and he felt the warmth of body, the smoothness of her skin, the scent of cotton candy and the tickle from her curly hair.

She is here with me. His unobtainable dream—how many people ever got a chance like this? He couldn't keep the smile from his face. Flesh, blood, bone, muscle, heart, and soul. The culmination of so many lonely nights and unspoken desires, but here she was. Like the Grand Prize. The Super Bowl of all his desires and dreams—Sassiere Crillon—was here. He thought his heart would burst from pride and joy. He closed his eyes and rubbed her breast gently until he fell asleep.

Sassy awoke the next morning and was quietly preparing to leave when Aidan awakened.

"Where do you think you're going?" He sat up. "It's

Sunday. Time for brioche, coffee, the paper, and lounging all day."

"And how many Sundays have you spent like that?" She teased, sauntering over to the bed.

"I'm willing to start a tradition."

"Oh, really. Well, I've got to go home and change and go visit Maman."

"Sassiere, let me go with you. I'm sure she'd like me."

"I wanted her to come yesterday. But the doctor called and said that the dialysis and getting dressed tired her out." She touched Aidan's cheek. "I did want her to meet you. I thought casually at the bazaar would be perfect . . . but."

"Let me go now."

"Nope. I don't think she needs any jolts or surprises. I don't want her worrying about me and you."

"Why would—"

"Trust me." She grabbed the teddy bear he'd won for her and kissed him. "Will I see you tonight?"

"Absolutely. Oh, I have something for you."

Sassy smiled watching his muscled body crane to reach something under the bed. He held up the present and said, "Open it."

"What is it?" She smiled, returning to the bed and giving him the teddy. "You spoil me."

"That's the idea." He smiled as she unwrapped the gift.

"Oh, Aidan!" She laughed as she held the snow globe of New York City. She flipped it so that it snowed all over the skyscrapers, one of which was Rockefeller Center and its Rainbow Room.

"So you'll always remember our first time in the Big Apple."

"I don't need this to remember. But, thank you, Aidan. It's perfect." She flipped it again and watched it snow.

"Play it here. Wind the key."

She obeyed and listened to the tune tinkle out. She cocked her head to decipher as Aidan smiled with satisfaction.

"'The Very Thought of You'?" she identified with a gleam in her eyes. "How did you find this?"

"Didn't. Had it made especially for you."

"You are such an amazing man." She cradled it to her heart and kissed him.

"Yes, I am. So you'll stay? A little while. I have something I want to tell you—discuss—"

"Really? What?" She stopped and aimed her eyes at him.

"It can wait. You're in a rush."

"I promise I'll come back." She kissed him. "I'll keep my snow globe with me for the drive up to Willowbrook and the drive back. It'll be like you're with me."

"I am, Sassiere. Always." He took her chin, lifted her lips to his and kissed her gently.

"Sooner I go—sooner I get back." She kissed him quickly.

"And next Sunday. I want a '*Sunday kind of love*,'" he quoted the song.

"You got it. My place. We can sleep as late and long as you like." She retrieved the teddy bear from him.

He donned a robe and walked her to the front door. "Drive carefully."

He watched her blow him a kiss, pull off, and wave. He would tell her this evening. There was really no rush. They were in love.

As Sassy negotiated the Interstate ramp, she clicked off her radio, wound her snow globe, placed it next to the teddy bear, and laughed.

"That man," she said as she cruised toward Willowbrook.

With arms open wide he invited her in and said "welcome" to the magic in your life. He seemed so right for her. Unlike Roux, Aidan was so easy. With Roux, her mind, heart, and soul suffered each time he left her—wondering, suspecting, rationalizing. Aidan satisfied her mind and heart *and* soothed her soul, which freed her to experience things with him she'd never experienced before, and she wasn't just talking about ice skating, either. Roux would always be the man-child who took her from dolls and double Dutch to lipstick and perfume. She supposed that some part of her would always love Roux, but she was *in* love with Aidan in a way she never loved Roux. It was a mature love. Aidan was neither threatened nor offended by anything she had done—so far.

There was the matter of the tape of her and Roux making love. Roux had a vindictive, razor-hot temper and could post fliers of their lovemaking trysts all around N'awlins. He'd feel justified plastering posters on the Interstate to embarrass her and Aidan. Aidan didn't deserve to have the woman he loved exposed in such a cheap, vulgar manner.

Sassy changed lanes, deciding not to belabor what she had no control over, although every now and again it seeped into her consciousness. Aidan could handle it until the sordid mess blew over, she thought. Aidan was just too good to be true. He must have some vices— some bad habits. Maybe he cracked his knuckles, ate crackers in bed, wore socks with sandals or white after Labor Day. He was too perfect. She heard Ivanhoe's words, "On the carousel of life you got a gold ring, chère. What'ya gonna do? Wait for the brass one? Not too smart, chère. Grab him and enjoy for as long as the ride lasts." And that's just what she intended to do. For as long as she had Aidan in her life, she'd enjoy him, she concluded as she turned into Willowbrook. Even if her days with him were to end tomorrow, the time they had shared was magic.

Sassy visited her mother, and the next week was devoted to catching up at work and correcting papers before Aidan came to her place for the promised Saturday-night movie, dancing, and cooking, to be followed by a lazy Sunday.

"I'll cook Saturday night," Aidan volunteered.

"You're going to cook for me?" Sassy asked, smiling. No man had cooked for her since her daddy.

"I'm an excellent cook."

"Everything you do is excellent."

"Absolutely. And I'm ready to prove that whenever you're ready."

"So what will you cook for me?"

"What's your pleasure? Make it something we can eat from on Sunday as well."

"Stretching a meal? You sure you didn't grow up in the ghetto?"

"I don't want to spend our Sunday cooking too. We have to lounge."

Saturday night they had a party for two as he cooked and she helped and they danced and ate before falling asleep to an old movie. At two-forty-five AM, she woke him, and they made love and fell back asleep. On Sunday, even the powers that be conspired by sending down torrents of N'awlins rain, which kept them close and cocooned in each other's arms. It was dark and wet as they relaxed, listened to music, and read the paper. The ceiling fan lazily rotated and captured humid air, cooled and then tossed its breezes across their scantily-clad bodies.

They were like an old married couple, comfortable, quiet, and happy to be in each other's presence.

Once Aidan looked over at her as they exchanged sections of the paper and he sang, "I got a *Sunday kind of love—*"

When he finished a few bars, Sassy said, "You've done both Dinah and Etta proud with your mellow, sexy voice." She checked out the TV guide and exclaimed, "Know what's on?" She flipped the remote and answered him with images of *The Long Hot Summer* and, a hour and fifty minutes later, *The Magnificent Seven.*

"Perfection." He grabbed her after the last scene and held her and then said, "It just doesn't get any better than this."

"Ain't it good to be alive," she quoted Orson Welles from the movie they'd just seen. "I could jus' live fore-ever!"

Chapter X

Sassy handed the wrapped rarity to the couple. "Enjoy it," she said.

"Oh, we will," the woman said just as the phone rang.

"Good morning, Rare Finds," she answered, then listened.

From across the shop, Ivanhoe glanced over and noted how Sassy's rich golden-brown coloring had turned pale. She hung up the telephone and stared at the receiver when he flounced over asking, "What's the matter, chère?"

Sassy aimed her watery eyes at him and said, "She's . . . gone. My Maman is—" she couldn't bear to say it.

"Oh, Sassy!"

She crumbled into his arms momentarily, then abruptly straightened up, wiped away her tears with one hand, and grabbed her shoulder bag with the other. "I've got to go to Willowbrook."

"Let me go with you," Ivanhoe said as he reached for his keys.

"No." Sassy stopped him. "I want to go alone."

"I don't like that idea at all. Let me call Aidan."

"No. She's my mother. I'll call him later." She made her way to the front door. "You can call Sebastien Funeral Home."

Ivanhoe watched Sassy leave, realizing that she didn't know that Aidan *was* the Sebastien Funeral Home. "Aw, sukey-sukey. It's gonna hit the fan, now." He made the sign of the cross.

Sassy didn't know how she got to Willowbrook, she didn't remember driving, but now she was being escorted by the nurse to her mother's room. "Sebastien Funeral Home has been notified as directed from your mother's records. They'll pick up the body once you sign the release."

"The body," Sassy repeated, as indelicately as the nurse had.

Sassy entered her mother's private room, her body covered with a white sheet. Sassy looked through the window and noticed how the sun danced on the lake, and the Spanish moss dripped romantically from the trees. This view was so far away from the one Maman had had in Gert Town or from her beauty shop; a pastoral view Maman would never see again.

Sassy stood on the side of the bed next to the window. She nodded, and the nurse carefully rolled back the pristine white sheet inch by inch, slowly revealing her mother's face. Sassy burst into tears. She wasn't prepared to see her mother—dead. She covered her mouth as if stifling a scream, but it didn't stop her cascading tears. It seemed as if water was pouring from every pore of her body—out of her eyes, nose, down the back of her throat, through her fingernails, her knees, her feet—

Sassy felt like she was disintegrating, vaporizing into thin air at the sight of her lifeless mother.

The nursed passed her a box of tissues.

"Could you leave us alone?" Sassy whispered as she took her mother's hand. It was ice cold. There was no life left in this body. She sat in the chair by her mother's bed as the nurse left the room.

Maman would die all over again if she saw how terrible she looked, Sassy thought. Gaunt, drawn, ashy, like a mummy that had been dead for centuries. Through her heart's eyes, Sassy saw her mother as she'd been when she was a little girl. When Maman would read to her, sing to her, fix her meals, sew her clothes, accompany her on school field trips, clap for her at dance recitals and comb her hair. And could she do hair! She worked so hard to get, then keep that shop—Alouette's. The patrons loved her, and often remarked that if Alouette couldn't do it with hair, it couldn't be done.

Like her dad, she thought her mother was one of the most beautiful women in all of Gert Town—certainly one of the most enterprising. He used to put on old records and the four of them would dance around the living room. When they were a family . . . and now with her mom, dad and CoCo gone—there was only one, Sassy thought. Me. Sassy felt so alone. She had nobody—no real blood relatives to speak of. In death she wouldn't claim cousins her parents didn't allow her to associate with in life.

With a sudden shiver, Sassy then realized that whether you're fifteen, forty, or fifty—when your mother dies? You feel like an orphan. Pain so deep, searing, and suffocating you don't think you can take another breath. Even though Maman had been sick for years and death imminent, Sassy had never been quite ready for the day it would arrive. The finality of it was numbing.

It was dark when the nurse reentered with the release papers. Sassy realized that she must have sat there for hours massaging her mother's hand, trying to revive her with sheer will and the warmth of her own skin.

"Sebastien Funeral Home is here for your mother, Ms. Crillon," the nurse said quietly.

Sassy signed the papers without comment.

"May they come in now?" the nurse asked.

Sassy shook her head, rose from the chair, backed away, and stood by the window. Her schoolgirl habit of nervously gnawing at her thumb returned, and she could hear her mother say, "Stop that! You're gonna eat off your fingerprints. Then who will you be?"

The men greeted her, and Sassy rested her chin in her hands. She watched them cover Maman's face with the sheet.

"She hates that!" Sassy blurted out, and realized that she couldn't remain in the room. She grabbed her purse and left, sprinting down the hall.

"Ms. Crillon," the nurse called after her. "The doctor left you these sedatives in case you need help sleeping."

Sassy took the bottle of little blue pills. She looked at them strangely, resting in her hand. Had she ever taken drugs?

Just beyond the vision her open palm, she saw the men roll the gurney with her mother's covered body out into the hall. An inexplicable pain she couldn't express or endure seized her.

Sassy left.

* * *

"Call me." Aidan willed the phone to ring as he paced in his office.

He wanted to be with her immediately, but he needed her, Ivanhoe, or somebody to call and tell him—Aidan, the man who loved her. After all he wasn't supposed to know Mrs. Crillon had passed until informed. He was sure someone had contacted Roux in the Bahamas—he just prayed it wasn't Sassy. In the hours Aidan had been waiting, Roux was probably already en route to her.

The grandfather clock chimed from the grand hall and he thought, *What a mess.* He was supposed to have told her who he was by now. She was so exhausted after the Christmas bazaar and then left so quickly the next morning, he didn't get his chance. He'd almost told her on the rainy, lazy Sunday they shared at her place, but the timing hadn't seemed quite right. He had wanted to meet her mother, not only to see her and thank her for raising such a wonderful woman, but to let her know that she didn't have to worry about her daughter. That he would take good care of her. He was going to ask Maman for her hand in marriage. But it was too late for that now. In all his years he had never botched anything so badly; in all his life he'd never been so in love.

He'd ordered his staff to give Ms. Crillon priority treatment and the best reconstructive technicians. If Madame Crillon was like most clients, she had written all of her specifications out, and Mr. Leveaux, the funeral director, was not only to attend to Sassiere Crillon personally, but to see that she was given *everything* she wanted for whatever amount of money she had.

Aidan paced the length of his office again and again. "Ring, dammit!"

Finally, the obstinate telephone rang.

"Hello," he said evenly.

"Aidan," Sassy said in a distance whisper.

Aidan closed his eyes with relief. "Sassiere, where are you? We were supposed to—"

"Maman died today."

"Where are you? I'm on my way."

"No. I'm afraid I wouldn't be good company. I'm just going to take care of a few things and go to bed."

"I don't think you should be alone." He looked at the clock, it was almost nine-thirty.

"I guess I'd better get used to that, huh?"

"Not as long as you have me, Sassiere."

"Well, not tonight, okay?"

"Sassiere—"

"I'll call you tomorrow. Okay?"

"Or later tonight if you change your mind. Anytime. I'll be there."

"Thanks, Aidan."

"Remember I love you, Sassiere."

"Me—too—you. Night."

As she hung up the telephone, Ivanhoe appeared in her doorway. "Ready, chère?"

"As ready as I'm going to be. I just want to get it over with. I didn't know funeral homes stayed open this late for business."

"Imagine," Ivanhoe said, knowingly.

They rode in silence to the funeral home and Sassy was grateful for the quiet. Ivanhoe knew her, so he offered her no platitudes or clichés, just a comfortable silence. As they drove up to the funeral home, Sassy noted how much it looked like a fabulous estate—the likes of which many people in life could not afford; but they wanted it in death, and Sebastien's was there to provide it for them. The parking and entrance to the office was around back. Being in the plush-carpeted hallways conjured up thoughts of when she'd accompanied her mother here to make arrangements for her father. Now she was here for her mother and would be alone if it were not for the man who shared no DNA with her but was the closest thing she had to a blood relative.

"Ms. Crillon?" the man greeted.

"Yes."

"I am Mr. Leveaux, the funeral director. I am sorry for your loss."

Sassy shook his hand, and then Ivanhoe saw it. The ring! The Sebastien heirloom . . . the diamond "S" on the bed of rubies.

"Thank you. This is Mr. Fauchon." When Sassy turned to Ivanhoe his face was sallow and tears brimmed his eyes. He was visibly upset, pale and shaking. "Ivanhoe, you don't have to—"

"No, no. I'm fine." He closed his eyes and breathed in deeply. "I guess no one gets out alive, huh, chère? Let's do this. Mr. Leveaux, lead the way." He was thankful for any conversation that would take his mind off the ring.

As Mr. Leveaux escorted them down the beautifully appointed hallway, Sassy was thankful that the floor plan concealed the rooms of other mourners attending wakes. As they entered the office their collective eyes feasted on all the gorgeous antiques. Mr. Leveaux sealed them in with intricately carved pocket doors.

Once situated in the cushioned seats, Mr. Leveaux began, "We have Madame Crillon's list of what she wanted on record, and everything has been arranged. However—"

"Here it comes, chère," Ivanhoe interrupted and Sassy shot him a glare.

"We have several 'specials' in caskets of superior quality

to the one selected and we thought you might want to chose one of those."

"How 'special?' Like how much *more* money?" Ivanhoe asked with a smirk and one raised eyebrow.

"Same price. No extra charge," Mr. Leveaux said flatly.

"Sounds fishy, Sass."

Mr. Leveaux ignored Ivanhoe and continued, "Madam Crillon mentioned on her list that if she had saved enough money by her demise she'd prefer the Golden Chalice casket with the pink satin liner. That is available at the same price."

"Tsk!" Ivanhoe sucked his teeth in disagreement.

"May I see it?" Sassy asked.

"Certainly. This way please."

"This is where they get you, Sass," Ivanhoe hissed as Mr. Leveaux led them through another beautiful door into a showroom of casket possibilities.

"This is the one she selected, and this is the Golden Chalice she wanted," Mr. Leveaux said, stepping back so they could inspect it.

Sassy and Ivanhoe stood before the gleaming Golden Chalice casket with the satin lining, astonished by its impressive, tasteful polish.

"Top of the line," Ivanhoe said. "I guess I better start saving now. This is what I want."

Sassy ran her fingers across the gleaming satiny finish and asked, "How can this one be the same price as that one?"

"It's a 'special' we're running," Mr. Leveaux repeated as convincingly as possible, wanting to keep his job.

"An eight-thousand-dollar 'special'?" Sassy shot back.

"Don't look a gift horse, chère," Ivanhoe singsonged. "Your Maman would be happy."

Sassy eyed her all-knowing friend. "Funny. Even after

you die you can still catch a sale. All right," she agreed on the upgraded selection.

"Wonderful. This Golden Chalice also comes with a blanket of the flowers of your choice. What would those be?"

"Gardenias," Sassy said without hesitation; her mother loved them but always settled for sunflowers.

"Very well." Mr. Leveaux noted and then asked, "And the horses—black or white?"

"Horses?" Sassy asked.

"Yes. The Golden Chalice comes with a glass hearse drawn by four horses. Either black or white stallions?"

Sassy and Ivanhoe's mouths were collectively agape. She eyed him and he eyed her back.

Finally she said, "I smell a rat. All of this doesn't have anything to do with a Roux Robespierre does it?"

"I beg your pardon?" Mr. Leveaux had just the right amount of indignity in his voice. He had been fore-warned that she might balk. "I assure you, Ms. Crillon, that this has nothing to do with a Mr. Robespierre."

"Is this you, Ivanhoe?"

"Are you kidding me? If I had this kind of dough I'd spend it on living, chère. Trips, jewels, good wine— Ferragamo loafers." But Ivanhoe knew—it was Aidan. Prince Charming had taken up where Fairy Godmother could not. It was actually very touching. "But, chère. Wouldn't your Maman love to go out like this? It's so *Imitation of Life*."

Sassy smiled. "Yeah, she would love this."

"Short of Mahalia Jackson's singing, let's just do this, chère. Your Maman will haunt you from the grave if you don't. White horses," he said to Mr. Leveaux. "With those little plumey thingies on their heads." He crossed his legs flamboyantly.

Sassy laughed. For the first time since she got the news, Sassy laughed. She loved this crazy man. "Thanks for coming with me, Ivanhoe."

"That's what friends are for," he sang and rocked from side to side.

"Duly noted," Mr. Leveaux said. "We'll coordinate all with St. Gabriel's."

"Thank you, Mr. Leveaux." Sassy shook his hand.

Ivanhoe closed his eyes against the sight of the ring.

"I'll get her wedding dress to you tomorrow," Sassy continued. "I want this done as quickly as possible. When?"

"We can have the wake tomorrow evening and bury Madame Crillon the next day."

Ivanhoe couldn't believe it, but of course, Aidan would move mountains for his Sassiere.

As Sassy sniffed the reheated oyster po'boy, the garden gate bell twirled, and Ivanhoe came up her steps bearing a box.

"Oh, chère. Pee-uu. I told you we should stop and get something on the way back. That smell. You trying to join your mother?"

Sassy looked at him.

"Sorry. I can be indelicate at times. Speaking of which." He presented her with the box, and said, "Personal effects from Willowbrook."

Sassy took the box and held it for a few minutes while Ivanhoe flounced back downstairs in his caftan.

Is this what your life boils down to? she thought. A box of personal effects; things you can't take with you. Sassy had donated all of her mother's clothes to charity when she moved her to Willowbrook, and she'd kept Maman's good jewelry to pass on to her daughters, should she

ever have any. *What else is there?* She wondered as she
opened the lid. Maman's Bible, a crucifix, and a handsome, youthful picture of her father. Then there was the
image of the four of them frozen in time: mother, father,
and two cute daughters with looped, rope-thick braids.
The times were so good and plentiful back then. They
were smiling and standing around a Christmas tree.
Sassy hadn't even remembered this picture.

There was an envelope at the bottom of the box with
her name on it. *Sassiere.* She opened it.

Dear Sassiere,

*If you're reading this, it means my body, along with
a detailed list of what I want, is sitting in Sebastien's
Funeral Home. That list stayed the same, but I've written
this part over and over. What else I got to do while I wait
to die? I'm probably skinny enough now to wear my wedding dress when I'm buried next to your father. But unless
Sebastien's works miracles, and they have been known to
do so, which is why everybody wants them (rumor is they
have a plastic surgeon on retainer—which is why they cost
so much), I want my casket closed. I want the picture of the
four of us at Christmas to sit on top of it. The one with
CoCo in it. By this time I guess we've resolved any differences up here. Ha Ha! I want "Oh, Happy Day" by the
Edwin Hawkins singers playing during the recessional;
blast the part about 'When I get to heaven, He'll wash all
my sins away.' Everything else is the way we have always
discussed it. I know you got tired of hearing it, but don't it
make it easier now? Sometimes, Maman does know best.
Sorry all I'm leaving you is my good looks. Your father and
I planned to leave you so much more, but life just got in
the way. Life is so short, chou-chou. Too short to drink
cheap wine, and it's too short to be with someone you don't*

*want to. Someone you can't trust or forgive. Which brings
me to Roux. If he is truly not your heart's desire, then let
him go. If you can't be happy with him and will have peace
without him, then your time with him is up. So be it.
Which brings me to my last want. When it's all said and
done—I want you to be happy. You were the best daughter
a mother could have.*

*You notice I said my cold, ugly body is at Sebastien's but
my spirit is all around you and in you, Sassiere. I will always
be with you in your heart and in your soul. I am just a
thought away. Remember me to my grandchildren, and let
them know what a ball we would have had, had I lived.
I love you, daughter of mine.*

Always, Maman

Sassy went into the bathroom, gathered a roll of toilet
tissue and blew her nose. As she sat on the commode, she
read the letter again. And again, as she ate the po'boy.

Later, Sassy sat in the comfort of darkness, dialed
Yvette's number, and told her the news.

"Sassy, I'm on my way. I can cancel two meetings
until—"

"No, 'Vette. It'll all be over before you get here."

"I don't live in Timbuktu. I think I should be there,
Sass."

"You stay there and take care of your business, Gardner and that godchild of mine. You know you still have
Christmas gifts to buy."

"Are you sure?" Yvette had been her best friend all
these years because she knew how to read when Sassy
wanted space and time to herself.

"I'm sure."

"Well," she resigned, "Only because you have Aidan."

The sound of his name brought a smile to her face. "Yes. I do have Aidan."

"Call me if you change your mind, Sassy. I'm just a phone call and a short flight away. I'm going to call and check in on you tomorrow."

"Okay. Bye."

"I love you, girl."

"Love you too."

Sassy hung up the phone, placed it on the windowsill beside her, and suddenly the darkness wasn't comforting. It was cavernous and cold, like Maman's awaiting grave. A shiver traveled up her spine, and Sassy held herself.

Only because you have Aidan, Yvette had said. Why did Sassy always feel the need to push those she loved and those who loved her away? As if needing comfort was a sign of weakness instead of strength in a relationship. She wanted to call Aidan, and she knew he would come. But after the initial hug and kiss, she didn't want to be bothered. Did she? If she could just make him appear.

"Sassiere?"

Sassy looked to the threshold of her bedroom and saw a silhouette whittled against the deeper darkness on the other side. Had she wanted him here so badly she'd conjured up this mirage of him?

"I hope you don't mind. Ivanhoe let me in." He stepped into a stream of moonlight.

"Aidan?" She realized it was him in the flesh, and she flew to him.

He caught her and held her.

"Oh, Aidan." She held him tightly and began crying again.

"It's all right. I'm here for you."

"Just hold me please. Just hold me." He felt so good; so strong and solid.

"For the rest of my life."

That night, as Aidan held her in his arms, she slept the sleep of angels. She awakened late the next morning.

"I can't believe I slept this long," she said.

"You were exhausted." He kissed her forehead and thought about springing the skiing trip he'd planned for her Christmas gift to make her feel better. But like telling her who he really was—the timing seemed off. "You feel like eating? I can rustle up something while you shower."

"Thank you." She smiled at him weakly, water brimmed her eyes, and she said simply, "My mother's wake is today."

"I know." He held her tightly. "But you're not alone, Sassiere."

It took Sassy awhile to dress and eat, as if prolonging it would make it all go away. They arrived at the Sebastien Funeral Home at four, two hours before the wake began. Now, there were only two hours left for her to say her private, last good-byes to the woman who bore and nurtured her. Mr. Leveaux came and escorted her into the parlor for her private viewing. Aidan was by her side as Mr. Leveaux parted the pocket doors revealing her mother's casket almost dwarfed by the flamboyant floral display around her.

"Oh my," Sassy commented of the garden which curved to protect her mother's earthy remains. She reached for Aidan's hand and he walked with her slowly as she approached Maman's prone body, bracing herself for the hideous toll two days had taken on her already deteriorated flesh.

Sassy eased up on her; Maman's hair and part of her forehead came into view, the tip of her sharp nose. Sassy closed her eyes momentarily, tightened her grip on Aidan's hand, and took the next few steps which would reveal her mother's entire face. She opened her eyes and looked at her mother.

"Aw!" she gasped. "How can this be?" she asked Aidan without removing her eyes from her mother's face. "How? Maman," she whispered, as tears welled up and spilled like a waterfall down her cheeks. "She looks twenty years old. How is this possible?" She only glanced at Aidan before her unbelieving eyes returned to her mother. "This is a miracle."

Lying there in her wedding dress, Alouette Crillon looked like a composed bride, napping before her nuptials were to begin. Her skin looked sun-kissed and pliant, her hair coiffed, her makeup understated and flawless, her hands crossed and youthful with a rosary laced through her fingers. "Maman always said—Sebastien's was the best. They did her proud."

"Excuse me, Ms. Crillon," Mr. Leveaux interrupted quietly. "Do you still wish the closed casket?"

"Oh, no," Sassy said. "Maman would come back and kill me if I didn't let folks see her like this. She looks wonderful, Mr. Leveaux. Just wonderful."

"Yes, she is," Aidan spoke for the first time and exchanged an approving glance with Mr. Leveaux.

Sassy didn't know how long she had been standing there carrying on a private conversation with her mother when she heard Aidan trying to prevent people from disturbing her peace in the back of the parlor.

"I'm her Aunt Naomi," the woman said loud enough for Sassy to hear.

Sassy turned around and nodded to Aidan who let the woman and the three other people past.

"Sassy, I'm so sorry," Aunt Naomi squeezed her for dear life before she caught a glimpse of her dead sister-in-law. "Jesus, Lord preserve us! Look at her! She's beautiful!"

She looked at Sassy and asked, "How you holding up, baby girl? You need anything at all?"

"No, thank you."

"I guess not, since you got the 'head man himself' tending to her funeral." Aunt Naomi inclined her head to Aidan. "How did you arrange that? He hasn't been involved with this part of the business for over ten years."

Sassy turned to look at Mr. Leveaux, who was standing by Aidan. "I don't know, just the luck of the draw I guess. I want to thank you for going out and seeing Maman every month like you did. I know that was a—"

"Sassiere, no thanks necessary." She looked back at Alouette. "She does look beautiful. She always wanted a Sebastien Funeral."

"Well, she got it."

Aidan left as people stared coming in to pay their respects. Old neighbors, friends, clients, folks Sassy didn't know.

In the distance Sassy heard voices coming from the hall. Perhaps someone in another wake was having fits. Then Ivanhoe hurried into the room and scurried to her side. "Chère, you'd better come pronto," he whispered urgently in her ear.

"Excuse me," Sassy said to her mother's former employees and followed Ivanhoe into the hall then left into another parlor. "Ivanhoe, where are you going?" fell from her lips as she passed the alcove into the room and was stunned speechless by the sight.

There, squared off at one another, was Roux and Aidan.

Oh, crap. Her worst nightmare. *I don't need this,* she thought. *Not now. Not today.*

She stepped between them said, "My mother is dead in there." She looked at Roux, knowing his temper was the cause of it. She didn't know how he found out about Aidan so quickly. "I should think you'd show some respect for Maman. We can discuss Aidan later."

She looked from man to man. From her past to her future. When she looked at Roux she saw the most peculiar glaze claim his hazel eyes, she continued, "Maman said you promised you wouldn't show out at Sebastien's."

"What do you mean, 'We can discuss Aidan later'?" Roux hissed in a fit of controlled anger. "Since when do we ever waste our breath discussing a Sebastien?"

"I didn't say *Sebastien*, I said Aidan. Aidan Symonds."

"Roux—" Aidan began and advanced cautiously toward him.

A flicker of recognition flared in Roux's hazel eyes, and he said, "Oh. I get it. You don't know who . . . She doesn't know?" Roux addressed Aidan and loved seeing the panic in his eyes. "Oh, sweat, this is rich!" Roux laughed out loud. "Richer than a Sebastien!"

"Roux," Sassy was trying to calm him; he was cackling like a crazy man.

"But that's what you are, right? A Sebastien?"

"Don't do this now, man," Aidan pleaded. "For Sassy's sake."

"What?" Sassy looked from man to man and her head began to throb.

"Wait. I get it. Sass," Roux said without removing his eyes from Aidan. "Have you met this man?" he asked sarcastically. "Allow me to present to you Aidan *Sebastien!*"

"What?" Sassy repeated, looking confused from man to man.

"Oh, Lord, here it comes," Ivanhoe said, making the sign of the cross, then covering his mouth.

"Aw, man!" Roux yelled. "You son of a bitch—"

"Roux!" Sassy admonished him.

"Oh, no, that would be me," Roux said with a wicked chortle. "I may be a *bastard* but at least I'm not a liar. Am I?" Roux stepped to Aidan.

"What is wrong with you?" Sassy said, dodging between. "What are you talking about?"

Roux backed away, glowing with the knowledge he had. Powerful with his ability to smash Aidan's hope. "Go 'head, you tell her. She doesn't believe me," he goaded Aidan. "Tell her your last name, man."

"Sassiere, I can explain—" Aidan said quietly.

"*Sassiere?*" Roux spat. "What the hell is going on?" He flew hot again. "This man is a Sebastien, Sassy. This is Aidan Sebastien."

Aidan's eyes closed. Never had he hated his name more than when it dripped lethally, like venom, from Roux lips.

"What?" Sassy looked at Roux then at Aidan. "Is this true?" Sassy physically shuttered, a finger of ice grabbed her spine. "Your last name is Sebastien?" She was struggling to absorb what Roux was saying.

Drunk with the power of exposing him as a liar, Roux was slow to notice how Aidan reached for Sassy and tried to hold her. "Wait a minute. What the hell is this?" Roux had only intended to reveal what liars and cheats the Sebastiens were, and how, all these years, he was justified in exposing him as a lying cheat. But Aidan was *touching* Sassy, and she was letting him. Roux fought to wrap his mind around the unexpected visual he was experiencing.

"You're a Sebastien?" Sassy said, part plea, part cry, and all remorse. "Oh, God." Not only did Aidan lie to her but she knew this would send Roux over the top. She held her head.

Roux saw her hand. "What are you doing with my daddy's ring?"

"What?" Sassy asked.

"You gave her the ring?" Roux asked Aidan.

"I found this ring," Sassy said.

"What the hell is going on!" Roux shouted. "What are you doing with my daddy's ring?!"

"Roux, calm down," Sassy said, touching his arm.

"Don't touch me with that ring!"

Sassy looked at Aidan and wondered if Roux was so sick with grief that he was losing his mind.

Ivanhoe saw the wheels turning in Roux's hazel eyes and knew the worst was yet to come. He flew for Mr. Leveaux and security.

"Hold up!" Roux froze the room in a hushed stillness. Was the joke on him? "Is this the cat you been messing with?" He stared at Sassy.

"Listen, Roux—" Aidan attempted to approach him again.

"Step off, man. This ain't got nuthin' to do with you. Sassy?" He was breathing hard and his jaw muscles contracted and released as his nostrils flared.

Sassy was speechless as she watched Roux's features collapse in horror then rise in anger as his body trembled with rage. His raised his hand to hit her.

Aidan grabbed it mid air and said, "Not going to happen."

Roux jerked his hand away from Aidan's grip. "Get your hands offa me!"

Sassy was horrified. Roux had never raised a hand to her.

Roux held his fist to his lips realizing that he was about to hit the only woman he had ever loved. But she had betrayed him in the worst possible way. Roux grew lethally quiet. "No, Sassy," he lamented, as angry tears charged his eyes but didn't fall. "Sassy? How could you? With him?"

"I didn't know, Roux. I swear I didn't. I would have never spoken to him had I known he was a Sebastien." Angry tears spilled and streamed down his face. She began to cry too.

"But he knew," Roux cut her off. "You knew," he challenged Aidan. "You selfish son-of-bitch. Why? Because she belonged to me and you just had to have her?"

"Roux—" Sassy attempted to soothe him.

"It wasn't that at all," Aidan said, calmly.

"Yeah, it was. She's like your sister-in-law, man."

"What?" Sassy was confused again, the two men continued to ignore her.

"Who's the lowlife bastard now? Neither you nor your daddy could stand for me to have one minute's peace. One worthwhile thing in my life. You have to take it all. Even her."

"Let's not do this now," Aidan said quietly.

"No, let's. I know what else he didn't tell you, Sassy," he said to her, but his eyes bored into Aidan. "Yeah." He wanted Aidan to hurt like he hurt.

"Come on, Roux," Aidan plead. "Not now. Why?"

"Why not!" Roux hissed. "Know what else he didn't bother to tell you, Sass? Huh, he didn't tell you he's my brother!"

With the weight of the truth finally out, Ivanhoe collapsed on a nearby chair and fanned himself.

"What?" Sassy asked almost inaudibly.

"My brother," Roux spat and tore his eyes from Aidan to aim them at Sassy. 'We got the same daddy—Maximillien Sebastien."

Sassy blinked her eyes a thousand times trying to process what he was saying.

"How could you, Sassy?" he said, then tore from the room, passing security.

"You need help, miss?" the guard asked her. She ignored him running after Roux.

Sassy caught Roux in the hall and grabbed his hand. "Roux, I didn't know."

"Why not just rip my heart out, Sass? Why not just kill me, stab me, and watch me bleed?" he said and jerked his hand from hers. "Of all the men in New Orleans—in the world, why him, Sassy? Why him?" He stared at her for a few minutes before he turned and left.

Sassy hadn't seen Roux that tormented, that wild-eyed and crazy since they were kids. Since they'd cut school and gone to that big house, since they watched that limo with boy looking out the back window at them, since . . . "Omigod," she whispered. "It was Aidan."

"Sassiere," Aidan came out into the hall. "Are you all right? Let me explain—"

"There's nothing to explain," she said wearily as Ivanhoe came to her side. "The wake's over. Will you take me home?" she asked Ivanhoe.

"Sure, chère."

"Sassiere," Aidan implored.

"I'm not Sassiere—but you knew all along that my name was Sassy. I'm not Sassiere and you're not Aidan Symonds. Whoever we are or are not—the charade is over. I bury my mother tomorrow. I have other things on my mind."

"Sassiere. I love you."

"Love?" She shook her head. "Love has made liars of us all."

She turned to Ivanhoe and said, "I knew he was too good to be true."

Chapter XI

Later that night, in the still of darkness, Killer barked, and Ivanhoe went to the gate.

"Well, I've been expecting you. I guess it took longer for you to cool down."

"I want to see Sassy."

"She doesn't want to see you, Roux. Can you blame her?"

"I just want to hold her."

"Touching. This from the man who upset her mother's wake."

"That's all behind me now. I know it wasn't her fault that she ended up with—"

"You can't even speak his name."

"Can't, don't, and won't have to after Sass and I get back together," he sighed, growing irritated. "You going to let me in?"

"No."

"I love her too, Ivanhoe."

"Longer? Perhaps. Better? No. I wouldn't ever do anything to hurt her."

"What are you? Her watchdog?"

"No, that would be Killer, here. She needs somebody

to look after her. She apparently isn't any good at picking men on her own." Ivanhoe eyed the good-looking, angry man on the other side of the iron gate. "You going to the funeral tomorrow?"

"Of course I am."

"Will you try to remember why you're there? To mourn, not cop a plea with the deceased's daughter."

"I don't need you or anybody else to tell me how to act."

"Do tell. That was so obvious from your most recent display of emotion."

"Has *he* been here?"

"Not yet, but he's expected, and I'll send him packing as well. You both are certainly brothers . . . selfish and willful. Neither of you nimrods realize that this is Sassy's last chance to say a proper good-bye to her Maman. She's got more on her mind than two bucks fighting over her like she's a piece of meat."

Roux looked up to her dark apartment. "She's alone, huh?"

"Her choice."

"She's probably sitting in the windowsill looking out back," he said wistfully. "Tell her . . . I stopped by. And that I love her."

Ivanhoe arched an eyebrow in answer and watched Roux get back into his truck and pull off. "Just a man holding on to a woman letting go," he told Killer.

Forty-five minutes later, Killer was summoned to the gate with Ivanhoe in tow.

"Aidan Sebastien. Why am I not surprised," Ivanhoe said, drolly.

"Unlock the gate. I want to see Sassiere."

Both Ivanhoe and Killer took exception to his tone. "Down, boy," he said to both Aidan and Killer. "That was a ten on force, but you lost points on charm and charisma."

"Let me up, please, Ivanhoe."

"Better, but she's not accepting guests."

"I have some things to clarify."

"No clarifying tonight." He patted Killer and let him go back into the house. "Lies, especially big ones, always have a way of coming back and biting you in the butt."

"What else could I do? 'Hello, I'm Aidan Sebastien?' By her own admission she would have said, 'Good riddance.'"

"Aren't you playing Sassy cheap?"

"I prefer Sassiere."

"You'd take her if her name was Godzilla. Well, neither Sassy nor Sassiere is seeing you tonight."

"Listen—"

"C'mon man, funerals are your business. You know too well the emotional hell she's going through with death and dying—she ain't studyin' about you two Negroes. Being less selfish and more considerate is a start."

Aidan had never thought of himself as selfish. In fact, it was Sassiere and only Sassiere he was thinking about. "She shouldn't be alone."

"She's not." Ivanhoe's tone let him know he didn't appreciate the reference.

"She needs someone who loves her."

Ivanhoe just stared at him, one eyebrow raised in annoyance and a smirk twisting his pursed lips.

"I mean the way I love her."

"Oh, that's been a great elixir for her so far. I'll tell her you stopped by," he dismissed, leaving the forlorn lover at the gate. "If you don't show at the funeral tomorrow, we'll understand. It's not like you knew or even met Alouette Crillon," Ivanhoe threw over his shoulder. "Just coming to badger her poor grieving daughter could be seen as harassment." He closed the French door and listened for the slate-gray Ferrari 360 Spider to roar away.

Ivanhoe climbed the stairs to Sassy's apartment and found her just where Roux had said she would be. "Can I get you anything, chère?"

"No. Thanks."

"They've all checked in, chère. Quite pathetic and contrite."

"I hurt Roux so badly."

Sensing the dissolution of her reserve and some back-sliding, Ivanhoe answered, "He hurt you first, chère. A couple of times."

"He hurt my vanity and pride. I shook the very core of his existence." She wiped away tears as the moon rose high in the sky. "Brothers. They don't look alike."

"Thank God they take after their mothers."

"I don't ever remember seeing a picture of Aidan's father in the house." she realized.

"Probably not. That crazy Simone probably had them all trashed. Aidan looks more like Maximillien Sebastien. Especially about the nose. It used to be huge, but either he grew into it or Simone's side of the family kicked in during adolescence; her nose is so small I don't know how she breathes."

"I never made the connection with the house or that Aidan was the boy in the back of the limo—"

"Why would you, chère? It was over twenty years ago. None of it made any never mind to you then."

"He must have been something, that Maximillien Sebastien. Simone doesn't sleep in her bedroom, only comes to the first floor of the mansion and *never* goes to the guesthouse—whatever that means."

"Like the Spanish proverb says, 'For a good marriage to be happy, the husband should be deaf and his wife blind.' Simone's sight has always been twenty-twenty." Ivanhoe sighed and continued, "No one could blame Maximillien

Sebastien. Roux's mother had a face and body that stopped traffic; she certainly stopped the heart of the head of Sebastien Funeral Home. He bought her that house and gave her all the money she'd ever need, but in the end he chose his wife and child—Madame Robespierre didn't have Maximillien, and she lost her son."

"In all those years, Roux never told me any of that. Just that he hated the Sebastiens because they refused to bury his mother. Not that his mother was Sebastien's lover. Roux couldn't trust me with the details."

"No, chère. You were his perfect woman and couldn't be tainted with such seedy history. Besides folk seldom want to dredge up all that old stuff. They'd rather it just brew and stink and contaminate their every waking moment without telling anybody why. If they don't speak about it, it'll all go away. *N'est-ce pas?*" He turned to look at the moon. "I guess we all do the same thing. Hide our trauma-drama, childhood baggage, hoping the person we love won't find out all of our deep, dark secrets and then think we're unworthy of their love. We all got *stuff,* chère. Our parents love us too much and they're smothering us; our parents don't love us enough and they're neglecting us. We only have one parent. We don't have any parents. Seems to me when folk get to their thirties they ought to stop the bitch and moan routine and move on. Stop talking about what they don't have and what other folk did or didn't do and just get on with life and living—this ain't no dress rehearsal, chère. This time on earth is precious and finite. The whining and wallowing is so unattractive in a grown person." He looked at Sassy. "In other words it was time for Roux to grow up instead of covering up, and time for Aidan to 'fess up. Well," he said, rising from the windowsill. "Truth-telling makes me hungry. Sure you don't want anything, chère?"

"No thanks."

"Let me know if you change your mind." He walked to the threshold of her room and looked back at her sitting there. Well, with everything finally out in the open—the curse was now the cure; it was going to affect three lives. He wondered how.

Sassy sat in the first row of St. Gabriel's of the Sacred Heart and never remembered the church looking so beautiful. The sun shone electric through the stained-glass windows, illuminating the images in bright, prismatic colors. She fought hard not to think about the two brothers; every time she did, her head began to hurt at the sheer bizarreness of it. So far, she hadn't seen either of them to remember. She couldn't focus at all on the eulogy. Someone slid into the pew next to her. She refused to look. A female reached out her hand. It was Yvette. Sassy was never so glad to see one person in her life.

"Hey, Sass. How you holding up?" Yvette whispered, as they embraced.

"Better." Sassy smiled as tears brimmed in her eyes. "Much better."

"Where's Aidan?"

"Long story."

As Alouette Crillon had ordered, the choir sang "Oh, Happy Day" during the recessional. Sassy, Yvette, and Ivanhoe climbed into the limo behind the glass-encased, horse-drawn hearse. They sat facing the polished open doors and watched as they placed the gleaming gold casket weighted with a blanket of fresh gardenias into the mouth of the hearse.

Sassy said, "Maman would have loved this."

"No lie," Yvette chimed in.

"She *is* loving it," Ivanhoe said.

"Yes, she is," Sassy said, taking the hand of each dear friend.

On the slow ride to the cemetery, Sassy told Yvette about Roux and Aidan. Yvette found it hard to believe.

"Truth is stranger than fiction," Ivanhoe interjected.

"Bad fiction," Yvette said.

"Biblical. Cain and Abel," Ivanhoe concluded.

Sassy donned dark sunglasses and stood beneath the canopy shading the open crypt. It was a bright golden New Orleans day when Alouette joined her husband and Sassy glimpsed Roux from her peripheral view. Sassy kissed the edge of the Golden Chalice casket, plucked a gardenia from its top and returned to the limo. The second line paraded and led the mourners to the church for the *repasse*. While Ivanhoe played hostess, Sassy was treated to all sorts of anecdotes about her mother and father from their neighbors and old friends she hadn't known. It was a celebration of their lives, and Sassy hadn't expected the jovial, supportive fellowship, but she welcomed it.

After three long hours, Sassy went to the lounge, just for a break from people.

"Sassy?"

She turned and sighed wearily. "What, Roux?" He was still a gorgeous man in his black suit; his hazel eyes danced in copper skin.

"How are you holding up?" He walked toward her and stopped inches from her, but did not touch her.

"I'm a little numb now. I really dread the days ahead. I suppose I'll have good days and bad days." She hunched her shoulders.

"I am sorry, Sass," he continued, glad that she wasn't

throwing him out or running away. "The way I acted last night. Your maman was a special lady."

"Yes, she was. And she loved you, Roux," she offered charitably.

"I loved her too. I used to always think of your mother as mine. Your pops too. Remember how he'd take me around with him to the clubs?"

"You were two of a kind." Sassy remembered her daddy saying that Roux was the son he didn't have; nothing "pansy" about him.

"He looked out for me. But your maman would praise me when I did good and bury me when I wasn't." They both chuckled. "I hope her daughter is as forgiving."

"Roux—"

"I know now is not the time or place, and I want you to decide when. But—it's like I lost my mother too." Tears stood in his eyes, he lifted his chin and dared them to fall. They fell anyway.

Sassy and Roux stood facing each other awkwardly. Two people who'd meant so much to each other for so many years—two people who'd shared laughter, pain and lovin'. Best friends and confidants. Two people who'd suffered an undeniable, immeasurable loss. Roux hugged Sassy emotionally; a hug of comfort, not pleasure, like she'd given strangers all day. Human contact born from healing needed, not love lost, and in that brief awkward moment, they cried for their mutual bereavement in each other's arms.

At that instant, Aidan walked around the corner to the lounge in search of Sassiere and saw the embrace. He looked at the two of them, lovers with years of shared history almost as old as they were, clinging together, crying together. Feeling like an intruder, he backed away.

The sight ignited doubts. How could he ever compete

with that? Why did he ever think he could? The display of their genuine love burned his eyes, singed his pupils and blazed across his consciousness. He left without being seen.

Once outside Aidan stood at the top of the steps and thrust his hands into his pockets. He lifted his face to be caressed by the sun before he bowed his head in defeat and sauntered down the steps to his car. He got behind the wheel and realized how he'd missed driving her. He'd sacrifice his automobile for Sassiere. He would have given up anything for Sassiere. He glanced back at the church and realized that in place of Sassiere there would now be an emptiness from which he would never recover. But he'd had a chance with her he never thought he would, and he had given it his best shot.

"Okay, Roux," Sassy said, feeling the hug lingering too long. "Enough." Despite him feeling familiar and comforting she felt like she was cheating on Aidan.

"I need you, Sassy," he whispered in her ear before she pushed him away. "We need each other. I've missed you, Sassy."

"Roux, I will *not* discuss this now."

"Then when, Sass?"

She shook her head uncaringly.

"You and me. We've been together for so long, I can't imagine being without you forever. I can't even conceive of it."

His sincerity was piercing her reserves.

"In the middle of the night, I wake up to shadows. I reach for you—where you used to be. Where you are suppose to be. Next to me, Sass."

"Even in the Bahamas?" she said coldly.

"When I heard you were seeing somebody, I left because I couldn't bear to see you with someone else regardless of who he was." Aidan's name hung, unspoken, between them and he continued, "I had the time, money and opportunity to be with women but not the desire, I didn't want any of them. I wanted you—my best friend. You're *all* I thought about. I saw you everywhere I looked."

Always had an answer for everything, she thought as she walked over to the window, just in time to see a dark gray Ferrari clear the driveway and roar away. Absently, she wondered who in St. Gabriel's parish could afford such a car.

"I used that time by myself to think about what I had and what I wanted. I should have been a better man for you."

"On that we agree."

He walked over to her. "I made a mistake." He turned her to him. "Don't you believe a man can learn from his mistakes? That a man can change? I've changed the core of me, Sass. You never have to worry about another woman; they never meant anything to me anyway."

"I didn't have a commitment with any of them—I had it with you. And just because you know and they know and everybody knows that I'm your 'main squeeze'— didn't make it all right, Roux. We have serious, major differences in the way we think and what we value."

"But that's what I'm saying to you. We used to, but now I'm on board. I've changed. It's like I've had some life-threatening, near-death experience that made me realize what's really important. I've assessed and rearranged my priorities, and Sassy, you're number one. We can travel like you always wanted to. I can sell the bar and go—"

"Oh, Roux," Sassy scoffed, thinking, *He's going too far now.* "That bar is your heart and soul."

"No, Sassy. You are. The bar is a thing. I have a head

for business, I can be a success anywhere. We can move and live anywhere you want—"

"Roux, you'd give up your bar?"

"If that's what it took, Sassy, I would. *Nothing* means more to me then you. Nothing. Which is what I feel like these days. Nothing if you aren't with me. I need you like water, like the air I breathe, and food. Without you my life is incomplete."

Sassy looked at the sun cut across his handsome, chiseled face and listened.

"We have history—a past, and we have a future. I want to be the man you deserve. I want to prove to you that you are the most important thing in my life—until our kids come," he chuckled nervously for levity. "Give me another chance. Give *us* another chance. I promise, you won't be sorry. I love you, Sassy."

Sassy momentarily closed her eyes at the sound of those words dancing in her ears. Words she longed to hear from him for so many years. "Roux, I just can't absorb all this now. You've got to give me time to sort it out and think. And you've got to give me space. I've got a lot on my mind."

"What about Christmas? We'll spend that together. What do you want to do? Your call." He beamed, exciting himself by showing her consideration.

"Roux? I'm not thinking about Christmas now. I'm not celebrating this year."

"Maman loved Christmas. And she loved us. Separately and together as a couple. What better tribute to her? We can get together and swap stories about her in the place of your choice."

"No, Roux." He was still pressing her, not listening to what she was saying.

"Okay, okay," he relented. "Just think about it. You have an open invitation. Just call me, and I'll come running."

"Thank you. And if you've *really* changed, Roux, you'll respect that I asked for my space and not come until I call—"

"I got it, Sass," he said, recognizing that this was a test, and he vowed to pass with flying colors.

"Sassy," Yvette called from the doorway. "I've got to get going."

"Merry Christmas, Roux," Sassy said as she left him in the lounge.

"Hey Yvette," Roux said with a wave.

Yvette sent him a chilly smile. "I didn't mean to interrupt, Sass. I just wanted to say good-bye. Everything all right?"

"Yeah, actually, we had a nice conversation."

"Uh-oh," Yvette said. "You need me to stay?"

"No. But I'm taking you to the airport."

"No. You've got guests."

"It's been five hours. Does it look like they need me?" They looked at the folks having a great time; laughing, lying, crying and celebrating the life of Alouette Crillon. "C'mon. They won't miss me."

As they drove to the airport, Sassy told Yvette about her discussion with Roux, to which she answered, "I can call my office and arrange to stay another day."

Sassy chuckled and answered, "And what are you going to do, baby-sit me all my life?"

"No. But you can move to New York. Roux won't come to New York."

"I just don't know how we got so far apart on something as basic as fidelity. Unless I was so in love with him early on I couldn't see straight. Trusted him unequivocally despite my inner feelings. But the mature me finally realizes that I deserved better. I wasn't going to change and neither was he. Why should we change our core selves for one another?" She paced her car with the flow of traffic. "You know it was funny. He said all the right things—things I've wanted him to say for so long. Prayed that he would say. But hearing them now—"

"You still weren't convinced?"

"No. I believe him . . . but—"

"Too little too late. And you don't *trust* him?"

"Not like I trusted Aidan. I still get the feeling if a butt-naked woman came into a room, and Roux thought he could hit it and quit before someone discovered him? He would."

"And Aidan?"

"Aidan," Sassy repeated while thinking then said, "Aidan would be so repulsed that a woman would have so little regard for herself and think so little of him— he'd call security."

They laughed and talked about Gardner, the baby, and work for the next few miles.

"Well, this is the airport, I got to leave." Yvette stopped and looked at her girlfriend and asked, "What you thinking about?"

"If I go back to Roux—it'll be a totally different relationship. Roux was always top dog; his wants and desires always came first. That's just Roux. But now, I'm different and he's different. It's like we'll be starting over with two entirely different people. What if the new me and new him don't click?"

"I think you and Roux will always click on some level."

"But I got a man with the new me and we already click. But given Roux's recent epiphany, do I owe him a chance on the new us?"

"You don't owe Roux a damn thing."

"It's like in *Prince of Tides* when Nick Nolte left Barbra and went back to his wife and kids in North Carolina—because he *owed* her a chance with his 'new' best self."

"Oh, yeah. Real noble. And he's callin' her friggin' name every night when he crosses the bridge to go home. Girl, that ain't right."

They laughed.

"Let me tell you something. Roux isn't all bad and Aidan isn't all good. They're human males and flawed. But Sass, if you never ever date again in this lifetime, you will never—I repeat *never* find two more basically decent men, except for my Gardner. Believe me, chère. I've been out there. I know. You better pick the best of the best—'cause that's what you got here. Even with their 'specialness,' one thing these two have in common—they *love* some Sassy/Sassiere."

Sassy pulled to a stop by the terminal and said playfully, "Get out."

Yvette kissed her on the cheek before opening the car door. "Now, Sass, you call me if any new developments come about, or if Maman comes and sits on your bed tonight."

"Bye, crazy."

"Bye," she said and began to walk off. "Let me know what Aidan says."

"When and if I ever see him," Sassy called to her.

"You didn't see him at St. Gabe's?"

"What?"

"Probably while you and Roux were in the lounge."

"Aw jeeze," Sassy said, smushing her face and forgetting the most important thing at the moment. "Hey, Yvette." Her shout halted Yvette in her tracks. "Thank you."

"You know you my girl. Talk to you tomorrow."

Sassy then surmised that the fancy black car she saw

pull off was Aidan's. *This just gets better and better*, she thought sarcastically.

Later that evening, Ivanhoe sashayed up the steps as Sassy was coming out of the shower. "So are Killer and I on night watch again tonight?"

"I think you can go to bed and let the locks and alarm work for themselves."

"So, how you doing, chère."

"I'm doing." She removed the thirsty towel from her head and ruffed her curly hair with her fingertips. "It's going to take awhile."

"You take your time, chère. That's the perk that comes from living and working with your boss," Ivanhoe quipped.

"And Fairy Godmother," Sassy added.

Ivanhoe blushed and said, "You take all the time you need to grieve, chère. When you're ready to go back to work—then work. Your classes covered?"

"Yes."

"Well, Cyril and I are turning in. Holler if you need us."

The next three days were full of sobbing, picture viewing from the family album, and old records on the turntable. On the fourth day, Sassy was sick of herself and ready for a change of venue. She dropped off her papers and the grades to the dean's office and took lunch in the park. It was good to be out. She'd shut off her phone and answering service, which allowed her to call out but no one else to call in. She figured that by the end of the week, both Aidan and Roux would start to press Ivanhoe again. She missed them both for different reasons—but she didn't feel up to seeing either of them. Of course, there was the outside possibility that Aidan had taken himself out of the race altogether if Aidan had seen her and Roux. Sassy wasn't ready to deal with that either. She wanted to work, but not at the shop where she would be accessible to them both.

On the fifth day, Sassy went down to Ivanhoe's apartment. "Something smells good," she said entering the door and petting Killer.

"She lives!" Ivanhoe exclaimed. "Good Lord, when did you last bathe?" Ivanhoe said. "I smell you over the shrimp."

"I bathed, thank-you-very-much. I just haven't used deodorant recently."

"You are ripe, chère. Here, use mine or eat with Killer."

"Your tree is nice," Sassy said, fingering the gold bulbs on the decorated tree. "Maman loved Christmas," she mused.

"You're welcome to celebrate with us. Midnight mass, then the mother of all brunches."

"Actually, I won't be here."

"What?" Ivanhoe asked, racking his brain for when and which man traversed his security system and got to her. "Who will you be with?"

"I'll be working. Alone."

"On Christmas? Where?'

"In Napa. I called Taylor Quade Coleridge and asked her if she still wanted her great-greats restored, and she said yes. As luck would have it, they spend Christmas at their house in Maui. So I'll have the place to myself."

"Well, I want to go with you," Ivanhoe teased. "That's pretty remote."

"Remote is what I need. I don't want to be here for Christmas or New Year's; I'm not in the celebrating mood. There's a caretaker and his family who live on the property. With no one underfoot, I should be finished in a week."

"Well, well, well. I'm impressed, chère."

"And I'm hungry. When do we eat?"

"After you deodorize."

Sassy had to cut on her answering machine in case arrangements changed with Taylor.

It took no time for the tape to fill with calls from Roux and Aidan.

Aidan's were clear and linear: "Sassiere, I'm glad you're feeling better enough to turn your machine back on. I want to see you. We have things to discuss. Call me when you can." She was relieved that he was still interested.

Roux used the sound of her voice as a means to continue to come to grips with all that had happened in the past few months. "I'm going to give you the space you asked for, Sassy. But I still need to at least talk to you. Are you there? Pick up." He'd wait for a few seconds then continue, "I'm going over all this in my head and I'm thinking that maybe Aidan was sent into our lives to shake it up, so you and I could make some changes, some adjustments. Maman told me that I had to give you some time to experience another man; I didn't know it was going to be *that* man but she was right, Sass. Now we both know what we were missing, and we can get back to the way we were. Call me. I love you, Sass."

As she shopped for her oils and supplies to take with her, it felt odd that she was not purchasing any Christmas gifts for those she loved: Maman, Aidan, Roux, Ivanhoe. It was with great relief that Sassy left a Christmas-wrapped New Orleans and boarded the plane for L.A. It was the first Christmas to remember that she would not be spending at home with her mother and Roux. Her life had changed in minute ways that had gigantic consequences, and she realized that she had little control over much of it. *You can't control life, chou-chou. Only manage it,* her maman frequently said.

Strange, the farther away she got from the two men, the

clearer it all became, she thought as she climbed aboard the Napa-bound propeller plane. The groundskeeper was there to greet her, and after exchanging fifteen minutes of pleasantries, they rode the five miles to Kismet in silence. The ranch, which she had never seen in the daylight, was beautiful. On the right, the sign, KISMET in ancient script, and on the left, COLERIDGE WINERY in calligraphy. He steered the vehicle through the adobe pillars and the vineyard laid out before her in neat, perfect rows, like a soothing homage to order and tranquility. Harvested earth waited for its next turn to make seedlings into luscious grapes and eventually scrumptious full-bodied wines for the world to consume. Like life itself, it all had a certain rhythm. A certain timelessness and anonymity, and this was just where Sassy needed to be: in the bosom of nature and the ebb and flow of time. As they took the road to the house, Sassy noticed that tucked off into the distance, up in a sunny knoll were cattle, a reminder of the ranch's beginnings when two black people settled here. "History. Hold on to your past," she said, sotto voce. "Should I hold on to mine?" she mused.

The house was gorgeous in the setting remnants of day. The wrap-around porch where she'd met Aidan for the first time was studded with Christmas decorations. "Or embrace the future?" she wondered.

"*Que?*" The groundskeeper asked as he steered the car. "*Nada.*"

"*Buenas tardes,*" his wife greeted, coming from the house.

"*Buenas tardes. Feliz Navidad,*" Sassy said.

"Ah, Merry Christmas to you too. *Por favor.*" She ushered Sassy into the house.

It was as homey and comfortable as she remembered. The tree laden in gold and white twinkle lights was splendid. Sassy was shown her upstairs bedroom and brought back to the kitchen's refrigerator, where an assortment of prepared foods awaited her.

"Mrs. Coleridge say we are to leave you alone," the man said. "But we want you to come to dinner tomorrow. No one should be alone on Christmas."

"*Gracias, pero no.* You and your family enjoy the holiday," Sassy graciously declined.

"This house is yours. Here is my number if you need it. We are five minutes away and we can see this house from there. So not to worry. I set up everything in the den like you asked."

"*Gracias.*"

Sassy made green tea on the eight-burner industrial stove. She explored the house to get her bearings, then took herself into the den. She looked at the couple.

"Well, Promise and Hecuba, Merry Christmas. It's you and me for a while. Can't think of better company."

She rolled the ladder with the extended ledge for her paints and climbed up to inspect them. The couple's image was just as impressive as it had been at their first meeting. "Tell me, do you ever have problems with this guy?" she asked Hecuba of Promise. "Was it always him? How'd you know? Talk to me, girlfriend. Your secret's safe with me. No one else will hear. I promise you."

Sassy climbed back down, flipped on the stereo radio and lay on the couch to assess the entire picture before she set out to work on it. She studied them—the crease in his hat, the folds in his duster. Her exquisite face, the arch of her brow, the depth of her eyes. After satisfying her praise with the aesthetics, she mentally divided the portrait into sections. She then made two calls, the first to Ivanhoe to let him know of her safe arrival and swear him to secrecy.

"I'm offended, chère. I've been the keeper of the castle all this time; why would I cave now?"

Then she called Yvette, with whom she'd been "thinking out loud" all week.

"Did you make a decision yet?"

"No, Yvette. You'll be the second to know. It's ironic that I'm working on this old picture of two committed people—as old as Roux and I could be someday—yet I'm in the place where I met Aidan on the porch. My past is crossing my future."

"Ironic?" Yvette said. "I think not. I think it's *kismet*," she said dramatically.

"Good-bye, girl."

"On a serious note, Sass. I said it once and I'll say it again. The answer is who makes you feel the best about yourself and your situation?"

"What about sex—"

"I'm not talking about sex, Sass. Hell, push come to shove you can sex yourself. I'm talking about you and how you feel about yourself and who you are when you're with him. Men, even my Gardner, aren't the main course, they're desserts and you should *enjoy* being with them."

Sassy sighed and played with the fringe on the sofa's afghan. "Aidan restores my soul, but it was too quick. Too fast. Too soon after Roux."

"Well, you gave Roux over twenty years and you're still not sure about him. Time don't mean diddley. It's *feeling*, Sass. Coming!" Yvette yelled into Sassy's ear. "Gardner's calling me. We're going to a movie. I don't even know or care what it is. We going out, girl. Talk to you later?"

"Enjoy!"

By the third day, Sassy was into the portrait. She'd only used her bedroom the first night. Since then she had been sleeping, eating, and living in the den with her two new best friends. On occasion she'd take a walk around the property for a change of venue, but mostly she worked all night and slept during the day. She was enjoying restoring and absently thought that she'd love to tackle the ballroom in the Sebastien mansion; she and Simone could do it in no time. *That's not likely*, she thought. Before her mind returned to Aidan, she began to sing "*Dr. Feelgood*" with Aretha, then slopped to the kitchen for more delectables from the refrigerator. Here, life was uncomplicated and good. This paradise would be over soon. If only she could stay here forever.

Chapter XII

"Yvette?" the male voice inquired.

"Yes?" She put her book down on the nightstand and propped her pillow against the headboard.

"Hi. Happy Holidays. This is Aidan Sebastien."

"Oh, Aidan," Yvette said, eyeing her husband who looked up from his book.

"Hey, Aidan," Gardner yelled over to the receiver.

"Tell Gardner hey. I hope I'm not calling too late. Is Sassiere there?"

"No. She isn't," Yvette said guardedly, smoothing the comforter over her belly.

"Do you know where she is?" Aidan asked, and when Yvette didn't reply, he continued, "I know from Ivanhoe that she is out of town, but that's a good deal of territory. I was hoping you could narrow it down for me."

"I can't tell you, Aidan."

"I know that Roux has had the opportunity to talk to her, and I haven't. I'd just like to level the playing field before she makes any final decisions."

"I know. I saw you leave the funeral *repasse*. But I just can't. Maybe when she comes back, you two can—"

"That might be too late."

"Sorry, Aidan, but I was sworn to secrecy."

"She's in Napa, man!" Gardner yelled over to the phone.

"Gardner!" Yvette chastised her husband, slapping him with a small pillow.

"Sassy didn't swear me to secrecy," Gardner said. "Besides he deserves his turn to cop a plea. Not just Roux. Got to level that playing field."

"God, you men all think alike!"

"Tell Gardner thank-you. I know just where she is," Aidan said. "But Yvette, I'd like to swear you to secrecy—don't tell her I'm coming. Please?"

"What's he saying?" Gardner asked Yvette.

"Don't tell her he's coming," Yvette repeated to her husband.

"Sounds reasonable. All she'll do is bolt and then make a hasty decision. Do you care about the girl or not?" he asked his wife. "Go 'head, man. Handle your business!" he yelled over to Aidan.

"Aidan—" Yvette took control again.

"Yvette, you know I love her. I wouldn't do anything to hurt her. There are just some things I want her to know before—she decides, that's all."

Yvette sighed, rolled her eyes at her husband, and finally confessed, "She's at Kismet Ranch, and I won't tell her you're coming."

"Thanks," Aidan said, and continued, "and Yvette?"

"Yes?"

"I hope you keep my secret better than you kept hers," he teased and hung up. Drunk with the knowledge that he knew where she was, he smiled. He thought it a good sign that she'd returned to where they first met. Maybe he had a chance at "happily ever after" with her. He was going to give it his best shot. He snatched up the phone, called the hangar and told them, "Fuel up my jet and file a flight plan for Napa."

The Kismet Ranch den was lit up like the Christmas tree and Sassy sang along with Lou Rawls as she applied yellow ochre to the ridge of Hecuba's cheekbones. *"What are you doing New Year's, New Years Eve?"*

Sassy and Lou ended together and her paintbrush was poised in midair as she thought about the fine designer gowns she and Yvette had bought for New Year's going to waste. She fought the thought (and lost) that this was Aidan's favorite Christmas carol. *Something always reminds me of one of them no matter how hard I try,* she thought and then resumed painting. She hummed as she applied quick, feathery strokes with an almost-dry brush. Then she felt a presence. From her perch she turned and saw Aidan standing there, his hands thrust into his pockets.

"Aidan?" It was the second time he'd "appeared" to her. As if her heart summoned him even if her mind refused to budge.

"Hi. I didn't want to startle you and have you fall off that ladder."

"What are you doing here?" she asked with irritation as she scurried down the ladder. Once reaching the floor, she didn't know what to do with herself.

"What are you doing New Year's?" he asked.

She fought her emotions as she put her paintbrush on her palatte. She wanted to hug him; she wanted to yell at him; she wanted him to go; she wanted him to stay. "Who told you where to find me?"

"Don't get angry with them, Sassiere. They just thought I should have a chance to tell my side of the story."

"I came up here to be alone. To mourn Maman and sort some things out—"

"Is it working?" He watched her nervously fiddle with her paints. "We met right out here on this verandah."

"Why don't you just speak your piece and then leave me to mine?"

"I hope I'm not too late. I hope you haven't already made up your mind."

"Aidan—"

"All right, Sassiere." He walked closer to her and stoked his chin with his hand, thinking of how to approach this. To say all he had to say so she would get the facts of him—of them. "I suppose you feel you and Roux have a history." He noticed her flinch at the mention of Roux's name. "So do we."

She folded her arms protectively, impatiently.

"I'm sure you know about the first time I saw Roux, when my father and mother rushed me into the car, ignoring the little curly-headed boy who called him 'Papa.'"

Sassy had heard no such story.

"I could get no explanation from either parent, and my visiting cousin just thought the family was nuts. Simone then hustled the two of us off on a Caribbean vacation, but eventually I put it together. I had a brother. Me, an only child, had a brother. I relished the idea. I found out where he lived and went to see him. He did not share my enthusiasm and told me so in no uncertain terms. I left him alone as he asked but looked out after him as best I could. In an attempt to get to know him I became fascinated with his constant companion—you."

Sassy looked over at him.

"A cute little girl whose ponytail bounced with every step she took. A little girl who had a little brown freckle on the back of her neck."

Sassy felt the back of her neck. Did she have a freckle back there?

"Who liked Oreo cookies and hot chocolate without marshmallows, and hated her navy blue uniform—in fact hasn't worn navy blue since she graduated from the eighth grade. That's when I sent you a gold cross with SASSY in the middle."

"That was you?" Sassy asked and Aidan came a little closer.

"That was me. I saw Roux fume and toss it away, and I never sent you anything else because I didn't want you to get in trouble. It was a simple gesture, and I didn't want Roux mad."

Poor Bobby Weston, Sassy thought. Roux had beat him up and terrorized him with his hazel eyes for years after, thinking he was the one who'd given her that crucifix.

Aidan sat on the arm of the couch. "When you were sixteen—'legal'—my fascination turned more to love, and I had yet to hear your voice. I fell in love with your goodness, your loyalty, and I, who had everything, envied my brother who thought he had nothing but really had everything, because he had you.

"After my father died, I thought Roux's hate for us and the money would die with our father. I went to visit Roux, who let me know nothing had changed; he didn't want me or the money my father left him. I couldn't make him see that we were both victims; neither of us were responsible for the shared DNA in our veins," he mused. "Once I saw you approach in the distance and I left. I heard you ask him, 'who was that?' and he said, 'nobody.' That was only the second time I heard your voice."

"Second?"

"The first time, you were at the Jazz and Heritage Festival with some girlfriends—Yvette was probably one of them—and you dropped your purse. I picked it up for you and you said, 'Thank you.' I guess you were about fifteen. I don't expect you to remember."

Sassy stared at him like the stranger he was, and said, "All those years you were watching Roux?"

"My baby brother who wanted nothing to do with me. It's not as sinister as it sounds. Our paths crossed occasionally. Once I was playing at the Black Onyx on Royal. I'd been there about two weeks. I was blowing my trumpet and the crowd away nightly. After one set, old jazzmen and fans came up to compliment my 'natural ability,' and the last in line was Roux. I'd been in Paris so I hadn't seen him for a year or two. He stood there and I thought, *This is it. We are older and more mature, and he's finally ready for us to be brothers.* Then he aimed those cold hazel eyes at me without speaking and I knew nothing had changed. He finally said, 'What is it about you Sebastiens? You got the whole damned world and you can't leave me two streets in the Quarter. What, I can't have nothing, huh? This is my territory, my side of town. Can't you at least leave me that?' he spat and walked away. I finished out my engagement and never returned."

Aidan looked out at the still quiet of the black night and continued, "I will always believe that if the two of us had united as brothers, become friends, my father would have been forced to see us that way. But Roux was as stubborn as our father. And because of it, they both lost. We all lost. In the end Roux took the money, but we all missed the most important thing—a chance to know each other."

"He would have been a different man if his father had accepted him," Sassy mused. "What a waste."

"And I don't want that to happen to us, Sassiere. Missed chances."

"So you make a play for Roux's girl?"

"Is that what you are?" Aidan grew irritated at the very idea. "Is that how you see yourself now? Define yourself? If you are still his defender, then this conversation is over."

Sassy didn't speak. Her head spun.

Aidan calmed down and continued, "Don't you know me better than that? In all the years that you ran in and out of my life, I *never* made a move on you because you *were* 'Roux's girl.' I respected and envied you both." He got up from the couch and walked around in front of her. "But you became available. Or so I thought. I knew that eventually you'd get tired of his cattin' ways, him trampling the love you thought you had."

Hearing the truth that everybody knew caused Sassy's eyes to flash anger, but she realized that only Aidan had cared enough to say it to her face.

"I thought my time was over when you got engaged. But years passed and no marriage, which said to me that even you had doubts. Still I waited. Then like an exquisite, rare antiquity—you became available by a quirk of fate. You know how that works, Sassiere. You can covet and want something, but can't bid on it until it comes on the market; then you pull out all the stops. And I did just that, because you were the prize for me. And I pounced. But we had help because it was only Providence that you ran into me that night when I was on the way to the opera. You collapsed in my arms and I took you home."

"That was you?" Sassy asked.

"That was me . . . and also my ring."

Sassy looked at him and then looked away quickly, not trusting her heart to his gazing eyes.

"I sat beside my date that night—but couldn't think of anything but you—the opportunity, the timing, the possibility of us. And yes, I positioned myself in San Francisco, here in Napa and New York City so we could be together.

So what? I wanted you—not for just a roll in the hay in San Francisco—but forever."

He walked to the mantle and back again. "You surprised me when you introduced yourself as Sassiere. Then I relished the idea. Because that meant you were leaving the Roux-Sassy relationship behind. That you were freeing yourself and beginning to explore the world beyond what he defined for you. It was exciting for me to watch you take control of yourself—your life. I didn't do it. Roux didn't do it. Sassiere Crillon did it. You *chose* to expand your world, and I wasn't threatened, because I wasn't afraid of losing you to it—I wanted to be your partner in it."

Sassy mulled over what he said and to save her heart her mind came up with, "You could have told me you were a Sebastien."

"And we wouldn't be having this conversation now. You would have heard 'Sebastien' and run like the wind. So yes, I kept that from you because I wanted you to get to know me, the man—not the family name. I had planned to tell you so many times, certainly before your mother's death, but the timing was always off. I would have loved to go grocery-shopping with you that first day you cooked for me. I didn't like having to check and see if Roux was still in the Bahamas before I joined you for the bazaar. I'm not used to lying, and I'm not good at it. But it was a justified means to an end."

He looked at her and his heart ached. "I lied to you once. A lie of omission, and I guarantee you it will be the first, only, and last time. I have nothing to hide from you now or later. Remember on our first date you asked how I managed to not get married after all these years? Now you know. It was you. It was always you."

Sassy's heart melted and her body responded to the nearness of him. "I can't possibly live up to that ideal.

"You already have. In fact you've surpassed my wildest dream of who you could be." He aimed his eyes at her. "You are enough for me, Sassiere, just the way you are."

Sassy looked at him and closed her teary eyes on his handsome image. He overwhelmed her senses, rendering her completely immobile.

He mistook her stance for pain, and not wanting to cause her any further hurt, he then stood, but didn't approach her. "Sassiere, I just wanted you to make your decision based on all the facts. The most important one, which— You are the only woman I have ever loved, and I've loved you all my life before I knew your name, before I met you. And I don't *need* you to complete me, or motivate me, or to be a crutch, or to make me feel better about myself. I won't shrivel up and die if you don't choose me." He watched her posture change. "But, I do *want* you, Sassiere. More than you can ever know. I want the aliveness you bring to my life; your intelligence, humor, goodness, and values. Qualities I want to pass on through our children."

Sassy opened her eyes and looked at the dying fire.

"I made a promise to myself years ago that if you weren't available by the time I reached forty, then I'll go on and marry someone twenty-five." He chuckled. "Well, I'll be forty in three and a half years, and if I don't have you as a wife, mother of my children then I will move on. Maybe the time we had together is all we're allowed in this lifetime. What we had in that little bit of time, most folks don't get in their entire lives. Maybe that brief period of happiness we had was our quota. I know it was a slice of heaven being with you."

His voice broke, and he continued quietly, "I love you, Sassiere. I will always love you but if you won't have me, I will marry well. I will be a good and faithful husband

and an excellent hands-on father. I will be and give and do everything for my wife except one thing—love her as I love you. That will be impossible," he whispered, his voice strangled by emotion.

Tears sprang to Sassy's eyes. The words were as tender as the love he'd shared with her, and the thought of Aidan married to someone else paralyzed her further. The thought was as painful as Maman's death . . . and she felt alone.

"So," he continued. "If you decide to marry Roux out of habit, a sense of duty, or just plain love—I'll understand. I gave you my best shot and I thank you for the opportunity. At least I won't have to wonder what could have been. During my life, I had my unobtainable dream— it was magic.

"If you choose Roux, I will not bother you. If I see you on the street, I'll cross to the other side. Not for Roux, but for you. Despite what you may believe about me, Sassiere, I had the best of intentions. The only thing I wish for you now and forever is your happiness. I wouldn't do anything to cause you one moment of grief or anguish. Because you see, Sassiere Crillon—"

At the sound of her name she dared to look up at him.

He let his smoldering gaze bore into her soul and said, "I love you enough to let you go."

Sassy bit her bottom lip as Aidan stood by the French doors he'd used to get in. He stared at her as if this might be his last vision of her. As if he already knew she'd picked Roux. Then he left. Tears fell from her eyes.

Go after him! her heart shouted as inertia set in her body like a thousand-pound weight. He laid his feelings out like a splayed and gutted fish for all to see, and she had no defense for her love for him. Like her daddy used to say, "There's nowhere to hide when love calls your name."

* * *

"Welcome home, chère?" Ivanhoe greeted as Sassy descended the steps from her apartment. "You're up early to have gotten in so late."

"I've got things to do. People to see."

"So, you've decided. Who's the lucky man? For the wedding—shall I dress regally or to have a funky good time?"

"Nobody said anything about a wedding. One crisis at a time."

"You are not going to get out of this without one, chère. That's what the brothers Sebastien are bucking for. So who?" Ivanhoe pressed as Sassy opened the gate to drive her car out.

"I owe Roux—"

"Owe! You don't *owe* nobody nothing, chère. You are debt-free, Sassy-girl."

"Good-bye. I'll see you when I get back."

"Just make sure when you bury your love, chère . . . that it's dead," Ivanhoe said with a wave.

Sassy drove the familiar streets and turned left on Bourbon, then right into the long drive next to SASSY'S. She parked next to Roux's truck and cut her engine. As she climbed the stairs, she thought, *Maybe I should have called first.* She didn't want her feelings hurt or to find him with "company." Or maybe she was testing him— still. She bit her lip and used the lion knocker she had given him for one of his birthdays.

"Hello?"

"Hello," the man said then asked, "Taylor?"

"Yes. Who's this?"

"Aidan Sebastien. Happy New Year!"

"Oh, Aidan. Thanks. How are you?"

"Just fine. How was Maui?"

"Great, as always. I know you're a snow person, but you must join us for sun, sand, and fun one year."

"Thanks for the invite. When did you get back?"

"Day before yesterday. Good thing, too, or I would have missed telling Sassiere what a *magnificent* job she did on the portrait. Aidan, it just pops out at you—"

"That's great, Taylor. I'm looking forward to seeing it," he interrupted. "So your houseguest is gone?"

"Yes. She left yesterday evening, so she should have gotten home last night. Saturday night. Date night. You weren't supposed to pick her up or anything?"

"I guess we just missed connecting. Thanks. Tell your better half hello and Happy New Year—" Aidan hung up the telephone and glanced out to the garden where Simone was painting with her new young protégé, Monique. Since Sassy had introduced them at the bazaar, they'd been thick as thieves.

Sassiere was home last night, why didn't she call? Aidan thought. Unless, for the first time in his life, he had lost. If this were true, there was nothing worse then losing the most important thing in your life to humble you. He dialed Sassiere's number and got the machine. He hung up without leaving a message. He grabbed his keys and dashed to his car. He drove through the skinny winding streets to her house. He coasted by and saw that her car was missing.

From inside the house, Ivanhoe watered his plant and pinched off a dead leaf. He looked up and beyond the plants, and out of his window he saw him. He saw the Ferrari cruise by soundlessly.

"Sorry, chèr," he said to the silhouette of the man he thought would be perfect for his Sassy. "You are one man too late." Ivanhoe watched the car until it was out of view.

Aidan stopped his car at the corner. He had a sinking feeling that Sassy was with Roux. He didn't want to know and told himself to go home, but his car drove him over to Bourbon. He sat catercorner to the club. SASSY'S was hosting its Sunday jazz brunch, and the patrons lined up to honor the coveted reservations. The car behind him tooted, and Aidan coasted forward. He was about to pass the driveway beside SASSY'S that led to Roux's upstairs apartment.

"Lord in heaven," he prayed, "please don't let me see their two cars there."

As the car drifted, he saw Roux's headlights come into view, and he began bargaining. "Okay, Lord, Roux has a right to be there. Please don't let me see Sassy's red convertible."

As Aidan took his foot off the clutch and the car drifted mid-driveway, Roux's car came into full view. Aidan smiled. But the Lord must have been busy with all the churchgoers this Sunday because, stuck in the back near the gallery stairs, was Sassiere's car.

Aidan stopped his car. Like rubber necking a train wreck, he had to stare and make sure that it was *her* red convertible. He didn't want to make a mistake on something so important as seeing any red car and thinking it was hers.

But it was. A stabbing pain pierced his heart. A searing pain catapulted to his head forcing him to close his eyes

against the offending sight. A car behind him blew its
horn impatiently. Aidan looked at the convertible and
up to the apartment door with the lion knocker. He
didn't want to imagine what was going on inside.

"It's done. Be happy . . . *Sassy*."

He drove on.

Roux had swung open the door. Sassy wasn't prepared
for the sight of him—bronze and bare-chested with silky
brunet hair clinging to his taut abs, tapering down to his
navel.

His sleepy face broke into a wide grin. "Dreams do
come true. You're really here."

"I'm sorry. I should have called first. I woke you."

"You kidding? Come in." He pulled her inside and
closed the door.

She looked around at the house they'd decorated together, fully intending this to be their home once they
married. After the first child, they were to move into a
house with a yard. All those plans seemed eons ago. In
another life.

"The place looks surprisingly clean, Roux," Sassy
teased, noting that his bed beyond the French doors was
empty.

"See how neat I can be when you're not around," he
teased back, wanting to but not touching her. "Want
some coffee?" he asked, defusing his desire.

"No. Thank you."

"Relax, Sassy."

Sassy stood stoically in the center of the room, second-
guessing her coming. "This was a bad idea."

"Why?" Roux walked his muscular body to the big over-
stuffed chair. "You should have written your regrets?" His

hypnotic hazel eyes bored holes into hers. "A Dear Roux letter, perhaps?"

"Roux—"

"You've got too much class for that, Sass. I guess that was always our problem—the hoodlum and the princess."

"Hardly."

"Well, I was hoping you'd pick me. Thankful even, but I'm not surprised you didn't."

Sassy looked at him curiously. *Who is this new man?* she thought.

"What did you expect? Me to fling myself at you or lose my temper? Anger is a weak man's strength." He sat on the arm of the chair and slid into its seat, and the sunlight escaping through the louvered shutters painted itself across his face. "I told you I had matured. Grown from that adolescent boy who, deep down, never thought he was quite good enough, but acted like he had the world on a string. It was a long run, but the show is over. We can all go home. Go on with our lives.

"I'm thirty-four years old, Sass. It's time to let all that anger and resentment go. I'm tired of it; just weighs me down like a nine-hundred-pound gorilla. I had to face my past then exorcize myself of it. What's that your daddy used to say: 'The more you run from it, the more you run into it.' True that. Resenting everybody was eating me alive—like taking poison and expecting the other folks to die. It was blocking *my* happiness. Aidan forced me to accept some things; to come to grips with him, my father, even my mother. I guess I have Aidan to thank for killing some of my demons."

"Aidan is a good guy," Sassy agreed as Roux stood. Sassy grew nervous, not that Roux would lay a hand on her in anger, but in love.

"I may be a bad boy, but I'm a good man, Sass. Regardless of how I came into this world. I got nothing to prove by grabbing and getting with every woman that's offered to me. Especially when I had the prize all along."

He touched her cheek and a tear fell from her eye, rolled down her cheek onto his finger.

"Well, you haven't told me I'm wrong," he said softly. A tear filled his eye. "Letting go of all our years is painful. So please don't insult me with that 'let's be friends' crap, because we can't. Not the way I loved you and still do." He strutted away from her. It was hard saying good-bye. "I accept my responsibility in it. If I had settled down, then you would have married me and would have never met Aidan Sebastien. I can't blame Aidan for seeing in you what I didn't. I held on too tight and bulldozed your spirit. I thought loving you as fiercely as I did was enough. Instead of making us closer, I pushed you away, and I was too hardheaded to realize that." He hunched his shoulders. "Well, that and love is not a three-way street. I get it now."

"Roux, we had a great time."

"Yes, we did. But I don't think we could get it back, Sass. You don't trust me," he admitted. "I know that. I'm not sure whether I want to have to prove my fidelity to you over and over again, day in and day out. Be on the clock when I go get a pack of cigarettes—"

"You don't smoke."

"See. It's startin' already."

They chuckled.

"What's that your daddy used to say: 'If you got to buy your way into heaven, you need to go to hell.'"

They shared another laugh. "That's my daddy." She wiped away a tear.

"I don't want to see suspicion in those pretty brown eyes every time we're apart. I just don't want to cause you any more pain, Sass. I'm sorry I hurt you so much in the past with other women who didn't mean a thing to me—ever. It just wasn't worth it.

"You deserve so much more. So much better. I *can* give it to you—but now—I don't think you want it—not from me. You don't want to take another chance on me. I don't like it—but I understand."

"I never meant to hurt you with my decision, Roux."

"I know," he said then remarked, "I hate your hair like this." He ran his hand over it. "I can't even get a handful."

She play-pinched his side and was thankful for his sense of humor and making it easy for her, not the high drama, guilt ridden, gut wrenching goodbye it could have been.

"You're going to be a hard habit to break, Roux. You were my sister, brother, daddy, mama, friend, confidant—my first love."

"I'll *always* be your first love." He pointed his finger playfully. "And don't you forget it."

"And how many others' first have you been?" Sassy reminded him that she could give as good as she got.

"Don't go there. We're having a mature, adult conversation."

She chuckled.

"How about we go get some breakfast?"

"I don't think so."

"Yeah. I guess you got some good news to deliver. Or does he already know?"

"You do know me, Roux."

"The worst first," he recited one of Sister Claire Regina's platitudes about homework. "Besides, I've had almost twenty years of experience."

They stood there facing each other and the finality of the situation. Neither wanting it to end, but neither having a way to avoid it. From the first day of hooky right on up to this moment, they had been so interwoven—the other half of each other's heartbeat, intricate threads in the tapestry of one another's life, yet, when she walked through that door it would be over, gone forever. Never recaptured; only in memory.

"You're a good man, Roux."

"Just not your man, huh, Sass?"

"You were for a lot of years." She broke her gaze from him and glanced around what had been her home for a lot of years. "Well, I better go," she finally said.

"Yeah." If he could keep her there, he would. *Please stay*, his heart ached to say.

"Take care, Roux."

"You too." *I love you Sassy. Don't go*, his heart pleaded. *Gimme just one more chance.*

She walked to the door, and he followed her at a safe distance.

"One thing, Sass."

She turned to him.

"Don't invite me to the wedding. I'm not that mature yet."

Sassy chuckled. "Who said anything about a wedding."

"If I know that broth—" he stopped, before continuing, "There will be a wedding. Aidan Sebastien is no fool."

Sassy blushed and chuckled.

Roux didn't. He took the back of his fingers and rubbed them across her wet cheek. "I'll never stop loving you, Sass. You were my best friend."

"Bye," her voice cracked with emotion. She cleared her throat.

Sassy stood on his porch and listened to the door close gently behind her. Closing on her past, securing it from her. More tears quietly cascaded from her face. As she descended the stairs to her car, she cried for the time they'd shared. She cried for the time they would never share again. She hadn't expected this to be so hard.

Sassy went home, thankful that Ivanhoe wasn't there to clock her comings and goings. She shed her clothes, stepped into the shower, and her tears flowed like the water. The hot water and cool tile against her skin were as conflicting as her thoughts and feelings. Did she make the right decision? Roux had changed. He had become the Roux she thought he was all along. Fair, rational. The tape. She forgot to get it. The Roux she just left wouldn't do anything to hurt her or Aidan. Should she give Roux just one more chance? Could she trust him with her heart again? Did she love Aidan only because he was a stable Roux? Well, now Roux was stable. Or was he? For how long? Nothing was ever black-and-white for her. She hated that. When the hot water ran cold, she stepped from the shower. She'd made her decision, why was she second-guessing herself now? She entered her bedroom, drying her hair with a towel. She spotted the teddy bear sitting next to the New York City snow globe and turned its key. "The Very Thought of You" tinkled out and she sang. She grinned. And she knew—unequivocally, she knew.

Aidan was her only thought. He had looked deep inside her, bypassed the heart Roux betrayed and headed straight for her soul, caressed, nurtured, and nourished it, and given it back to her. All he wanted in return was to be part of her life and do more of the same. Now, that was a love she could feel, Sassy thought. She felt no duty or obligation with Aidan, only pure desire and need. She *wondered* with Roux but she was *sure* with Aidan—as sure as the sun rose in the east and set in the west. Aidan was her man. Roux was not all flawed and Aidan was not all perfect, but he was perfect for her.

She missed Aidan. She yearned for his essence and

longed for his touch. She laughed out loud as she
dressed, giddy with the integrated affirmation of mind,
body, heart, soul, and spirit. She glanced over at the
Cajun moon beginning its rise, and the sight sent a stab
of pain to her heart. This time it was the fear of never
waking up with him beside her each morning. She
didn't want to live in a world without Aidan Sebastien.

Chapter XIII

Sassy was still singing "The Very Thought of You" as she drove through the gates up the long driveway and parked under the portico. Lavinia's opening the door caused her to stop.

"Good afternoon, Lavinia. Is Aidan in?"

"Well, no. Hughes took him to the airport about three, four hours ago."

"Airport? Shoot. Do you know where he went?"

"Ms. Crillon, we're close but not that close. Mr. Aidan probably told Ms. Simone."

"Is she in?"

"All the time," Lavinia said with a roll of her eyes, and stepped back to let Sassiere in. "She's out back, as usual," Lavinia offered as she peeled from the grand hall into the kitchen.

Sassy walked toward the Gone With the Wind staircase, veering right, through the beveled glass door to the garden. As she negotiated the brick verandah and the five flat steps, she greeted, "Well, hello!"

Both Simone and Monique turned from their canvas and paints to glance at the intruder.

"How are you?" Sassy approached.

"Look, Ms. Crillon," Monique said excitedly.

Simone did not speak.

"This is lovely, Monique," Sassy said, viewing the girl's magnolia blossom.

"She's got real talent, this one," Simone said, looking at neither of them.

"She certainly has," Sassy agreed as Monique went back to painting.

"How are you, Simone?"

"Been both better and worse."

"That is beautiful," Sassy said, watching Simone dab in feathery strokes.

Obviously Simone did not enjoy the interruption, so Sassy just said, "I'm looking for Aidan. Do you know where he is?"

"Of course I do. Not much goes on around here without my knowledge, approval or consent," Simone scoffed; the big hat shielding her face bopped with each word she spoke. "Why now?" she asked, applying a touch of orange to the center of her blossom.

"I want to speak with him," Sassiere said.

"Oh, really?" Simone cut her eyes at Sassiere and returned to her painting.

"Do you know where he is?" Simone repeated, not falling for Simone's fishing expedition.

Simone let her hands fall to her lap, looked up at Sassiere, and asked, "You meaning to hurt my boy?"

"No. Quite the opposite, actually."

Simone looked at her for a long time. The tinkling from the fountain commingled with the loud chirp of birds seeking their refuge for the night. Sassiere held the woman's gaze in hers. Neither of them blinked.

"Humph," Simone finally grunted, and went back to her painting. "He went skiing."

"Of course. Where?"

"Aspen. Not enough time for Cortina or St. Moritz. He'll be gone a week."

"Do you have a phone number or address?"

"Tsk!" Simone let her aggravation show and said to Monique, "People who are not artists don't understand peace, quiet, and trains of thought." She aimed her eyes at Sassiere and asked, "How do you know he is alone?"

Simone's question wiped the smile from Sassy's face. "I don't. I hope he is. But I have to see him."

"Go humiliate yourself then." She resumed painting.

"You do all sorts of crazy things when you're in love, Simone."

Without looking up, Simone said, "In the office." She mixed just a hint of zinc white on the tip of her brush and sarcastically added, "He leaves me notes in case of emergencies."

"Thank you. Bye," Sassiere said, as she turned the doorknob. "Simone, please don't call him and let him know I'm coming. I want it to be a surprise."

"I have better things to do with my time, chère." Simone offered dismissively.

There were no flights out that night, so Sassy was forced to spend what she considered her last night apart from Aidan. After a fitful night's sleep, the next morning she sat in first class with a permanent goofy grin on her face. The plane spirited toward Colorado. Knowing Aidan's persistence, she imagined that they'd be married within the year. She twirled the heirloom ring on her finger and hoped that she'd have at least a year with him all to herself before she had their first child, but it was negotiable. Then she laughed out loud at all the plans she was making without Aidan, and the man next to her smiled.

She was so happy. So sure about Aidan Sebastien, like she had never been with Roux Robespierre. Roux was trying to *become* the man she wanted—deserved. Aidan *was* him. She loved them both—but differently. Roux was her fun-filled past, but Aidan was her death-do-you-part, man-of-her-dreams future.

She'd spent too many years lying beside a man she couldn't trust—that was the loneliest existence in the world, and she refused to subject herself to that pain ever again.

She cherished nothing more than the simple pleasure of lying in the circle of Aidan's arms, where she felt such freedom. Free to be or do or say anything she wanted without fear of judgment or reprisal. With this freedom, there was no place else she wanted to be but living inside his love. Aidan freed her to think of Roux without anger or hope, without resentment or interest. Aidan freed her to think of her possibilities that, with his love and support, were endless and divine.

Sassy arrived at the chalet, and a maid dressed in a gray uniform welcomed her at the door. How did she know to expect her? The only answer was Simone; maybe his mother did believe what Sassy already knew—she and Aidan were perfect for each other. Once alone, Sassy surveyed the expansive A frame edifice with the mammoth two-story fireplace and the breathtaking view of the snow-covered slopes. She flicked on the component set and smiled when someone's smoky sax played an instrumental version of "The Very Thought of You."

"Trying to get over me, huh?" she said. "Not going to happen."

She ascended the open staircase to the bedroom and

touched his silk pajamas; she let her fingers caress the fabric then inhaled his scent. She rubbed its sleeve around her neck and between her breasts. His leather bedroom slippers peeked from beneath the bed. His comb, brush and manicuring set were arranged in an arc on the dresser. In the bathroom she fingered his shaver, the bottle of lotion and soap he'd brought with him, and thought, *Neat freak.*

She opened the other side of the closet. A woman's hot pink ski parka and winter clothes hung in a neat row.

"Breathe," Sassy told herself.

She couldn't bear to think Aidan was here with another woman. She grew jittery trying to will the thought from her mind. The practical, savvy Sassiere told her there was no other toothbrush or cosmetics, and told the emotional Sassy to calm down.

If he was there with another woman, Sassy would just have to confront them both. She was saying her piece—professing her love—just as he had done in Napa. She had nothing to lose and everything to gain.

She ended up back in the hall, stood in the "A" of the frame, and watched skiers in the distance carve trails on the powdered white, like flicking fingers on the white icing of a cake. She strolled back downstairs and went to the window where his laptop computer was set up. She cut it on and pressed ENTER; the game Solitaire lit up.

"Yeah, you miss me," she said and looked up through the plate-glass window.

In the distance she saw one skier break from the prescribed trail to blaze one of his own. He skied effortlessly, poetically towards the house in wide "S" swirls.

"It's him," she said, identifying him as only someone in love can do.

She watched him rhythmically glide from side to side,

hunched down for speed, forging deep burrows, frothing up snow in his wake. "Smooth," she said, "regardless of what he does. He is the best at it."

She pulled on her coat, cursed that she hadn't thought to bring or buy boots, and then panicked. "Oh, God, please let him still love me," she prayed as she opened the front door, carefully negotiated down the steps, and walked up to the embankment, apparently there to protect the chalet from avalanches.

She watched his wide graceful swipes across the frosting come to an abrupt stop. Dressed all in black, he stood there. She smiled at the sight of him, her heart beating uproariously. Then she realized he was close enough to see her. She froze and breathed in the cold stinging air.

"Oh, God, oh, God—please, please, please," she prayed as he skied toward her then stopped again at the top of the incline. He just stood at attention, like a soldier awaiting marching orders. As if he didn't believe what he was seeing. There was nothing identifiable about him; a man in a black ski suit, with gloves, goggles, hat, and a mask covering what she knew were the most perfect lips in all the world.

He finally perched his goggles on his forehead, revealing the penetrating eyes she'd grown to love, but they were cold and distant now. His handsome form whittled itself against the dull, gray sky, but he didn't speak.

This wasn't the response I expected, she thought. To break the ice, Sassy asked, "What are you doing New Year's?"

"We missed that, didn't we?" he said, as coldly as the frigid air that began to sting her ears and toes.

"Well, what about the rest of your life?" She chanced with a grin.

He popped out of his skis and said, "Listen, Sassy—"

"*Sassy?*" she challenged. "What happened to 'Sassiere'? I kinda liked her."

"I loved her," he said and hoisted the skis over his right shoulder.

"'Loved.' As in past tense?"

"She doesn't exist anymore." He slid down the slope and looked into her eyes.

"Oh? Here I am." Only then did she see the hurt and rejection registered there. It broke her heart. She never meant to hurt the man she so deeply loved.

"You came a long way to deliver bad news." He shifted his skis over his left shoulder and began walking.

"Hey, hey!" She tried to run to catch up with him but the snow held on to each of her bootless feet. She yanked at his arm but missed. "I don't have that kind of money. You think I came all this way to tell you we're over?" She had to use his footprints as a guide and gage every step she took so she wouldn't fall. "Boy, you've got some opinion of yourself, Mr. Aidan Maximillien Sebastien. The best I'd do is send you a 'Dear Aidan' letter as a keepsake so you could torture yourself over and over by reading it." Sassy ranted on, not realizing that Aidan had stopped a few paces ahead of her.

Aidan looked at her with a hint of recognition as to why she had really come.

"Or I'd wait until you got back to N'awlins," Sassy said, watching her feet sink into the snow with each labored step. "But I wouldn't waste my money and my time to give you bad news." She stumbled to a halt when she realized he'd stopped walking and had turned to listen to her.

"So why did you come?" he challenged.

Sassy thought she saw a spark of playfulness behind his soulful eyes. She hoped she did. She'd take any bit of encouragement he had to offer. "I came . . ." she began, "to return your ring." Sassy offered it to him.

Aidan looked at the heirloom in the palm of her hand, looked into her eyes, took the ring, and slipped it in the zippered compartment of his parka.

Not being able to read his facial expression, Sassy thought, *He must be dynamite at poker.*

"Is that it?" he asked. "You came to give me back the ring?"

"And . . . to . . . say . . ." she dragged it out and stopped where she stood. "That I'm not twenty-five, but will I do until she comes along?"

He stared at her. Emotionless. *I'm too late,* she thought.

That parenthetical smile she so loved and thought she would never see again gradually reappeared, framing his sculptured lips. Sassy relaxed a little, letting her warm breath blow in one stream of relieved smoke.

His eyes danced in his handsome face. "Just how old are you?"

"Not twenty-five," she chuckled, and he laughed.

"You look young and spry enough. But are you any good?"

"Oh, I'm good. I'm real good. Although ninety-five percent of it depends on my partner."

"It only works if you're in love," he said, then asked seriously, "Are you in love?"

She grinned and said, "Absolutely. Hopelessly."

Aidan hesitated, searching for sincerity in her eyes. This was too important for her not to be positively sure.

"What I had with Roux was habit and adolescent illusion." She stepped closer to him so he couldn't mistake what her heart and soul were saying. "What we have is deep and wide and all-consuming. Aidan, I have never been so in love—where I feel like I can touch the moon. That's what I have with you."

He dropped his skis and gathered her in his arms and the kiss they shared warmed them to a spontaneous combustion that could have melted all the surrounding snow. "Oh, Sassiere."

"You're the only man my heart beats for, Aidan."

"Me too, you. And when I thought I'd lost you—" His words became buried in another kiss. "I've missed you, Sassiere."

They stood forehead to forehead trying to catch their breath and he said, "Let's go in and get you out of all these cold, wet clothes."

He picked her up and carried her back to the chalet, kissing her again as he opened the door. They shed their clothes as they made their way to the couch in front of an unlit fireplace. They made love borne of a thousand nights of deprivation and desire, then lay spent and satisfied in each other's arms. Aidan lit the fireplace into a roaring inferno before gathering her in his arms again.

"I just want to hold you forever," he said.

"Good. Then we both want the same thing." She giggled and snuggled near him. "I love you, Aidan. To the moon and back."

They slept the sleep of the content and awoke while it was still light.

"I need protein," Aidan said, "How about I make some eggs?"

"I'll make some cheese toast." She rose slightly from his arms. "Is there a store somewhere near here?"

Aidan chuckled. "As close as that kitchen. It's fully stocked—you make a list when you rent the place."

"Oh. Well, excuse me."

"I have all of our favorites. Haven't had much of an

appetite until now." He kissed her temple. "First, I'll turn the thermostat up to eighty-five."

"Turn on the shower and we'll be back in N'awlins."

"Hot and steamy. One of my greatest pleasures is to watch you walk around in your panties and a skimpy tee."

"Oh?" She watched him, and the source of her most recent pleasure, dart to the thermostat and return in a flash. "I packed light and don't have any of those sets with me."

"I do. I brought a few things for you with me." He extended his hands to her. "They're upstairs—along with a hot-pink ski outfit and skis. Merry Christmas."

"Oh, Aidan, I didn't get you a thing."

"What you have given me is . . . priceless. If I live a thousand years I'll never be able to repay you, Sassiere."

"Oh, Aidan."

He kissed her nose and said, "I'm glad I don't have to leave everything here—the food, clothes—because when I left here, I was going to be over you."

"Oh, really? Just like that?"

"I was a man on a mission. But my private hell turned into paradise when you came."

"You know I saw those female clothes upstairs."

"Oh? You snoop?"

"Absolutely. So you better remember that for future reference."

"Go ahead. Like I told you—I got nothing to hide. Not now—not ever. When you're with the One True Love of your life—there is no need."

"Smooth."

Over the next week they made love, cooked, ate, cuddled, sang, and danced with the stereo as Aidan taught her how to negotiate the chess pieces across sixty-four spaces. He became her ski instructor and lead man on

the toboggan, but she became top dog on the snow-
mobile. They only ate at the lodge twice, preferring the
cocooned intimacy of their chalet. The days and nights
sped by like wind through a latticed trellis on a N'awlins porch; then they returned home *together*—the way
they'd always be from now on.

The couple settled into a familiar rhythm. Sassy resumed working at Rare Finds, teaching one course at
Tulane and completing the final research for her thesis,
but nighttime belonged to Aidan. They were inseparable
spending their time between the two houses; content
eating, sleeping, and hanging around basking in one another's presence. They slowly became the most sought
after twosome in all N'awlins, but successfully remained
a much-desired but low-profile couple who had few
friends and fewer social obligations. For Mardi Gras, he
escorted her to the elegant and prestigious Original Illi-
nois Ball and she took him to the Claiborne Street festivities before they left the city to tourists and went sailing
in St. Barts.

Aidan worked at his desk and heard Sassiere's voice in
the garden followed by his mother's echoing laugh. He
stopped. He hadn't heard Simone laugh in years. It was
a lilting laugh that warmed the corners of this grand
house, chasing all the cobwebs and ghosts making a way
for the light. And the light was Sassiere. She'd brought
life back into the stoic mansion, connecting all who lived
here, past, present and future, making it a home, and
everyone delighted in her presence. This house no
longer appeared huge and ominous to its inhabitants or
to those who began to visit. Whether Sassiere, barefoot
and dressed in linen overalls and a tank top, yelled

"Aidan!" from the upstairs gallery, or was dressed in a designer frock hosting an open house for a charity tea, she was the reason Sebastien mansion was born again. She'd brought an energy to the stuffy Sebastien name, and they were all the richer for knowing her. Aidan had told her he wanted her, but the reality was he didn't know how much he, in fact, needed her—they all did.

"Aidan!" she called in to him through the open window as a few of the children from St. Gabriel's of the Sacred Heart began their Easter-egg hunt in the garden. "C'mon. All work no play now makes Jack get no play later," she threatened with a wink, her fuchsia and hot-pink sundress as sultry as she was.

When he came out onto the back verandah, he shoved his hands into his pockets and looked at the flurry of activity. Sassiere and Lavinia were setting up the refreshments by the guesthouse as Simone supervised the egg hunt. She nodded and winked at her son, knowingly.

"Sassiere," Simone called, "You have to look too."

"I'm a little old for Easter-egg hunts," Sassiere said.

"C'mon, Ms. Crillon," Monique urged her on.

"All right. I'll give mine to you," Sassiere whispered, as she pretended to hunt for eggs.

She bent over and saw Aidan eyeing her appreciatively. She shot him a long, sultry seductive look and Simone stepped in between them. "*Mon dieu!* There are children here!" she scoffed. "Sassiere, go over there for your eggs."

Sassiere sauntered past Aidan licking her lips and went where Simone told her. She looked near the palm and saw purple foil peeking from the sphagnum moss. *How pretty,* she thought and pulled the box from the ornate planter. Her name was on it.

Aidan and Simone exchanged looks and eyed Sassy with interest.

She sat on the rod-iron chair near the fountain and undid the gigantic bow. "Ahhh!" she exclaimed as she opened the extravagantly wrapped box to reveal a Fabergé egg in pink enamel with twenty-four-carat gold borders set in a thousand individual Austrian crystals. "Oh, Aidan!" She ran to him. "This is the most exquisite Easter egg ever." She kissed him. "No wonder you didn't want to help us dye the others. Does a Wells Fargo guard come with this?"

"In a manner of speaking. It's a 1890 reproduction from Limoges, France."

"I can't keep this in my apartment. It costs more than the whole building."

"Open it."

Sassiere hesitated and held it to her heart. "Oh, Aidan." She began to cry as Simone joined them.

"You going to start crying before you open it?" Aidan asked. "I could yell 'psyche,'" he teased.

"Oh Aidan, I know what it is." She hugged him. She kissed him, wetting him with her tears.

"You might just embarrass yourself, girl," Simone said. "Better open it."

Sassiere was so nervous she was trembling. Aidan wiped away her tears with his thumb, then kissed her again. She unhinged the egg and let the top fall away to reveal a gorgeous, pink, Austrian six-carat diamond. "I love you," she held onto him and cried. "I'm not supposed to be this happy."

"Who says? That's my job: to make you happy for the rest of your life—if you let me." He kissed her salty lips, "And I take my job very seriously."

"Eh," Simone said to Sassy. "You were right. I was

wrong. Welcome to the family." She turned back to the children.

"Sassiere Crillon . . . will you marry me?"

"Yes, yes, yes, yes!" she showered him with kisses as he held her.

Later that evening, as they lay in the hammock on the little balcony off his bedroom, Sassiere listened to the familiar sounds and inhaled the fragrances knowing that, now, they would become a permanent part of her and her children. She looked at her ring sparkle and dance in the moonlight. "I just can't believe it."

"It's no secret that I love you and you love me. This is just the natural progression of love, Sassiere."

She grabbed his hand, looked at the Sebastien ring on its rightful owner, and said, "Now we both have exquisite rings."

"I'm passing mine on to *our* son."

"Our son," Sassy repeated, relishing the sound of it. She grinned, all sunshine and light. "My mother wanted me married so badly."

"Well, you've gotten this far before—engaged for years. I want you to set a date."

"Next year," she teased.

"Funny. Try again."

"Just not June. June is too cliché and common. Are we going to live here?"

"Of course, it's my house. We'll move into the front bedroom—"

"No. That's your mother's room."

"She doesn't care. She hasn't slept there in over thirty years."

"And neither will we."

"Okay, how about one bedroom for each of the children?"

"Good lord, Aidan. Do you remember how this room made you feel?" She rocked the hammock into motion with one bare leg. "We can divide the second bedroom into two huge rooms and put a bathroom between so they can share."

"That'll work. And right through there." He pointed towards the hallway to his bathroom and dressing rooms, "We'll make an inner hallway so we can get to them—"

"And them to us—in a hurry."

"Ummm." He snuggled closer and squeezed her derriere. "We'll talk about that one. Sometimes we won't want them to get to us in a hurry."

"Oh, Aidan. One of my fondest memories was when we'd all pile into bed together on the weekends and read—the comics, books—"

"That sounds nice. I'd like to have that. Look how great you turned out." He kissed her nose. "We'll take at least two vacations a year. One with and one without the children."

"One place hot and sunny for me and one place cold for you."

"Yeah? Well, I've got some hot lips for you right now."

In just six short weeks, the elegantly engraved invitations with the garden motif were selected and sent, the caterers booked, and the orchestra secured for the small, tasteful wedding of Sassiere Crillon and Aidan Maximillien Sebastien on May fourteenth. Many desired the coveted invite, but few would garner the privilege of witnessing this prince of the Sebastien dynasty finally take a princess.

The day had come and Sassy sat in the room that would be hers after the wedding; the vanity had been one of the many additions Aidan made to their suite. She saw the assemblage of family and friends in the white chairs facing the garden fountain where they were to exchange their vows as man and wife. An ornate Victorian gazebo had been constructed for just that purpose.

Yvette helped Sassy with her dress, a beautiful ecru French silk, a designer gown that was "simple, but elegant, so as not to detract from my future wife's face," Aidan had offered playfully one night in New York as they looked through a bridal book. The bodice, studded with a million seed pearls, looked like liquid sunshine as it shimmered in the light; the veil was an exquisite cacophony of tulle and flowers.

"Aw, a vision, chère," Ivanhoe gushed as he entered. "I so wanted to wear the ecru, but I understand you get first dibs."

"Ivanhoe! You look awful."

He dabbed his swollen eyes; the mascara dribbled in rivers down his round cheeks. "Just because you're the bride doesn't mean you get to dog the mother of the bride," he hissed playfully. "Okay, going for more cold water." He left the room.

"He's a trip," Yvette said. "He is so beside himself, escorting you today. Maybe the highlight of his life."

"He's a sweetheart. And I'm so glad you're here today for me, 'Vette."

"We always said we would be the maid of honor for each other," Yvette offered. "I was wondering if I'd ever get my chance to reciprocate for you," she teased.

"And with such big *breast-tises*."

"You can thank Gardner, your godchild and breast-feeding for that!" They chuckled.

Sassy stopped finagling with the heirloom necklace Simone had given her as "something old" to wear. "I thought all those years that I'd be marrying Roux.

I prayed for him to calm down, settle down; I made novenas but he just kept runnin'." She looked over at Yvette and grinned. "Then I met Aidan." She blushed and said, "Thank God for unanswered prayers."

"Amen!" Yvette hugged her friend. "I don't want to cry and mess up my makeup. I'll get your flowers."

"Thanks."

Before Yvette could leave there was a gentle knock on the door. Yvette opened it, and Hughes said, "Special delivery."

Sassy looked at the package. It had *Sassy* on it with Roux's handwriting.

"I wish you hadn't seen this," Yvette said. "Let me just throw it away."

"No. Let me have it."

Yvette sighed and handed it to Sassy.

Sassy opened the ribbon and chuckled at the way the tape overlapped the sides. "He never could wrap worth a damn." Her relationship with him seemed centuries ago.

Yvette didn't smile.

Sassy removed the lid, and there, on a bed of white cotton, were the charred remains of the tape—with the little heart etched into the black plastic.

"What the hell is that?" Yvette asked.

Sassy chuckled. "Just Roux's way of letting go." She took the card. It simply read, *Be happy, Sass. You deserve it.* "Now you can throw it away." She gave Yvette the box and stuck the card on the fireplace mantel under an urn.

"I'll go get the flowers," Yvette said and left.

Sassy sat there waiting for her time to marry a man she'd never had the capacity to even dream of. She was more sure about Aidan in this little bit of time then she was never sure of Roux in all those years. Aidan was comfortable and comforting. She heard the harpist clinks accompany the tingling of the fountain.

Yvette poked her head in and asked, "You ready, Sass?" She handed the bride her bouquet of orchids and gardenias.

"Yeah. I was just thinking about Maman."

"Wouldn't she just love who you're marrying?"

"She'd get a kick out of it."

Sassy walked from Aidan's room to the hallway. When she returned it would be *their* room. Across the expanse of the gallery she could see the frenzied movements of the caterer's setting up for the reception in the ballroom. This was pretty overwhelming. She loved Aidan so much, she never considered his wealth. His money had been such a part of who he wasn't to her; he was wealthy in so many nonmonetary ways. To think she had seen this house when she was eleven and never, in a zillion years, guessed that she would have ever gotten inside for a visit, much less live here. Only in America.

It was twilight as she descended the Gone With the Wind staircase for the final time as Sassiere Crillon. She took the steps slowly, deliberately, and her train dropped then slipped over each carpeted stair one by one. She rounded the corner, and through the beveled glass, she could see the flickering of the lit candles, so that the riot of flowers shimmered in their romantic glow. Hughes opened the door for her and Ivanhoe stepped up to her, crying and dabbing his linen handkerchief to his eyes.

"You look beautiful, chère."

"Thanks." She smiled nervously.

"You're trembling. Why?"

"I don't belong here. I'm just a girl from Gert Town—"

"Who stole the heart of a Sebastien. Twice," Ivanhoe said with a chuckle.

Sassy smiled, and they both missed their cue.

"C'mon, chère. Buck up. It's showtime. Let's do this!"

As they stepped onto the brick verandah, French horns sounded, announcing her. She smiled at yet another surprise from her husband-to-be, who remembered how much she loved the pure, regal sound of them.

"My little black Cinderella," Ivanhoe quipped as they stepped down on the flat brick step.

Sassy and Ivanhoe glided past the white garden chairs, every row punctuated with alternating bouquets of fresh gardenias and sunflowers . . . for her Maman. "She'll be there too, Sassiere," Aidan had said when ordering them.

As Sassy turned the corner to the fountain she saw him. Her husband-to-be, standing tall and handsome, waiting for her. The sight of him, of his parenthetical smile, immediately calmed her, and she saw no one else. She loved this man and thought her heart would burst from the pure joy contained there.

"You stopped trembling, chère," Ivanhoe whispered as she reached Aidan and took his extended hand.

Aidan wrapped her hand over his arm and secured it with his own, and they stood side by side, as close as they could, lost in each other's gaze. Speaking their own silent language; missing the promptings of the priest as their own secret vows were exchanged.

"I give you Mr. and Mrs. Aidan Maximillien Sebastien," the priest announced and the couple turned to the clapping congratulations of their guests.

As the newlyweds' pictures were snapped for posterity, the guests dined on sumptuous hors d'oeuvres, exotic canapés, and flutes of champagne circulated by liveried waiters. Ivanhoe approached the guesthouse and slipped inside. Compared to the harmonic raucousness outside it was eerily quiet inside. He looked around and couldn't tell where the old rooms had begun or ended. In this incarnation, it had been gutted and reborn just like the inhabitants. There were no tangibles left to this building, not from old slaves or anyone else. There were only memories of the long-dead that rattled around not anchored by bricks and mortar, but only feelings. Ivanhoe heard the chime that meant that the orchestra was ensconced in the second-floor ballroom balcony, and the reception was about to begin.

"Now is time for the living," he said to the ghosts, and left.

The six-course, sit-down dinner for one hundred and fifty well-wishers was a breathtaking symphony of elegance. The ballroom reflected the garden motif, as round tables of eight framed the gleaming mahogany dance floor. Candles cast a romantic patina over the ancient frescoes as guests dined and danced; "A reception in the palace of Louis XVI couldn't have been any grander than this one at the House of Sebastien," a reporter who was not a guest would later write. "Magically elegant—gand style."

He continued, "The couple's first dance as man and wife began with "The Very Thought of You," followed by "A Sunday Kind Of Love," "At Last," "What Are You Doing New Year's?," and "What A Difference A Day Makes"; an unconventional repertoire throughout which they never sat down. A one-month honeymoon is planned in the South Pacific—Tahiti, Mooréa, and Bora-Bora—after which they will reside in the Sebastien mansion."

* * *

"I wish I knew who leaked this," Simone fumed the next day at this breach of privacy as the newlyweds just cooed and cuddled under the portico, waiting for Hughes to finish loading the car for the airport.

"I bet it was that Ivanhoe person," Simone continued, and glanced at her son and new daughter-in-law, who could not have cared less. "Eh—" she dismissed. "Happy honeymoon," she said, and went into the house.

"I love you Mrs. Aidan Sebastien."

"Me too, you."

Epilogue

A Year Later

The Cajun moon sat high in the sky; its neon beams shone down on the skinny streets of the French Quarter, casting its amber-orange patina on all who ventured beneath. Roux Robespierre pulled his car up in front of SASSY'S. He hopped out and went around to open the passenger door, and a pretty young woman took his arm. Her hair was long and she resembled, in physicality as well as in values and morals, her predecessor—Sassy. They rushed into SASSY'S trying to beat their guests to the back room which had been set up for the celebration: a cast party for her sixth-grade summer schoolers who had just brilliantly performed *The Wiz*, and their parents.

Across town, in the Sebastien mansion, Aidan and Sassiere swung in the hammock off their bedroom, watching Simone snip orchids from her garden.

"I'm turning in," Simone called up to them. "*Bonsoir.*"

"*Bonsoir,*" the couple replied, as they watched her carry the bundle of fragrance into her studio.

"Look at that big, pretty moon," Aidan said as he held Sassiere close.

"Hummm," Sassiere answered, rubbing her cheek next to her husband's smooth skin.

"So which is it tonight? Popcorn or frappés?" he asked her as they let the sway of the hammock transport them.

It was so peaceful and quiet, they were content until the grandfather clock struck.

"Better hurry," Aidan said. "*The King and I* starts in twenty minutes."

"I'll set up the pillows and turn down the bed," Sassiere said as she took her husband's extended hands and lit from the hammock.

"I'll miss you." He kissed her as he left for the kitchen.

"Crazy man." She laughed and swatted his behind.

As she rolled back the comforter and placed it in the chest at the foot of the bed, she listened at Aidan whistle "Shall We Dance?" down the hall to the steps. She chuckled with anticipation.

The whistling Aidan entered the kitchen from the backstairs entrance, pulled down their special, oversized float glasses and set them on the counter. He went to the freezer and got the ice cream, then the scoop from the drawer.

He opened the gallon of ice cream and said, "Perfect. Nice and soft around the edges." He sunk the scoop into the frozen confection and twisted three rounded scoops into each glass. He put the ice cream away and grabbed the tray, then the Oreo and Fig Newton cookie canisters and went into the pantry for the sodas. He set the sodas on the granite counter with a click and then noticed an envelope propped up on the napkin holder. *Dad*—it read.

Aidan opened the card and read beyond the printed verse: *Enjoy this Father's Day Eve because next year we'll be here and your whole life will be changed. We know you're going to make a great father. Our Mommy told us so.*

Aidan stood there and his smile turned into a full-blown, teeth-baring, ear-to-ear grin, and he yelled. "Sassiere! Sassiere!" He ran out to the front hall around and up the Gone With the Wind staircase, bolted left to their room and slammed open the doors.

With a mischievous grin, Sassiere turned around and asked, "Where are the frappés?"

"Sassiere. Are we?" He was breathing like he'd just run a marathon.

"You're not but I am—"

He yelled and swooped her up twirling her around and around in the middle of the room. He stopped abruptly and asked, "You're not playing. Are you sure?"

"I know better than to come to you half-stepping, Aidan. I'm sure. We're going to have babies."

"Babies?" His deep penetrating eyes questioned.

"Well, the doctor said since you're so old, he'd give us two at once," she teased.

"Twins?" He grinned and tears brimmed his eyes. "Oh, Sassiere." He held her close to him.

"You better put me down and conserve your energy, Dad. We'll be alternating those two o'clock feedings."

He placed her gently on the bed as if she were made of porcelain. He couldn't take his eyes from her. "Can I get you anything? Anything at all?"

"Well, some workman to break down the room next door into two, a hallway in here like you promised—and my frappé."

He sat carefully on the bed beside her.

"We're going to be parents, Sassiere."

"Yes, we are Aidan." She laid her head on his shoulder. "Twice."

"Alouette Simone for the girl and Maximillien for the boy," Aidan verified.

"Just like we decided."

"Max Sebastien—swoosh! Three points—all net. The boy is bad!'" Aidan said in his announcer's voice. "And for the record, Sassiere."

She raised her head to look at him.

"The doctor had nothing to do with it. It was all me."

"Oh, Aidan—" She hit him playfully and giggled.

"I *am* smooth—"

They laughed and laughed and laughed.

Ivanhoe took a full glass and a bottle of champagne and sat in Sassy's old bedroom in her favorite windowsill seat. He sipped and looked at the Cajun moon beyond the cistern.

"Hey, big, bright, and beautiful," he said. "Just like me." He chuckled, toasted and sipped. "So whose life are you shaking up tonight? I'm not mad at you—those lunar rays you sent to my Sassy a while back were right on time. I do miss her."

Like a father whose daughter had gone off to college, he kept her room unchanged in case she came back. He had begun using other parts of the apartment, but he kept her bedroom as it was. She didn't take anything but clothes and some pictures, but hell, she was moving into the Sebastien mansion, for chrissakes.

Clearly, she wasn't coming back. He really didn't expect her to. Aidan was good for her and she for him. It was a match made in heaven, spawned by the Cajun moon. Sassy'd turned that stodgy old house and the people in it around. She even managed the impossible by pumping life into that bitter old crone—Simone. Her bad grade of good hair wasn't the only thing that had straightened out.

Sassy and Aidan remained a quiet couple who preferred their own company to others'. But at least Sassy gave out candy to trick-or-treaters on Halloween and decorated the mansion beautifully for Christmas. She held the Second Annual Christmas Bazaar for St. Gabe's, had Easter-egg hunts and rolls for the children on the lawn, hosted a Valentine Sweethearts' Ball for heart disease in the ballroom, Daffodil Ball for cancer in the spring, the Harvest Ball for the Lupus Foundation in October and the MS Luncheon in the winter. He was invited to them all. Who would have thought that he would ever be invited to the Sebastien mansion as a welcomed and honored guest? But he was a constant staple there. *Life is full of ironies,* he thought and sipped again.

With each invitation, he was able to purge more of the old feelings and replace them with good ones. Seeing Sassy with the Sebastien ring at the funeral home when they were making arrangements for Maman's funeral was surreal. Guilt grabbed him by the jugular when Aidan confided how lonely he was because his father didn't spend any time with him—Ivanhoe knew where his daddy was, and with whom. But none of the visits were as traumatic as when he first returned to the house after thirty-some years for that first Christmas Bazaar. He walked up the long driveway and tears sprang to his eyes. He hated being back there. It was painful, but he loved Sassy, so he went. He hung onto the iron gate, peering at the once workshop—now guesthouse—and the memories of making caskets as an apprentice flooded back. He

could almost hear Maximillien's voice, and when Aidan
touched his shoulder, he had jumped. When Aidan asked
if he would like to go in, Ivanhoe stuttered and bolted
like a crazy man to get away. And when he and Simone
came face to face . . . he thought he would collapse. Their
eyes had locked, and despite their mutual torture, age
had treated them both well, even if Maximillien had not.
They had loved the same man; and he them.

"Well, My Love," Ivanhoe toasted the Cajun moon.
"You can rest easy. Both of your sons are straight as a
board, not a hint of tendency. You should be proud of
Aidan, who has parlayed the funeral business in all sorts
of delicious directions that I can't begin to comprehend.
He is consummately masculine and Roux is seemingly a
reformed Don Juan . . . only time will tell. Aidan has married his perfect woman and they live a perfect hetero life
that you couldn't quite pull off. Sorry, no pun intended."

Ivanhoe sipped his champagne. "In the end whether
hetero or homo—we all want the same thing. Someone
to love and someone to love us back." He drained his
glass and poured more from the bottle at his feet.

"Aidan and Sassy will be fine. After the trauma of losing
Sassy, Roux may actually treat this schoolteacher he's been
dating for eight weeks like a lucky lady and settle down. It
took him awhile. Almost a full year, like he was waiting for
Sassy to come to her senses. Seeing she'd moved on, so has
he—finally. But in those quiet moments of the day and
night when the Cajun moon hangs low, Roux will always
love Sassy, as I will always love you.

"You wanted the best for Aidan and I wanted the best
for Sassy. We both got our wish."

Ivanhoe sipped and said, "I miss you madly, Maximillien.
But in the end, we have to thank God for unanswered
prayers . . ."

Acknowledgments

Special thank-yous to my mother, Evelyn Gunn-Horad—I am who I am because she allowed me to be; to my husband, Marvin E. Gunn II, for all his technical assistance and support; to my agent, Cheryl Ferguson, for her unflinching belief in my literary abilities; to my unwavering champion, Gwendolyn Osborne; to my insightful editors, Pittershawn Palmer and Natalie Weber; to Ophelia Jackson and Clifford Johnson for exuberantly sharing their native N'awlins with me; to my linguist, Otello "the Professor" Jean; and to Andrea Bray for her musical company and inspiration.

For serendipity, thanks to: PVM—Pat "Thelma" Mitchell, Charles R. Drew, Jr., Juanita Jones, Bertie Bryant, Scheryl Price, and self-proclaimed Number One Fan Diane Moreno, and everyone who reads and enjoys *Cajun Moon*.